UNBURNABLE

UNBURNABLE

Marie-Elena John

Amistad *An Imprint of* HarperCollins*Publishers*

UNBURNABLE. Copyright © 2006 by Marie-Elena John. All rights reserved. Printed in the United States of America. No part of this book may be used or reproduced in any manner whatsoever without written permission except in the case of brief quotations embodied in critical articles and reviews. For information address HarperCollins Publishers, 10 East 53rd Street, New York, NY 10022.

HarperCollins books may be purchased for educational, business, or sales promotional use. For information please write: Special Markets Department, HarperCollins Publishers, 10 East 53rd Street, New York, NY 10022.

FIRST EDITION

Designed by Betty Lew

Printed on acid-free paper

Library of Congress Cataloging-in-Publication Data

John, Marie-Elena.
Unburnable/Marie-Elena John.—1st ed.
p.   cm.
ISBN-13: 978-0-06-083757-0 (acid-free paper)
ISBN-10: 0-06-083757-8 (acid-free paper)
1. Women—Dominica—Fiction. 2. Dominica—Fiction. 3. Domestic fiction. I. Title.

PR9275.A583J64 2006
813'.6—dc22   2005053658

06 07 08 09 10 ❖/RRD 10 9 8 7 6 5 4 3 2 1

For Donna Boyd Oflaz,
who was, among so many wonderful things,
a natural storyteller

This is in your memory,
and the memory of that magical time
we all had in Dominica

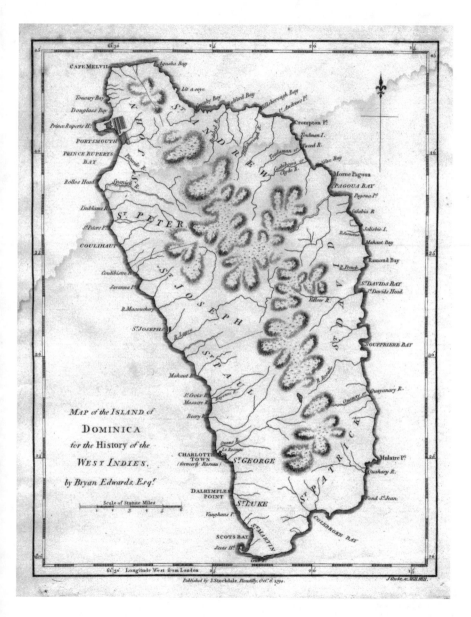

MAP of the ISLAND of

DOMINICA

for the History of the

WEST INDIES,

by Bryan Edwards, Esqr.

Scale of Statute Miles

CAPE MELVIL
Agucha Bay
Lill a soye
Toucary Bay
Douglass Bay
Prince Ruperts Hd
PORTSMOUTH
PRINCE RUPERTS BAY
Rollos Head
Dublane R.
St Peters Pt
COULIHAUT
Codibiere R.
Savanna Pt.
R. Macouchery
St JOSEPHS
Mahaut R.
St Croix R.
Masacre R.
Boery R.
CHARLOTTE TOWN (formerly Roseau)
DALRYMPLES POINT
Vanghans Pt.
SCOTS BAY
Scots Hd.

NORTH
ANDREW
 St PETER
St JOSEPH
St PAUL
St GEORGE
St LUKE
St MARTIN
St PATRICK
St DAVID

Douby Bay
Blenford Bay
Killsborough Bay
St Andrew Pt.
Crompton Pt.
Toulman I.
Tweed R.
Cachibena or Clyde R.
Woodax Bay
Morne Pagoua
PAGOUA BAY
Pagoua Pt.
Salubia R.
Salisbio I.
Entamouna
Mahaut Bay
R. French
Ramond Bay
St DAVIDS BAY
St Davids Head
Yellow R.
SOUFRIERE BAY
R. Rouble
Quanry or Quayanary R.
Quaquary R.
Mulatre Pt.
Quahary R.
Fond St Jean.
COLEBROKE BAY

61 30'
7 5
2 0
1 5
45
46
35
30
25
26

61 30' Longitude West from London

Published by J. Stockdale, Piccadilly, Octr. 6. 1794.

J. Cooke, sc. Mill Hill.

1

UP THERE, NOAH

Lillian's mother, Iris, was known throughout the island for a number of distinct characteristics: the women would say that chief among them were her uncommon beauty, the fact that her skin was reputed to actually glow in the dark, and the nasty cussing she directed at anyone who crossed her path when she was drunk beyond a certain point. Others insisted that Iris was known best as the daughter of Matilda, who had been tried, convicted, and, on one typically rainy Dominica day in 1950, publicly hanged. Men, though, would laugh at that and say it was the quality of the sex Iris offered that was the thing, for her mother had taught her a number of tactics for keeping her vagina in pristine condition, despite the damage that had been done to it many years before by a broken Coca-Cola bottle. The elasticity was not only due to the tightening exercises she performed for twenty minutes daily, drunk or sober; she also knew about the enhancing properties of alum and such substances, and was never without a supply of these aids.

But beyond all this, the men—men of all classes, town men and country men—were astounded by the passion of their encounters with Iris. Several of the fainthearted were too cowardly to face it a second time, but for the most part this was what kept her steady stream of visitors coming. None understood that the intensity that left them shaken was actually the aggression of an otherwise powerless, disappointed, and very angry woman, who was, in fact, molesting them with her body as she threw them onto their backs and attacked them brutally. But they were oblivious to this dynamic, and left with their chests out, proud of their potency, which they felt had aroused her to such an extreme response.

Without fail these men brought with them a bottle in a brown paper bag, and took care to leave behind "a little something to help out." While the high-class town people from Roseau referred to her as "the half-Carib *salop*," it is to the credit of the country people, islandwide, that none of them, woman or man, considered her to be a prostitute. The villagers, as villagers often do, exhibited a sophistication beyond their time and place regarding the options left for a woman who had suffered Iris's fate, and they understood the practicality of what is today called, in certain circles, the sex industry. The women, in particular, beyond acknowledging her historical place as the daughter of the infamous Matilda, had a definite appreciation for Iris: she kept their men from bothering them when they were too occupied with raising their children to be concerned with the effort of sex; and especially in the areas around her house, she kept their young boys from experimenting on their young girls, thereby keeping down underage pregnancy.

Iris died in 1971 in a Roseau jail, where she was being kept overnight for the crimes of disorderly conduct and disturbing the peace. She had lived in or just outside of Dominica's single town for most of her life, from the time she was fourteen years old until her early death at the age of forty, but she was born in a very different environment, at the top of one of the island's highest mountains, on a plateau. The isolated place where Iris's navel string was buried didn't appear on a map until 1950, after it had already ceased to exist, when it was recorded as "Noah." Before that, it was known only as "Up There"—with the rest of the phrase, "where Matilda lives," left unspoken, understood.

Up There was where she was born to Matilda and Simon the Carib, a short, red-skinned, flat-faced man with slitted eyes and straight, heavy black hair, a kind of person the inhabitants of the place that came to be called Noah had never seen before. He had walked out of the surf onto the black-sanded beach dragging his canoe along the rocks, asking around the coastal villages if anyone knew where to find a woman named Matilda.

The technology to build roads by blasting canyons through mountains had not yet reached Dominica. The rains that constantly washed away the attempts at roads insulated them from the rest of an island so inaccessible and impenetrable that Columbus had bypassed it, describing it to Isabella and Ferdinand back in Spain, it is said, by throwing a crumpled sheet of paper at their feet. The people who lived Up There, every last one of unadulterated African descent, knew that not even sixteen forested and mountainous miles opposite their enclave, over on the Atlantic side of the island, lived a small group of people left over from the time before the white people and before the Black people. But while most other Dominicans were accustomed to seeing the red people with the dead-straight hair, few of those who lived Up There had ever set eyes on a Carib until the middle of the 1920s, when one appeared in the person of Simon.

The underlying red hue from her father's Carib blood made Iris glow. Matilda's West African features melded with those of the indigenous Caribbean people to give her a mouth wider than they thought possible; slits for eyes that slanted upward at almost half of a right angle, and cheekbones that slashed high across her face. The nose, however, was the thing, a replica of the one on Matilda's face: a dominating piece of work set broad across her narrow face, the bridge dipping down and staying low to the plane of her face, the nostrils rising high, finely carved and perfectly curved. Nowhere had the secluded people seen such a captivating combination of features. Her singular, iridescent looks convinced them that there had been some kind of otherworldly intervention in her conception, and they took this to be confirmation of Matilda's powers.

From infancy Iris had been badly spoiled by her unusual beauty, but Matilda didn't know that her daughter was worshiped, her every wish indulged. She had no idea that Iris suffered no consequences when she transgressed. The other children of their community were deliberately raised without individual attention, except when they stepped out of line. They were cared for meticulously as a unit, a large tribe of small people-in-training. The main lesson of their childhood was that, outside of their protected world, they would only find a limited lower space within which they could exercise their ambitions, and that they would be better off staying where they were.

It was a sensible socialization, one that did not promote mobility, but that gave them a clear understanding of who they were and where they belonged. It first and foremost protected the children from the disappointment of destroyed dreams.

Matilda was too busy to notice that the others were not raising her child in the same way as the ordinary children, otherwise she would surely have seen what was coming, and tried to save her daughter from her future.

2

PREPARATIONS, HOPE

Let him say yes, let him come with me. This was the only thought, a prayer, really, that Lillian would let through as she looked at herself in the mirror.

She took off the ankle-length sleeveless sheath. Although she'd chosen it so she might match him, sitting up in his Georgetown town house in casual Armani because one never knew when a camera crew would show up looking for a quote, the black dress had fooled her on the hanger. She had not anticipated what the bias cut would do, and now the effect was all wrong, the fabric sticking to her, following the exaggerations of her torso before falling to swirl frivolously above her feet. A caricature, she thought. Waists were not that small, hips not that round. Breasts that size did not sit so high. And the neckline was too low.

Even though that would have been the appropriate thing for her to do, to present herself in those terms, given what she wanted of him and given her clarity of purpose—her intent was to seduce him—she still took off the dress, just as she had removed the black lace bra-and-thong set she'd also bought for the occasion, exchanging them for her everyday cotton whites. She had physically recoiled at her image, pulling back from the mirror, yanking down the strip of shiny hundred-percent polyester in a single reflexive movement. She had looked, she thought, whorish, like an underwear model in the kind of catalog with which teenage boys occupied themselves in locked bathrooms; and in any case, the string of a thong could rest harmlessly in the shallow space between the flat cheeks of a white woman, but caught inside the rolling depth of a Black behind, it was nothing but an instrument of torture.

She ironed a pair of black slacks and put on a white shirt, although it could be called a blouse thanks to the sueded silk of the fabric and the French cuffs of the three-quarter sleeves. She dug under her sweaters for her jewelry box. She lifted the hinged lid and her hand stopped, suspended before she touched the gold cuff links, the only items in the simple wooden box apart from a heavy gold cross on a thick, long chain. Had anyone been watching, it would have appeared to be a moment of reverence.

She'd had them made for him for his twenty-first birthday. They were taking the same African history class together, and he'd asked for "something from Africa." He used to show his affection for her by mimicking the French undertones in what he called her island accent, and he had said *"som-feeng from Af-ree-ka"*—that she remembered clearly, as she remembered most things from when they were in college—the last chance, it is said, for people to make true friends; for Lillian, it had been her only chance.

"Nice French accent you got there." That was how Theodore Morgan had approached her, his own accent deep New York.

"I don't speak French," she'd had to explain to him twenty years earlier. She could place the moment exactly. It was the first class of freshman English, a get-to-know-you session; she could even remember what he was wearing, the gray Class of '87 Columbia sweatshirt with the hood, baggy sweatpants.

He was insistent. "But that's a French accent."

"English is Dominica's official language, see? And we also speak

French *Creole."* Over the course of that first year, as he persisted with his efforts to draw her out, she'd ended up giving him his first de facto course in Third World history, describing how many times the Caribbean islands changed hands between the fighting Europeans.

For his requested gift, three years after he spoke his first words to her, she'd found a small shop in New York's West Village where the jeweler had apprenticed in Dakar, his certification of training ornately framed and hung above a counter displaying his trademark amber-and-gold creations. Written in Wolof and French, the certificate proclaimed him to be a master goldsmith. She'd chosen to have the cuff links made in the shape of one of the dozens of Adinkra symbols that represent the Akan worldview. From a wall poster she had picked it out purely for its swirling symmetry, and the jeweler had allowed her to watch him make the mold and pour the gold. The design **છ**, in Twi, was called *Hye won Hye;* in English, "that which does not burn," he explained. It was a symbol of the permanence of the human soul.

But when the time came to give them to him, she couldn't part with them. Their heaviness in her palm comforted her somehow, anchored her, and she had kept them for herself with the excuse that they turned out looking like a pair of abstract gold butterflies, too feminine for a man to wear.

From an African art studio on the Lower East Side she bought him a mask instead, one that cost much more than the gold. She had spent a full afternoon there, persuading the owner to allow her to purchase it in installments, and eventually she had presented Teddy with a mask—neither one that had been hastily carved at the back of some craft center in West Africa, shining with shoe polish, nor one made in China and buried in dirt for a few weeks to make it look old. She bought Teddy a mask that had once been worn, a mask that had been danced, that had once represented a spirit.

৪৪৪

S he spoke aloud to her mirror. *I wonder if you would like to come with me?* She sounded laughable, pitiable. *Come with me!* Then, *Come with me?* A different approach, carefully: *I think you'd enjoy Dominica.* She noticed her evened-out accent, not exactly American, but the singing quality had long disappeared.

She finished her toilette with lipstick, also a special purchase, just one level up from a gloss. Once, when she was younger, she had braved a rich, heavily pigmented brick-red, liking the effect, but she had received unsolicited comments all day, mostly from men she did not know. She had since used only Vaseline, which, along with powder, was all she normally put on her face. Basic eyeliner was also rejected—she would never emphasize her eyes. In America, their yellow-brown cast was called various exotic and complimentary names: hazel, tawny, gold-flecked; but where she came from, her feline eyes had a different association. "Pussy-Eye!" schoolchildren would sometimes dare to call after her in the absence of the teachers, maintaining their safe distance, running away if she turned around to look at them. The eyes, indeed not much different from those of a cat, gave further credence to the story of how Lillian came to be born, and were a constant reminder to the children that they should heed their mothers' warnings.

She spent time choosing her watch; she had a small collection laid out on her dresser, all of the same basic design, functional men's watches with big faces and wide bands that bore no resemblance to jewelry. The delicate one Teddy had given her as a thank-you gift after his book came out—more a skinny bracelet than a watch—had been exchanged for the one she now selected, snapping the catch and swinging her left hand in a downward arc, shaking it, adjusting to the weight of the stainless steel and gold.

Standing in front of the full-length mirror again, she reached up and back, pulling out the hairpins, finding her look too severe. She almost never wore her hair out: it drew so much attention, double takes from strangers whose first glance required another to accommodate the amber eyes on the amber skin. Adding the jet-black, dead-straight hair to the mix made them stop, turn around; it sometimes made men follow her. And not only did she dislike what the fly-girl hair implied—that she was the kind who wasted half her morning in the company of a blow dryer and a flatiron—but that type of hair simply did not match her African features. When her hair was out, it made her look fake, she thought, like a Black Barbie doll. Still, it was her only inheritance from her mother, Iris—the Carib hair—and she didn't have the courage to cut it.

Today, she thought, shaking her hair back, swinging it around white-girl style to fall heavy over one shoulder, she would make an exception.

With that thought, her body sank. She felt no pain as her knees crashed to the hardwood, she still stared into the mirror as she tried to up the ante of her prayer: *If you make him come with me, I will…*

And then with the realization that she had no chip with which to bargain, the familiar slow panic began, the kind that ends in profound despair. She closed her eyes as she finally folded, and she stayed curled on the hardwood until there was no longer any danger of recalling exactly what she had found the night she had gone digging, when, long ago, she had done six feet worth of digging all by herself.

3

MATILDA

Lillian's grandmother was hanged long before she was born, and Lillian had never seen a photograph of her, although once, as a child, she had looked into a mirror and seen her swinging from a rope. The story of Matilda—what the songs said she was, what they said she did—consumed her, obsessed her.

People said many things about Matilda. Above all, they said she had Obeah powers, which included the power to heal at will. In the early 1920s, before Simon entered her life, people along the length and breadth of Dominica came to find Matilda for her to set their bones, usually the broken ribs of women whose current lovers believed or at least claimed that they had no better way to show their love than to fly into a fit of jealousy, anger, or general irritation. She drew teas from the various inflammation bushes, these being effective against the symptoms of gonorrhea, particularly the blockage of urine. She boiled roots that helped women to conceive, and brewed teas to wash away a fetus. She successfully treated high and low blood pressure, sugar, and hearts that beat too fast or too slow. And, most famously of all, she treated unidentified medical and psychological conditions, all of which people were convinced had been caused by an enemy "working Obeah" against them.

Matilda handled all these physical afflictions—and psychological ailments, too—with "potions" of a scientific base: aphrodisiacs, sedatives, stimulants, and narcotics: double and triple compounds of the extracts of plants, and occasionally of animals, insects, sometimes fish. And in the many cases where her patients had been poisoned (which was often the case with victims of Obeah), she was at her professional best, because she had been taught how to compose their antidotes— wherein lay her greatest expertise.

She treated her patients with medicine and she treated them with prayer and sacrifice and ritual, because for her there could be no clear separation of the physical, the mental, and the spiritual. To the many people who came to the bottom of her mountain, the base of Up There, to wait for her to climb down to them, she always insisted that she did not work Obeah, but this denial was expected, Obeah being illegal and clandestinely practiced. As far as Dominicans were concerned, she brought back people from certain death, from illnesses they believed were supernaturally derived, and her methods were identical to the kinds of things an Obeahwoman would do—the drinking of foul-tasting mixtures, application of powders, herbal baths, incantations, and other rituals.

Many years later, after she was arrested and convicted, after she was hanged, people forgot that before Simon came, she had always refused those women seeking potions and powders that would tie their men, and she chased off the men who beseeched her to give them "something" to avenge their broken hearts, their wounded pride. She knew she could develop any kind of poison that, slipped into the food or drink of a client's enemy, would cause instant or prolonged death, blindness, barrenness, intestinal dysfunction for life—the possibilities were practically limitless. She would never promise wealth or happiness or good fortune in exchange for money. That, she maintained, would involve adding the elements of fear, mind control, and charlatanism to her relationship with her clients. She didn't doubt that she held the psychological power to have any of them gaze into a mirror and see whatever they most wanted, needed, or feared, but she had no desire for that. Matilda already had enough to handle when she wore the mask and took power over life and death.

4

DESPERATION

The ringing of her telephone brought Lillian back. It would be someone from the twenty-four-hour switchboard at her work, passing on the details of another urgent appeal that had come in from somewhere in the world. The sharper pitch of the ring of Lillian's second line meant that somewhere in the world, a woman had found herself in trouble when she had tried to stand up to the expectations of her culture, or the dictates of her government, or the demands of the social order under which she lived. The insistent sound of the dedicated line told her that she would need to get money to a woman who was in deep trouble somewhere in the world, money that would keep her out of jail, pay for a lawyer, or allow her to flee her country. This was Lillian's job, as far as it was possible to verify that the appeal was genuine and worthy, and to use all the means at the Urgent Appeal's disposal to get the money to Asia, to Africa, to Latin America, although it often did happen that she could take a train or a bus, even a taxi, to the woman's hiding place, and deliver the cash herself.

Lillian did that for a living, and she also designed the Urgent Appeal's fund-raising campaigns: the one that raised money to buy girls in Ghana from the fetish priests to whom they had been enslaved had won her an Amnesty International award.

She normally never let the second line of her phone ring over to her assistant, who, like Lillian, was on twenty-four-hour call. She had learned that the strongest firewall against her flashbacks was to work herself to the point of physical and mental fatigue. From that day, though, she was on vacation, she just hadn't told her colleagues yet. She was preparing to go back home.

L illian was finally ready. She went back to the mirror and made a three-quarter turn to check her back view before going in for a last close-up smile, but there was nothing vain about the gesture. She checked herself one last time to make sure she stepped out into the world with a clean face, neat clothes—that was the stocktaking she did, even though other women of her station might have been using that last look to reassure themselves that there was still time left before old age. Lillian behaved like the women of the world on behalf of whom she worked, destitute or desperate women who lived without the promise of a tomorrow, women whose condition left no time for frivolity like preoccupation with looks, or concern with the inevitability of getting old, or the business of staving it off.

She was not destitute, but she did think of herself as desperate as she backed away from the mirror, put on her shades, and left her apartment. The attention she paid to her reflection in the mirror left her with no idea of whether she was good-looking, and in this case it didn't really matter, because Lillian did not plan to seduce him with her face, nor with her body. She would seduce him first with all the unacknowledged things he had felt for her. She would remind him of that one particular moment from their past.

After, she would sustain the seduction with her story, with the sheer magnitude of her grandmother's alleged crime. The sex would be just an inevitable and, she believed, unfortunate by-product, because in the softhearted, generous conceit of his gender, he could only understand what she needed from him in those terms, and she hoped, she prayed, that he would not have the heart to deny her.

The mask on the foyer wall directly behind him, just to the left of his own face, was the first thing Lillian saw as he opened his door. A sign, perhaps. She pointed to it after they touched cheeks in greeting. "As you get older, the resemblance gets stronger," she said.

They were laughing as they walked through his living room, which had been professionally redone in the few months since she'd been there for his celebration party, thrown for him by the journalist girlfriend to mark the point at which Teddy officially become famous—not just to the urban, BET-watching, morning-show-listening, *Essence*-reading crowd. The homemaker in Minnesota, the farmer in Iowa, also knew his name, since DNA confirmed what Teddy (and several others) had argued since he was a first-year graduate student in 1989—never mind their confessions: those five boys did not gang-rape that white woman.

Lillian hadn't stayed at the party, there had been too many beautiful people positioned artfully around Teddy's eclectically tasteful furniture, holding champagne flutes in limp-wristed poses. The circling professional photographers only heightened the sensation of being part of something orchestrated, a tableau. Now, she stopped as they passed his Bearden, stepping back to catch its full impact. She hadn't seen it in a while; Teddy often loaned it to exhibitions. "I can't believe Diane let you keep this." It was an earlier piece, from the artist's Harlem period. Newspaper photos of black-and-white faces with huge eyes jumped out from the collage's brilliant background, big colorbursts of fabric and foil.

"She had no choice," Teddy said. "It was a gift, remember? You give somebody a gift, it's no longer yours."

"I remember," Lillian said. She had been there nine years earlier when, with great fanfare, Diane presented Teddy with his wedding gift at their rehearsal dinner on an Antiguan beach. The ceremony lasted almost as long as the marriage, which was declared null and void within five years. But she barely remembered any of it. She hadn't expected it to have been so difficult; difficult to watch Teddy profess his love for another woman, and difficult to be back in the Caribbean. It had been fourteen years since she left Dominica, enough time, she would have expected, for her to handle being in the vicinity.

Yet there had been that terrible feeling when she stepped off the plane: even from the airport, the island appeared to be laid bare. No canopy of trees, no range of mountains, no big-belly clouds hanging low, no hint of drizzle or mist to give a sense of privacy. No sign of rain falling in the distance, soft-focusing the horizon. No feeling that maybe your lesser transgressions might be hidden from God by nature's benevolent spirits that were looking out for you and willing to give you a little break—Antigua was open flat. Standing so exposed, Lillian had felt obliged to close her eyes, like a woman yet unaccustomed to a new lover at the moment of apprehension when she opens her legs and waits.

As Lillian walked through Teddy's house in Georgetown, she could only remember how, to make it through his wedding in Antigua, she'd called upon all the tricks which, at fourteen and fifteen years old, she had used to convince the psychiatrist that there was nothing wrong with her head.

Teddy could remember every small detail of his wedding. When the plane approached Antigua, he had looked out of the window to discover that the island was everything the tourist brochures said, even from the sky. Beach after beach—tiny, fluffy, white-rimmed indentations. The water started out a deep shade of blue from where the sea was still ocean, changing and becoming pale and translucent long before it came close to shore, revealing darkened coral formations beneath. At the coastline, he couldn't tell it was water but for the shimmer and the froth: it was so clear as to be completely transparent.

In Antigua, what happened on his wedding night was of course his strongest memory. He still got goose bumps when he thought of the deliberate way Diane had laid out the snapshots on the bed. But before that, the clearest recollection of his time in Antigua was actually a feeling: the sense of dread brought on by the simultaneous knowledge that he could still do something about the mistake that was about to happen, and the understanding that he would make that mistake anyway. He remembered how busy Diane was kept by her mother and the hotel's wedding coordinator, and the amount of time that left for him to be in Lillian's company, even though they were mostly in a large group—loud, excitable members of Diane's family, and a few of his, in high American-tourist mode.

He remembered the day before the ceremony, when an overbooked catamaran day-trip to Barbuda, Antigua's sister island, left him and Lillian alone at the beachfront hotel. He had known her for over a decade by then, but it was the first time he had ever seen her in a swimsuit. Side by side on lounge chairs on the sand, Teddy was forced to keep his eyes closed for much of the time, not wanting to risk being embarrassingly caught in one of those disgraceful ogles where a man's eyes, despite all efforts, are unable to hold normal eye contact and keep sliding down to a woman's chest. He used to see men do it all the time, scornful of their lack of self-control and their bad manners, but now he understood. The alternative to closing his eyes would have been to fix them directly,

unnaturally, in the middle of Lillian's face, without blinking, because it
was in the blink, he discovered, that the slippage occurred.

He'd been pretending to read one of Antigua's tourist brochures, a
glossy magazine with a cover that featured the flat, sleek, thonged
behinds of three white women lying on their bellies in order to blacken
their bottoms.

"They say here that the sand in Barbuda is pink," he had said to
Lillian. He was thinking that she had developed a skittishness since
arriving in Antigua, and some other quality he could not identify.

Teddy—twenty-eight years old, about to get married, and fighting a
strong urge to bolt—had been wanting to explain to his old friend Lillian about the kind of love he had for Lady Di, as he called her, with her
grace and dignity, born on Washington, D.C.'s Gold Coast, from a family
of firsts: first Black female doctor, first Black dentist, first Black lawyer
to defend a civil rights case successfully, first Black bishop in a white
mainstream church. She was a distant relative to names like Adam Clay-
ton Powell and current family friend to any number of famous Black
musicians, artists, and political figures—her grandfather and Romare
Bearden had been close.

He had wanted to talk to Lillian about something he'd once heard a
frat brother say: that he laid eyes on his wife, just seen her, a stranger,
one day walking down a street, and knew she was the one, that he would
have to find a way to meet her and marry her and have children with her.
He'd heard this in other, slightly milder versions from many others, too,
the trite idea that a soul mate was already out there, premade for you
and waiting for the right moment. It was a tall tale. He knew from experience that love was a very rational thing.

He had tried but was never able to have that conversation with Lillian. He had turned his face away from her and contemplated the large
bushes of blazing pink, papery petals that grew just beyond the sand, all

over the hotel grounds. He was a man who could initiate and sustain a conversation with anybody, even the hotel gardener, who had told him that the bougainvillea did so well in Antigua because the lack of water made it think it was always about to die; to stave off death, it sent forth its most abundant flowers, its most brilliant colors. He could have a twenty-minute discussion with a semiliterate horticulturalist who spoke a dialect so thick it could not be called English, but he couldn't start a conversation with Lillian about love.

Instead, he offered only this: "Barbuda's got pink sand, and seventeen miles of unbroken beach."

5

SIMON

Before he found Matilda, Lillian's maternal grandfather, Simon, used to wake up each morning and behave as though Columbus had arrived the day before, though it all had started some four hundred and thirty years earlier. Everyone else, it seemed to him, had failed to understand the magnitude of it all. They did talk about it among themselves from time to time, and Caribs were generally described as brooding and sullen and reserved, but it felt to him like he was the only one who went through the day unable to concentrate on anything other than the statistical fact that they were extinct, notwithstanding the four hundred of them now living on a little rectangle of coastal land in the northeast corner of Dominica.

They were the very last. It had been all over for the Island Caribs since the early 1800s, when, after fighting the Europeans up and down the Caribbean chain, they had finally succumbed to disease and fire-power, leaving only two islands with any significant number of Caribs: Simon's people in Dominica, and the Black Caribs in St. Vincent, who had been smart enough to team up with African escapees. When the British finally defeated these Vincentian Black Caribs in 1796, five thou-sand of them were shipped off to an island off the coast of Central

America, where, Simon heard, they had spread, settling in different countries and now numbering in the tens of thousands.

But the numbers of the Dominican Caribs had dwindled steadily until 1903, the year of Simon's birth, when a kindly, anthropologically minded British administrator took pity on the remaining four hundred or so. He got the British government to guarantee their permanent ownership of the five and a half square miles on which they then lived.

Simon, as much as he loved to be surrounded by his beautiful people, woke up one morning and decided to leave the Reserve for good. He would go to town, to Roseau, to find work, and although there were a few Caribs there, he would not be surrounded by the defeated faces of his people. He recalled that the entire Atlantic Ocean had been his ancestors' property, and the two percent of Dominica where he lived was not enough for him to call his own. His people had moved in their numbers from island to island in long canoes, all the way from Trinidad in the south up to Puerto Rico, Jamaica, and beyond in the north. To him, the tiny piece of land they had been cornered into was no different from a pigpen, a fowl coop. And even though his people begged him, argued that he was their best healer, and that so much time and training had been invested in him, on that particular morning he knew for certain he would lose his mind if he stayed.

It was not so much that the Europeans had come and had conquered that bothered Simon, because, after all, so had the Island Caribs, come up from South America in their canoes only a few hundred years before, fighting the Arawaks bravely and viciously, creating a new homeland for themselves. But these white people did not think they had to earn the land by fighting for it, they did not expect to spill their blood over it. This was the unbearable thing for Simon, that white people had shown up and told his ancestors that they were entitled to land not theirs, entitled to enslave other human beings simply because of their God, a special kind of god who would not tolerate other people's gods. And in spite of all the killing they did in his name, they said he was a good God, a God of Love.

To leave the Reserve for Roseau, Simon could have gone by foot, knowing the complex network of Carib trails they had used for hundreds of years to traverse his island, *Wai'tikubuli*—he never used "Dominica," holding on as best he could to what little remained of his lost native tongue, and thinking of the island as feminine. True to her original name, Dominica's body was indeed tall, her height deriving three-dimensionally from the mountains. She was also shaped like a limbless woman's long torso; with shoulders, with a head; twenty-nine miles long and sixteen at her widest point, more tapered lower down.

His home was on the northeast coast, high up on the tall body near the right shoulder, with Roseau down in the southwest, diagonally opposite from where Simon had lived all his life. It would have been easy for him—for any Carib—to trek by foot, though dangerous for most others, except for the escaped slaves of old, the *Nègres Marrons*, who had also used the trails to wage their wars against the whites, and who, like the Caribs, had been vanquished by the early 1800s. The only difference was that there were still a handful of Caribs left to tell their story, while the Dominican Maroons had been history for nearly two hundred years, totally exterminated. We should have done like the Vincentians, Simon often thought. We all should have fought the white people together—the Caribs and the Maroons.

Simon rejected the trails and went instead by sea, his preferred method of travel, reminiscent as it was of the glory days of the Caribs. He regularly circumvented the island by canoe for no good reason, just for the swelling feeling of it. He considered the route he would take: he could have gone to Roseau by heading north, quickly crossing the head and shoulders, and then all the way south down the west coast to

Roseau, but then most of the journey would have been along the coast of the Caribbean Sea, where the water was calm and unchallenging. He opted to go south first.

For a while, he stayed far from land, so that out in the Atlantic's deep swells he could give his imagination free rein. He was overwhelmingly tempted to hold his course. He imagined passing Martinique, St. Lucia, St. Vincent, and Grenada. He might stop in St. Vincent and spend some time with the remaining Black Caribs. Perhaps in Grenada, too, he could go to the village called Sauteurs, where he would stand at the very place on the cliff—the point called Carib's Leap—where the cornered warriors had jumped to their death in the sea in the early 1600s. Certainly he would be able to feel them if he stood there, he would be able to connect with them.

He would continue, still keeping south, and if the handed-down stories were correct, he would enter South America at the mouth of the Orinoco. He would travel deep into the interior, finally going eastward via the river's many tributaries, and would arrive at the place where his tribal ancestors still flourished. Eventually he would move on to Central America, to find the descendants of St. Vincent's Black Caribs.

Such were Simon's dreams as he left his home for Roseau.

6

FEELING HISTORY

They settled upstairs in a section of Teddy's study, originally the master suite. The town house was a new one, in a small development designed for childless professionals. The second bedroom was but an afterthought, the master bedroom and its sitting area taking up almost the entire upper floor. He opted to sleep in the tiny bedroom, and converted the larger space for his other needs, soundproofing it against the Georgetown traffic to accommodate his morning-radio telephone interviews and lining two perpendicular walls with mahogany built-in bookshelves.

Several shelves along one wall were packed tight with no-name detective books where the readers were given clues designed to mislead—books whose writers apparently stayed in business thanks only to the patronage of cult readers like Teddy. "My little hobby," he called it, light reading, his distraction from the heavy business of being an expert on racism in America. Right above the tattered paperbacks, though, were the shelves with the collectibles, almost everything Agatha Christie ever wrote, all first editions, along with the auction-acquired works of some late-nineteenth-century crime writers. On the bottom shelf, DVDs. Season compilations of the kinds of prime-time police dramas where profilers solved murders by developing psychological descriptions of the killers, or by sheer deductive brilliance.

The history books, including his own, the early ones he had written on the Underground Railroad, and his latest one—Lillian had practically written it for him—took up another wall, along with the tomes on the present-day state of the African-American condition. At the intersection of these two walls was Teddy's workstation: desk piled with reference books and file folders of clippings; computer, printer, scanner, and the full array of research-oriented technologies.

A pair of fishtail palms next to Romanesque pillars marked the end of the library and an entrance of sorts into another kind of space, one that worked well for informal interviews and tête-à-têtes—for his armchair strategizing, as Lillian called it; and also, a number of seductions had taken place there, where the sleek outward curve of three concave walls, warm with sepia-toned finishes and exotic indoor plants, created an intimate alcove, and he had worked hard on getting the right feel. He was slightly embarrassed to admit the amount of money he had paid for the Pakistani carpet; he could have bought a small car for the same price. Two distressed tobacco-colored leather armchairs faced each other, deep and comfortable and almost forcing one into a position of semirecline. Between them was one of Teddy's prized antiques, a low-sitting teak Chinese daybed, typical of the ones used in opium dens a hundred and fifty years earlier.

I t was the first chance Lillian had to look directly at him, and she noted, as she always did, how he had transformed himself from a physically unremarkable, intellectually gifted boy. When he'd presented himself to her nearly two decades earlier, he had a puppy-dog approach to making friends. It had not been too long, though, before the overeagerness was polished away, buffed down into the smooth holding-back that African-American men wear so well. But still, there was nothing distinct about him. He was of average build. His skin was a brown that could only be described as brown. Perhaps if you really needed to specify, you'd have to say it was the color of a paper bag. The texture of his brown hair—too light, really, practically the same shade as his skin, was simply everyday kinky, with no other descriptive element to classify it. The features of his face were strong, evenly spaced, well designed, and complementary. But back then there was nothing distinctive about Teddy, nothing that could create an impression long enough for someone to even remember having seen him, much less remember what he looked like.

He had known all this about himself, and he set about to ensure that he would not become the kind of man who melted from memory. Hence the bodybuilding, the shoulder-length, dyed-black dreadlocks—always worn loose, never in a ponytail. Teddy calculated that once his ordinary features were contained and given structure by the falling dreads, their perfect symmetry would be highlighted, creating a sum of parts that was way more than the whole. As usual, his math was correct and he morphed into a sensual and very good-looking man, who was at that moment engaged in building a following for himself among Americans of African descent.

He was a man of great confidence, of great intellect, although he was careful to cultivate an aura of accessibility. He excelled in both the sciences and the humanities, but in graduate school he turned to history, to the disappointment of his physics and calculus undergrad professors, who genuinely believed that the only people who took advanced degrees in the humanities were those without the intelligence to do any better.

To a large extent, Lillian agreed with them—not with his choice of history, but that Teddy had aimed low. "All that brain," she would say, "going to waste, working so hard on nothing but your own self." The betterment of his people, she said, was only a nice fringe benefit of what he did; he was out for fame, for pure self-aggrandizement, he was looking for adoration. He had once confessed to her that his ultimate vision was for his own greatness—and then he had amended it. "No, what I mean is, I want to be *known*. I want people—*Black* people—to know my name." That was during one of those soul-searching conversations that can only take place during the college years, requiring a level of sincerity that disappears long before graduation.

"It's all about your ego," she would tell him. "You don't really feel your history." The truth was that Teddy *did* feel his history, but it was his own personal and recent history; it was his parents' unheralded life of isolated dignity, their absolute satisfaction at having been able to take themselves and their son out of crowded city poverty into a stable middle-class community far into suburbia.

It had been a shock for Teddy, at seven years old, to be so suddenly and completely surrounded by people who looked nothing like himself, whose slippery hair grew straight down, whose skin could turn from pink to bright red without warning. They even had a different smell, like wet wool, and they spoke like television actors, with clipped, precise diction. One of the first memories of his new life was of standing in the playground in front of a long line of classmates, who had queued up in order to touch his hair. He remembered how carefully they would place their palms on his oil-sheened and picked-out Afro, pressing down gently and whispering their impressions and reactions: *Wow! Soft! Springy! Cool!* And he could remember the one girl who had poked her finger down to his scalp as she rubbed the finger against her thumb, her face puckered in disdain at the grease she'd found there.

Over time, he learned how to comport himself in this new and sanitized world. He learned to change the rhythm of his speech, to remove the bounce and the lean from his walk. He had to figure out the new rules for forging friendships, which involved complicated and unspoken restrictions and boundaries: his parents had made a sacrifice for the sake of their gifted son's future—they had chosen to live among white people, but this did not mean that they would stoop to living *with* them, there was too much history for that. Teddy noted his parents' example, how they sat alone in their comfortable home in the evenings, forced to make do with each other's company because there was no other company to be had. They never had to explain to him that he could play with the white children all he wanted outside but he could not bring them inside their home, neither could he enter theirs.

It wasn't enough for Teddy to know that his family could not be counted in the statistics of poverty—among those who did not rely on government subsidies of any kind: they went to work; they owned their own home; their sons did not go to jail; their daughters got married before they got pregnant; there were few drug addicts and alcoholics among them—and those who succumbed did so in the privacy of their homes and not on the street disgracing everybody.

As he played outside in the safe and quiet culs-de-sac with the white children, Teddy did not have the right words—cultural deprivation— for what he felt, he only felt a sense of something lacking, he knew a feeling of anonymity that fully resolved itself when his parents would drive for an hour or so to the towering apartment buildings teeming with Black people. And it was here that Teddy would feel comfortable in his skin, during the time spent in the small living rooms, around Thanksgiving dinners or Christmas lunches, or at the brunches after Easter service at restaurants with names like Sylvia's and Copeland's— in all the loudness and laughter, thick bodies pushed together, with old matriarchs holding court, with drunk uncles and strident aunts, and cousins getting public spankings for their smart mouths, and the smell of the kind of food his mother no longer cooked.

He had, in fact, been lying on the grad school essay when he stated that his life's goal was to better the lot of his people—that was secondary. That was just the means by which he would be totally and constantly surrounded by Black people; and it was the means by which they would all know his name.

7

HEALERS, APHRODISIAC POLICY

Simon did not follow his fantasy of going to South and Central America. He went as planned to Roseau, where he sought and found work as a gardener, and the ultimate irony, he would think every morning as he sharpened his cutlass in preparation for his workday, was that he actually liked the priests and the nuns for whom he worked, and the God they had used to wipe his people out was the same God he himself worshiped. One should never blame gods, he believed, for the use to which human beings put them.

Simon found his employers, most of them, to be kind and good-hearted, and as he tended their gardens, as he worked the grounds of the presbytery and the convent, as he fertilized their flowers and pruned their fruit trees, he was grateful to them. Outside the Carib Reserve, as he knew, there would be no work healing any sick, as no right-minded Dominican would patronize him in that capacity, so he was grateful for what the missionaries in Roseau offered him: an education, in addition to employment. They taught him to read books that in turn taught him to think more deeply about his situation and to feel deep pride in his heritage.

And at least these descendants of the original conquerors were not as openly disdainful of the Caribs in the way the Black Dominicans were. He did not hate them, he could not blame them at all, the African transplants, for their attitude. He understood that after they had been slaves for hundreds of years, it would help them, help their broken souls, to in turn have the Caribs to look down upon as depraved, to scorn them and accuse them of eating human flesh, or perhaps it was not an accusation but a historical fact, Simon did not know—he only knew that the Caribs were now more mythologized than real.

Simon did not hate the Black people at all, he only envied them deeply, even wished to some extent that he had been born a Negro, because although Africa was now lost to them, they had survived, and now they had a new place to call their home, even if it was his home.

And then one day, as Simon trimmed some bushes near the window of the convent, he heard a whispered conversation about a woman called Matilda. He had heard her name before, that she was good with bush medicine, a healer like himself. But this was new information, something so dangerous and taboo that the bearer of the rumor had only dared to whisper it to the nun; it had been so dangerous that the nun had thrown back her head to laugh and shout it back at the woman in order to disperse it.

Simon did not wait out the day; he put down his gardening implements and left Roseau by his canoe, going north up the flat Caribbean coast in search of Matilda. This time his fantasies were of a different sort, and he stayed close to land and paddled hard, only heading out to sea out of respect when he approached the village of Massacre, where scores of Caribs were massacred in the 1600s. He preferred the ocean on the other side, but here along the east coast, many of the villages had retained their original Carib names. He enjoyed reciting them as he passed: Mahaut, Layou, Mero, Batali, Coulibistrie—and then he came to the village where people said he should make his inquiries: Colihaut.

It was love at first sight for Simon, who had never seen anything as beautiful as the woman who was his polar opposite, the tall, thick Black woman with the grainy woven hair, and although Matilda first looked down at the small red man with a kind of amused dismissal on her face, his intensity won her over, and she listened to his talk about how, with their combined knowledge of the forest's secrets, they could outheal the few white physicians in Dominica—or in any other island for that matter.

Matilda was not interested in the world beyond her village. But for a while she fell under the spell of the small man with the large vision. For a short time she behaved like any other woman who thought she was in love, following somebody else's dream.

Together they recorded exact proportions, precise combinations. And while they were coming up with ever more powerful compounds, more accurate dosages, they tested their findings on their patients with enormous success. They healed and cured and mended. When they worked together, there was little in the medical realm they were unable to handle. And with Simon's special expertise in narcotics, if they couldn't cure, they would stone their patients out of their minds so their last days on earth were also their happiest.

I ris was born while they were in the throes of an extensive process of documenting, of experimenting and testing, and they barely noticed the newborn, handing her over to the communal child-care system.

They were oblivious to the fact that the women—who should have been at least a little selfish about sharing the milk that belonged to their own infants—went against instinct and would never cut Iris off when she'd had enough, happily allowing her to suckle them empty, and they would then find themselves irritated at the hungry tugging and the wailing of their own ordinary offspring, would all of a sudden develop a dislike for the accustomed feel of their children's woolly hair, scratching their skin as they rooted in vain for their food. Two women had come to blows one day over whose turn it was to feed Iris. Another, about to go dry when her toddler shifted to solids, borrowed other babies, nursing them for seven consecutive hours until her milk came back, all for the pleasure—she did not realize that she was seeking an honor—of feeding Matilda's bright-colored and glowing baby with the soft hair through which, amazingly, her fingers could easily pass.

That would not have been enough to spoil the child, though, because she soon enough would leave the women's care for the company of the other children, who stood prepared to terrorize her back to normalcy, to slap her back down to their level, to drag her back to her place. If all things had been equal, Iris, faced with the prospect of the children's hatred and malice and scorn, would have quickly relinquished the superior position to which the women had assigned her by virtue of her difference, in exchange for the goodwill of her peers. But Iris had been born with the kind of generosity that is called a big heart, and she was also cursed with a desire to please and to be liked—a combination that propelled Iris to pass her privileges to the other children, who, seeing their lot in life improve so drastically thanks to her, proceeded to overlove her much worse than the women had.

M atilda and Simon saw none of this. Their fame was growing; their reputation spreading. People came not only from Roseau and all the villages in Dominica to be seen by them, but they also started coming by boat from all the small islands: St. Vincent, St. Lucia, Antigua, St. Kitts, Anguilla—even from Guadeloupe, known for its own powerful Obeah practitioners, second only to Haiti's voodoo priests and Cuba's Santeria priestesses. Then big-island people came too: from Barbados, even Trinidad.

It was inevitable that these sojourners, having come so far, would want more than to be cured, however. For these descendants of slaves, remnants of the African worldview guided their understanding of what caused sickness and health, misfortune and death. And so it was only a matter of time before those who had been cured looked at that powerful team, African woman and Carib man, and insisted on protection so that their enemies would no longer be able to harm them. They begged the couple to vanquish those who had caused their sickness and bad luck. Letters with money and strands of hair, bits of fingernail, swatches of cloth from worn clothes, started coming from as far north as Jamaica and the Virgin Islands with written requests to kill, protect, maim, avenge. The letters containing the most money generally contained pleas to obtain the everlasting, faithful love of a certain man, a certain woman.

Matilda was used to this. When people from Colihaut would bring her mail to the foot of her mountain, she brushed them away, sent the envelopes back to the post office for return to their senders. But Simon's big plans for a future had hit a wall. For making them healthy, people compensated the couple with food, livestock, raw goods, along with gratitude, but little cash. On the other hand, poor people would readily go into debt to pay for protection against those who sought to bring misfortune upon them, for the promise of wealth, and most of all, for wreaking their vengeance against foes.

Simon was a man with imagination, and he saw the possibilities. Reports began to reach Matilda that he was taking people's money and making impossible promises. There were even rumors that he was now

dealing outright with the devil, and he admitted to her that he, despite
having no capacity to summon any power, be it good or evil, had indeed
made such claims. "Go back to the Carib Reserve," she first ordered,
then pleaded. "Work all the Obeah you want there."

He ignored her. He could work any amount of Obeah by himself,
but he would have no patronage from any clientele but for the four hundred Caribs left; he was only viable attached to Matilda.

The feelings Matilda had for him broke down. The day it was over
between them was the day he violated her sacrosanct policy on the protocol for handling aphrodisiac requests. Matilda's clients had long made
her understand important facts about the nature of human sexuality.
They soundly refuted the scientific allegation that female human beings
are unique among animals by virtue of the absence of alternating periods of rut and sexual dormancy. In their nonscientific words the women
who came to Matilda made it clear that, like any bitch or cow, they too
entered into periods during which they had no desire to mate. Some of
these dormancies were more prolonged than others. They were triggered by a host of physical and psychological causes—most of which
had to do with the responsibility for bearing and raising children without the assistance of men. Matilda was also made to understand clearly
by the men who visited her that male human beings underwent no such
cycle and, like any dog or bull, were ever ready to jump in between an
available pair of open legs. She learned yet another critical fact, which is
that those male animals have the good sense to interfere only with
females in heat, but that men lack the sexual intelligence or instinct to
leave their disinterested women alone.

As a young general practitioner, she learned a devastating lesson in
sexology. One day she had given an extremely old man a very strong
enhancer, and soon thereafter his equally old woman, exhausted and
terrorized by his advances, cutlassed her overprescribed man into pieces.

His death, the old woman's attempt to cover up what she had done, and the resulting social turmoil caused by the scandal scarred Matilda for life, left her hypersensitive to the power of sexual dynamics between couples, and after such an experience she laid down the law: any man seeking bedroom assistance from her would have to come with the woman who would be the beneficiary of the strengthened libido, and that woman would have to verify that she was in favor of the treatment. Those who were uncomfortable with that policy were forced to go to town and try their luck at the "pharmacy" run by the island's only Chinese inhabitants, a couple who claimed to have an herbal remedy, a natural pill, or a special tonic to fix anything. The Chinese people would sell them, no questions asked, as much China Brush as they could afford to buy.

So when the mother of a five-week-old came, baby on her back, and respectfully complained to Matilda that Simon had given her husband "something" and that he was breaking the unwritten rules governing when he could resume relations with her—Matilda packed Simon's belongings along with the bed they had shared, and put them outside their house. He refused to take them away, so she burned them. The night after the bonfire, he took action. When he stood erect, the top of his head did not make it past her shoulder, but by starting off with a length of pipe while she slept, he beat her such that she was confined to a bed for three days.

Afterward, people speculated about how he could have underestimated Matilda to such a degree. He constructed a new bed and continued to live in the house. Matilda quietly, almost meekly, waited for two months, and then she dropped a fingernail's worth of powder into his morning tea. He disappeared after that, and it was generally understood that Matilda had killed him.

8

NO JUSTICE

"I missed the interview last night." Lillian paused, fingering her Adin-kra cuff links, tracing the spirals of each of the four whorls, the wing segments of the butterfly. She considered additional words, discarded them. She would say nothing else because something might slip—as it had a few months earlier, in an e-mail, triggering one of their digital debates—something about the fact that, in the five years since his divorce, he was choosing girlfriends as a part of his professional development, and he moved on and up after a few months, often with over-lap. There was the well-placed media executive, a legislative director, the journalist; usually someone with a little power, or the potential for power, or better yet, access to power. Unless they were his other genre of women, the model types, the jazz singers—some quite famous—and those whose claim to fame was based on nothing but absolute beauty, and even those had a purpose, so photogenic on his arm.

Even before the convictions of the five boys were belatedly thrown out, Teddy's rise had steepened sharply thanks to this legion of girl-friends. His latest and most regular was the television correspondent, Stephanie somebody, a near-celebrity. Lillian had seen him being inter-viewed by her before, and their involvement was obvious, their quid pro quo blatant as he fed her sophisticated preambles to her questions, obvious as he answered in his effortless way. Teddy's women, Lillian thought, poor things, were but rungs on his ladder, his foot always on their necks. "She's doing a series on sentencing disparity, right?"

He shook his head. "That was last week. This was more on the gang-rape overturn."

"What angle?"

"The usual rehashing, you know, why would they have made false confessions—what made me so sure they were innocent—I called your name, by the way."

"I told you not to do that."

"Yeah, but I wrote a little grad-student article for the school paper. You, on the other hand…" Teddy got up and walked back into his library, returning with a book, his most recent, published just over a year earlier. He placed it on the table between them. His face on the cover was serious for the camera. *No Justice*, it proclaimed, speaking of America's criminal justice system as it related to African-Americans. It had largely been Lillian's concept, something they had cooked up together by e-mail when his dean was pressuring him to publish "something a bit more academic than your usual fare"—and they had developed the idea of a compilation: reprints of his articles, transcripts of some of his radio discussions, and a few speeches—most of which she had written in the first place, or at least, she had given him the outline he would transform with his trademark rabble-rousing rhetoric.

She had insisted, overruling him, that he should not lead with the more current fatal police shooting in Harlem; the two-page article on the five convicted boys, she argued, captured more of the issues, and not only should it be included, it should be the opening chapter. She had suggested that the concept embodied in the title of his short, idealistic student effort—*No Justice*—written over ten years earlier, should be the book's overall theme. She helped him write the chapter links, managing to make the same connections in each section. She demonstrated how White America's assumptions and fears about Blacks were institutionalized in laws; she showed how those laws were interpreted, how they were implemented, how history kept being repeated. It was not just the academia his dean had requested; it was much better than that, it was accessible. Lillian's name appeared prominently in the acknowledgments.

"I didn't want to use that article," he said. "I was a student when I wrote it, I thought it wasn't sophisticated enough—"

"It was brilliant, actually, the simplicity of it. The way you laid it out: the confessions had to be false because a, b, c—no jargon, just common sense. You couldn't write something so powerful today, you'd screw it up with your sophistication."

"That's the thing I love about you, Lilly, how I can count on you to keep my feet on the ground." Keeping his feet on the ground was becoming difficult for him these days. He had only been an insignificant one of many who believed—knew—that the boys may have been part of the forty-strong gang of wilding youth that night, but they had not committed that particular crime. His opinion twelve years earlier meant nothing, but when another man confessed in January of the previous year, with DNA to back it up, Teddy's stars had all been lined up. None of the others (the Black talking heads, public intellectuals, activists, politicians, race spokespersons, religious leaders, and so forth) had a new book out that just happened to resurrect that very case. By the time the boys' conviction was overturned at the end of the year, *No Justice* was a bestseller and his face was on national television every night for two weeks, until his publicist advised him against overexposure.

"What your girlfriend should be doing is a series on the culpability of the press in that whole mess," Lillian was saying, "instead of more fluff."

He didn't answer, not taking her bait. He unconsciously looked past the pillars and the palms toward his desk, where her one-line e-mail remained on the screen of his laptop. There were aspects of their relationship that reminded him of an old married couple, the way he tried to keep certain things hidden from her—the fluff—things he felt would not meet her approval. The way he lived, for example, in overt luxury, taking such pleasure from material, costly things. When she admired his plants, complimenting his green thumb, he did not tell her that a local florist came monthly to his house to exchange the fishtail palms and the orchids and the bromeliads in the bathroom for fresh ones.

It had something to do with her self-imposed austerity, the way she was so strict with herself—so different from the kind of women he associated with, women who were enamored of themselves, who pampered themselves guiltlessly.

She often called him vain. *Vanity, thy name is Theodore,* she wrote him a few months earlier in response to his making the cover of *Essence.* This time, her e-mail was as spare: *I need to see you,* it said. *I have a big favor to ask.* That she had not named the favor was significant and made him curious if not concerned; these days their communication was straightforward: *Have you heard of Women for the Promotion of African Concepts of Beauty? Do you think you could mention their campaign the next time you do morning radio? What you need to say is…*

Of course she had a favor to ask: high-level professional favor-trading was what they did, it was now the basis of their relationship and had been for many years. He might need her to read a ten-page document and e-mail him a summary and a position in half an hour. She invariably asked him to support a cause. They had their system. Her volume of requests was higher than his, but Teddy made up in magnitude for the relative infrequency of the favors he needed. Some, like his book, went well beyond their simple quid pro quo formula. But generally, they were the kind of thing that could be easily spelled out in an electronic note, easily answered in a few keystrokes. *No problem* would always be the answer to whatever she requested, because in the end he was happy to do what she needed. It was like a secret language they shared, their ordinary e-mails, it was like their code for what they might have had if he had not known exactly the kind of woman he wanted.

"So, Lillian." He leaned toward her and used both hands to take off her shades before settling back in the armchair and putting his feet on the opium table. She usually visited him at his office when her favors needed face time; unaccustomed to one-on-ones with her in his home, he opted for small talk. "Tell me about your love life these days." It was a joke. His sex life, indirectly, was a standing topic of discussion, one of the many ways she was able to score political points against him, but any reference to hers was and always had been strictly out of bounds. Lillian never spoke about her lovers, and anyway he knew that she was too busy dealing with whatever it was that ate her up to do more than fall passingly in love with a bleeding heart with a cause (actually she fell in love with the cause, the man would just happen to be attached to it). And Lillian would always pick one who lived far enough away to necessitate a long-distance relationship destined to be unsustainable for more than a few months.

He let his thoughts follow an idle path to a recurring theme: Was she still a virgin? Impossible, not at her age. They were born the same year, although he was six months older, which made her almost thirty-seven. In college she had certainly behaved like one, but there had been many a wishful story circulating about what she was like in bed. Yet the colorful descriptions never rang true to the kind of girl he knew her to be, and he had known her very well. His fraternity brothers were in the business of ruining reputations back then, although in the context of back then, putting out the word that a girl was a freak mostly served to elevate her status. Neither option, he decided, was possible. She was just one of those private women, a throwback to an era when women were socialized differently. It was one of the many places where her cultural difference was tangible, this protectiveness with her sexuality, which was why he had never simply asked her outright.

He repeated his question. "Your love life?"

"Same old, you know. Nothing out there. All the good men are gay."

"What happened to the brother from Atlanta?"

"You said it. Atlanta."

"Ever visit?"

"No."

Teddy was suppressing a smile as he remembered how his nearly twenty-year-old relationship with Lillian had been forced down the platonic path following her reaction to his initial attempt to get some when he first met her. He was eighteen. One hand straight to the breasts and the other inside the panties had been his standard reaction to finding himself alone with any girl. She had bitten one of his hands and clawed the other. The memory came back with a hard jolt, how the body of the silent West Indian with the gold eyes and the dark shades sent every Black man on campus deep into fantasies that involved resounding hard slaps. There had been a flock of brothers that seemed to follow her around, brothers who did not stand a chance but who nevertheless made up and circulated fantastical stories of how hot she was in their beds.

She had changed little since then, the same body the college boys used to call lush, pronouncing it with an overemphasis that turned the word into something obscene. The same face, with the large lips, the dominant nose, and those eyes, their color matching her skin. No makeup, then or now, but her bare face lacked the tired look that women past a certain age acquired without the foundation, the concealer, the eyeliner, the highlighter—Lillian's features were so pronounced, so structured, that they produced their own contouring and shadowing, they created their own emphases. She still had the same expression, too, the voluptuous face held impassively, nothing given away. The chin slightly raised, tilting her face up and back so she could keep her eyelids lowered, the lashes covering what the lids did not, so that she could see without, it would appear, being seen.

It was this, he thought, that was so striking about her when they'd first met: how she seemed to hold herself in a kind of isolation. It was this appearance of complete inaccessibility that had made her so appealing to potential suitors, himself included—himself most of all. "Think she too damn good-looking to speak to somebody," the Deltas and the AKAs and even the Caribbean Student Organization sisters used to say about her, and it was something of which he had been vaguely proud, that she spoke to him, that he had been among her few friends, even though he knew it wasn't that she had picked him. She had ignored him, as she ignored everyone else. It was not a matter of a beautiful woman's arrogance—looks did not feature in Lillian's world. It was that she had no understanding of the social exchanges involved in forging friendships, she'd somehow missed out on the basics of socialization, and he understood that.

He ended up becoming one of Lillian's few friends because, for some reason he had never sought to analyze, he had kept going past her apparent rebuffs, he had refused to give up.

9

PROTECTION

Lillian was raised in complete ignorance of the details surrounding her identity. Her stepmother, Icilma, saw to that, although everyone else over the age of five or six knew the full details, thanks to all the songs.

"Matilda the Great," Lillian's grandmother was called in Dominica, among other things, a name coined by one of the *chantuelles* who "sang on her." That was among the first set of songs, and there were many more to follow, not only about her but also about Iris, her daughter. They continued to inspire *chanté mas* songs long after they were both dead, some of which became famous throughout the Caribbean: rare folk classics sung spontaneously word for word even by generations who had not yet been born when the events that made them infamous took place and who had no understanding of the true meaning of the lyrics.

A schoolteacher, Icilma naturally used the school system to protect Lillian. She carefully considered which school her stepdaughter would attend, and rejected the government schools immediately, knowing from firsthand experience that children of the lower classes, even the very young ones, would be unable to resist the joy of bringing down a light-skinned child whose parents were said to have money (although all they had, really, was land, and Icilma's salary). That left the two Catholic schools.

In those days, before the advent of a certain Jamaican-born bishop who would take on the task of decolonizing the Catholic Church and schools in the small islands under his jurisdiction, there was a Catholic school for the poor and another for those who were not. The difference was a simple matter of wealth and class: the ability or inability to pay school fees, and the attendant prestige, or lack thereof. Icilma could well have managed to pay for Lillian to attend The Convent School, but she opted for the free Holy Family Day School instead. The children of poor Catholics, she knew, were ruled with an iron fist by the mother superior of the Sisters of the Holy Virgin, a literal fist which regularly landed across the jaws of children who forgot their place. The poor Catholic children, severely schooled in submission, would never disobey an order from a nun.

Icilma first presented herself to the mother superior, who fully supported and encouraged her plan. One month before Lillian was to have started kindergarten, Icilma began her legendary visits to the school's parents. She sat formally in the tiny salons of the women, women who lived in poverty without the men whose offspring kept them there. Icilma always noted that their poverty never ran so deep as to prevent them from beautifying their surroundings: white eyelet lace curtains at the windows, doilies crocheted by hand on the table, beaded strips of cloth taking the place of doors between the rooms, small, dome-shaped, water-filled plastic ornaments which, when shaken, would rain tiny specks of snow upon small-scale models of Big Ben or the Statue of Liberty, sent no doubt by relatives who lived in cold places. And in the most central place on their largest wall, without any other object to distract, would be the framed picture of the Sacred Heart of Jesus, serene-faced and indicating the crown of thorns around his exposed and bleeding heart.

The women listened carefully, faces sad and serious, crossed themselves numerous times while she spoke, and promised Icilma that Lillian would never hear the story from their children, that their children would never sing any of the songs to Lillian. It was a ritual that would continue each August for years, until Icilma realized that her request had become institutionalized. In the years to follow, mothers who sent their children to Holy Family already knew what to tell their children without her instructions.

As a result of this intervention, there was not a single child at Holy Family School brave enough to play with Lillian. She walked through the playground seemingly protected from the swarm of helter-skelter colliding children by some kind of reverse magnetism, an invisible field that repelled contact and surrounded her with a circle of untouchability. Icilma's heart would collapse in her chest at the sight of the left-alone child, and she would wade into the playground to push Lillian into one or another group of playmates. But she couldn't have it both ways. Not only did the children have their instructions to sing her no song, but knowing what they knew, they were also very afraid of her.

Lillian, by the time she had enough awareness to realize that she was not a part of the playground culture, was so used to her solitary status that at first, as a very small child, she assumed it to be normal. Later on, after she knew it was not, she learned that it was less painful to just let go of any hope for the privilege of friendship.

10

FIRST COMMUNION

Although the details were not provided until much later, if Lillian were asked to identify one defining moment in her childhood when her sense that she was somehow untouchable was crystallized into fact, when she knew that her isolation was not happenstance, she would have said that it happened on the day of her First Communion.

Preparations had begun many months before, although the dried fruit for the First Communion cake had been soaking in wine for an entire year. All the paraphernalia had been shopped for in New York by the newly immigrated Auntie Margaret, put into a barrel, and shipped home well in advance. White everything. Patent leather shoes, sheer stockings, gloves, white pearlized rosary. Prayer book with white leatherette cover embossed with a gold cross. But the dress Margaret selected was rejected by Icilma as too simple, the veil as too short, and both of obviously synthetic fabric.

She traveled to Trinidad to purchase silk and the lace and the voile herself, and designed another dress, bridal in scope and proportion. Every evening for two weeks, she went to the home of the seamstress to supervise and assist with the lace insets and the hundreds of tiny pearls sewn by hand to the bodice. The skirt's three tiers of lace-edged flounces stopped an inch or two above floor length, and the veil, falling from a wreath of silk roses, came down past Lillian's waist.

At that time, in the early 1970s, the demystification of Catholicism dictated by Vatican II a few years earlier had not yet trickled down to Dominica, where the people had great appreciation for the rituals and customs from which the Church was attempting to distance itself. First Communion celebrations still carried their full, pre–Vatican II weight, all the pomp and circumstance, and preparation for the event was no small matter.

The cooking for the party always started days in advance, with extra maids and cooks borrowed from friends for the occasion. The homes of the celebrants would be prepared for their most significant party yet, with milk punch and rum punch mixed up and chilled, abundant quantities of sherry, whiskey, and rum, the crates of bottled soft drinks and soda water piled behind the homemade bars, the bartenders hired and uniformed. There would be records playing, there would be dancing.

There would be gifts. From friends and protégés of the lower ranks—market women and maids and agricultural laborers, past and present—would come the prayer books, the children's Bibles, and the painstakingly signed cards, the outside of which would be adorned with embossed hosts emerging from gilded chalices, the inside lettered with long verses of religious rhyme. From family friends and relatives there would be gold, enough eighteen-karat to carry a girl child through to her twenty-first birthday—crucifixes, crosses, medals of patron saints, of the Blessed Virgin; chains, bracelets, and earrings of every style, with the orchid design being the favorite. Perhaps even a dress watch to put up for when the child learned to tell time. There would be cash, too, in brand-new crisp bills smelling of air-conditioned banks, enough to give a solid boost to the obligatory savings account, opened seven years earlier with the money from the baptism.

And then the Sunday morning would finally arrive, and the children would all stand lined up outside the cathedral at the bottom of the steps. They would be nervous, but still ready for what was ahead, because there had been such preparation: the correct way to walk slowly in procession up the cathedral steps, one little veiled girl matched with one little white-suited boy, like brides and grooms, like a mass wedding, the tiny ones in the front drawing the sighs and the tears and the camera clicks, the unfortunate tall ones straggling, largely ignored except by their own parents, in the back. In the long trek up the center aisle in the semilight, the high ceiling was far enough away for it to resemble heaven to the seven-year olds, most of whom would not really understand the concept of the miraculously transformed body of Christ, but who still understood that this was a Day of Days, that this was what they called Religion, something that was not to be deciphered, but like Santa Claus, and the rat that had taken their first-fallen tooth, leaving money in its place, it was something not far from magic, it was miracle.

My Miracle Morning, is how Lillian had been thinking about the day she would receive her First Communion. When it came, she was ready. At the final rehearsal in church the previous day, unconsecrated communion wafers had even been used, so that all the children could practice with the bland stickiness as their saliva turned it into thin paste. They had been disappointed, expecting the texture to be crunchy, or at least crumbly, expecting the taste to be one of strong peppermint, so closely did the blinding white host resemble Extra Strong, eaten out of common paper bags along with pear drops and sugarplums, bought by the children from old ladies on the sidewalks of Roseau pushing trays on top of abandoned baby prams.

Forbidden to touch the body of Christ with their teeth, and understanding this concept of absolute sacredness, if not the overwhelming rest of it all, they learned at that last rehearsal how to work the flats of their tongues against the roofs of their mouths, how to discreetly stab at the stuck pieces with the tip of a stiffened tongue, how to gather their spittle and shoot it in sharp jets into the difficult spaces where gum and teeth met to form pockets where the most stubborn morsels would collect. Lillian mastered that, the tricky part, and did not think much about the first part, the part where the priest would transfer the host to her waiting tongue.

"The Body of Christ," the priest would say. "Amen" would be the answer, and they would shut their eyes tight, extend their tongues as far as they would go, and wait. Truly easy, this part, simplicity itself, because the wet tongues with their suction-cup taste buds were like flytraps for the host. One touch and the spittle would start an immediate meltdown, the precious cargo safely glued, held so fast that not even a chance scrape of an overlong new front tooth would dislodge it on its way to purify the souls of the little children.

L illian was ready. She had taken her first confession seriously, and even before she learned the words of the Act of Contrition, in which all the children whispered to God that they had sinned and deserved hell, she had determined to make doubly sure that she was worthy. After she had come up almost empty-handed from her examination of conscience through contemplation of the Ten Commandments, she invented a long list of sins for the occasion. She had not killed, stolen, coveted her neighbor's wife or his goods, neither had she disrespected her parents. She had not considered that there could be any other god but the one Icilma taught her to worship, although at times there did seem to be three of them. But because the sixth commandment remained unexplained, she began her confession by telling the priest that she had committed adultery. Although he assured her that she had not, she was undeterred, and having concluded that there was no commandment against bearing false witness against her own self, she confessed to lying, to stealing, to cheating, to fighting, and to entertaining bad thoughts in general, and, dissatisfied with the puny penance the priest gave, walked around for days chanting continuous decades of the rosary.

She was taking no chances with what she knew would be the end of her exile. She could tell that there would be a miracle in it for her, too, quite apart from the body and the blood. She knew this from Icilma's state of euphoria, from the way she touched the large crucifix that hung around Lillian's neck down to the place where she imagined her soul resided, the spot on her chest in between what would later grow into breasts. Lillian understood that while she was only protected externally by something powerful, soon she would have the protection where it really counted, on the inside, and she believed that whatever prevented people from looking her in the eye, whatever was tormenting her father and making Icilma love her with such fierceness, it would all be over.

On the morning of her First Communion, she stood outside the cathedral, lined up with the other children, sweating in her stockings and gloves, waiting for her miracle.

After the last-minute confusion outside the cathedral—the picture-taking, the final parental kissing and well-wishing, the wiping of lipstick from the children's cheeks—the adults made their final rush up the steps into the cathedral. The children clasped their gloved, rosary-draped hands at the level of their chins, prayer book in between, and on signal the procession began. As she began to walk slowly, Lillian focused on the back of her father disappearing into the dark church, and she registered a number of firsts: the first time she'd seen him in a suit, the first time she'd seen him near a church, the first time he'd ever kissed her, the first time she'd seen him hold Icilma's hand. It was also the last day he would sleep in the same house as his wife and child.

It started out well, without warning, and when Lillian thought back on it, she could only remember one other thing, when the smell of the incense, swinging on its metal chain ceaselessly toward the children, its black smoke ominously pouring out of the thurible, triggered a nausea that would have made any other child vomit. But she would not allow it, she swallowed it back, clamped her throat shut, and made the feeling go away by the force of her will.

She remembered little else of the mass until consecration, the best part, began. The part where she would participate in the miracle, the moment at which, with the ringing of a bell, a thing that looked like an Extra Strong would become the flesh of her God turned human. Not the representation of flesh. Flesh, and blood, too. Lillian was the only child that morning who understood what it was all about, and who went to it with any expectation.

And then, she arrived at her moment. She closed her eyes, extended her tongue.

What she heard first was a series of tight, incomplete sounds. Hissings, breaths drawn in too fast and then held; measured exhales that took too long. A cry, cut short, and then several other aborted exclamations. Someone began a whispered recitation of the Hail Mary. It was not the droning sound, the dull incantation, of a supplicant who has settled in for the long haul of a rosary—but harsh and fast, an urgent appeal. Her eyes were still closed, but she knew that these sounds came from her immediate surroundings, because she could hear them over the singing of the choir. And then the organ faltered, the singing died out, and there was silence. She opened her eyes. The priest was looking down at the floor, where the host lay at his feet.

The Belgian-accented voice of a nun spoke at her ear. "Put your tongue back inside your head," and she was led back to her pew to kneel with the other children. She might not at first have understood the abomination of God's flesh falling on a dirty floor, so defiled that it could no longer be touched but now had to be burned where it had fallen, but she saw the looks in the eyes of the adults around her, looks that should have been angry but were instead afraid. She saw the children in her pew scoot away, raising and lowering their thighs in tiny increments along the wood of the bench, sliding away, leaving her surrounded by space.

Lillian understood that for some yet unknown reason, she was so polluted that the body of Christ himself would not dare enter into hers.

On the day of her First Holy Communion, she did not receive her miracle, but she certainly saw the signs. At her party, Icilma's red eyes, her father's absence. The uneaten food thrown away. The subdued way the few guests collected and talked, standing in bunches, the way they touched Icilma's arm, as if offering condolences. People making the sign of the cross with precision, not the careless shoo-fly way they did before a meal or when passing a church, but with the deliberate motion they used in the vicinity of a cemetery.

11

MARY-ALICE

Lillian's mother, Iris, was too young when Simon left to have realized the existence of a father, much less to have missed him. She continued to be raised by the adoring villagers to understand that she was special, so special that the Council persuaded Matilda to send her to town to school.

At fourteen years of age, Iris found herself at precisely the wrong moment in history: 1945, immediately postwar. A few years earlier, and the notion of sending one of their daughters away to live among strangers would have been inconceivable. Born several years later, and a secondary school would have been built close enough for her to walk to her education—a walk of more than an hour, but she would have climbed back up to her village to sleep at night. She would have continued to believe in her beauty, she would have turned down most of her suitors and borne children only for the most coveted man: the one with the strongest arms, the one who showed the greatest courage and the deepest compassion. At a different moment in history, she would never have known that she was poor, or that she was Black, or that she was anything less than royalty.

Had Iris stayed in place, she might have had the chance to realize her father's vision before the idea of glory for his people became corrupted. She might have been the one to take the knowledge so carefully transcribed by Matilda and Simon, to give it greater access to other worlds.

Had Iris been properly grounded by those tasked with her upbringing, she might have had a chance to fit properly into the slot for which she was made. But they had failed her. They filled her head with a sense of her own importance, warped her mind by making her aware of the difference between her looks and theirs, between the color of her skin and theirs. Her spirit was doomed to be broken by her mistaken belief that she could bestow a smile upon someone and, by virtue of that, be granted anything she so desired.

The arguments of the Council were strong and they prevailed. In the aftermath of the war, following six years of food shortages and of general stagnation, everything was beginning to boom. Full independence for Dominica and the other small islands was still more than thirty years away, but the nascent local political class was finding a footing, along with a vocal new elite—Dominica's first local doctors and lawyers had begun to replace the British. The clamor for development was strong. Demands for roads to connect the island were loudest of all. Telephones. Electricity in remote corners. Words like *progress, education, anticolonialism, trade unions*—such words were beginning to circulate and resound, even to the outer reaches.

The Council had the vision to see that their isolation from the rest of the island could not last much longer; that their ways would have to shift and adjust. More and more of their young people were showing signs of restlessness, of wanting to be part of a bigger world.

The Council eventually convinced Matilda, and Iris went to Roseau for an education, but it was not Matilda who took her daughter to town.

She would have been instantly recognized, even by those who had never waited for her at the bottom of her mountain, never set eyes on her, who only knew that she was "very black and very tall." Roseau people would be able to identify her not by her color or her height but by her walk: haughty, with her head back, as if she did not come from slaves. Matilda would have caused too much commotion and ruined Iris's chance to be boarded with a respectable family.

Regina was selected for the task because she was one of the few who went to Roseau on a regular basis to supply the nuns with fowl. "She is a very bright girl, Mother," said Regina, who knew the right way to address the old shriveled white woman who looked like nobody's mother at all, not even like a human being, but rather like a specter, something that was already dead to this world. Regina lied: "She can read and write already, Mother, just some extra lessons and she will catch up."

All the people in that dark, cool house were strange, stern beings, ostensibly female, with faces but no heads, hands but no bodies; who did not walk but who glided around their mysterious house full of statues in grottoes and candles and repetitive chanting whispers that never seemed to end; members of a fearsome women's secret society with access to an all-powerful three-pronged God and a seemingly unlimited number of influential spirits, the saints. It was called the convent, the same name given to the school they ran. Regina kept her courage up. "We want her to have a Catholic education." She had practiced the words carefully, and she said them with feeling, knowing that the success of the mission depended on her capacity to deceive. And then she remembered to add the obligatory acknowledgment of human frailty and lack of control over life: "God willing, Mother."

The request was a common one, to help a bastard country child find a family with whom she would lodge and attend school in exchange for housekeeping and child care, and the convent provided the service. They felt an obligation to assist in this way, because few if any of the children from the country were legitimate, and their strict order was still holding fast to their rule that children from illegitimate families could only attend the Convent School if they were removed from the corrupting influence of their mothers and lodged in a family with married parents.

The mother superior, a Belgian who had taken the name of Elizabeth, had no choice but to agree to keep Iris until the arrangement was made, but she wished she could have given Regina the advice she was obliged to swallow. Elizabeth's mission in the small island, cemented by her vow of obedience, was clearly defined: to improve the lot of the Catholic population through education. But had she not been bound by her vows, she would have told Regina to take Iris back as fast as possible and allow her to continue her uneducated life among her own kind.

She looked at Iris's glowing skin, the pliability of her adolescent limbs, the remarkable features of her face. And Elizabeth knew that, as a boarder in any of the elite homes that took in such children, Iris would be pregnant within a few months—either by the husband of the household or by a son.

It was something that Elizabeth and the sisters of her convent struggled with spiritually, and which had often been discussed in the night when the habits and wimples were off, when they were women among women and not nuns among the flock, when they sat passing their fingers through their short hair over the evening's final cup of tea. She had seen it first, although in a more extreme form, when she was stationed in Haiti, where such children were called *restavèk* and were accorded a status little different from that of a slave. In Roseau, they enjoyed better conditions than in Port-au-Prince, and often were able to secure homes in which they assisted the mistress of the house with her workload in a manner that was fair and manageable. But in many cases, it was not. And Iris was far too beautiful to escape the appetite of the men—or the expectation of the women, seeking respite from that most tedious and taxing of their household duties.

Over the night's last tea, the nuns would speak frankly among themselves, and the night Iris came to the convent they raised the issue of the school's boarders again. No one would have believed that those women with their vows of celibacy and their existential aura could analyze the issue in such worldly and practical terms. That night, the discussion was hot.

"They've been doing it since slavery." Sister Mary-Alice was not a member of the same order as the other teaching nuns. She was from Texas, responsible for social welfare, a new concept in the convent, and was on loan, so to speak, from an American order. Her primary responsibility was to lower the illegitimate birth rate among the Catholic population through the propagation of the teachings of the Church on the subject, a responsibility she ignored. She believed they were in much greater need of prenatal care than of catechism, and so her focus was on raising money for maternity clinics in the more remote villages. "It's a way out of poverty for the servants," Mary-Alice explained. "They are not fools. A bastard son of a rich man will help his whole family."

"Sister!" her mother superior reprimanded her. "Surely you're not suggesting that the child upstairs will plot and scheme to bed her mistress's husband?"

"Mother, Iris is a child." Mary-Alice knew the mother superior and the older Belgian nuns took quick offense at her frank American way. She always spoke cautiously, hoping that the careful tone would imply deference. "I'm talking about something general that women here do. I'm saying that many of these women make conscious decisions about their children's fathers. They do it to give their children a chance at a better life. But Iris is a child. That would be something else. Child abuse." She checked the softness of her delivery. "Perhaps it's not the best idea to board these young girls. What about if we ran a kind of boarding school for the country girls?"

Elizabeth's voice was cold. "We thought of that already, of course. We couldn't raise the money."

Mary-Alice knew that she could get the money in a heartbeat from any one of her father's Texan friends or business associates. Pure of body and of mind, she nonetheless instinctively believed that the end—God's work—justified any means. But she would have to wait until she was sent on home leave, which was six months away. Then she would present herself to her prospective funders. The habit she was obliged to wear would hide almost everything, but she was only twenty-one years old, and she had her lips and her eyes to work with; and her hands. She would show up at the office of the aging oil-money men, and she would place her chair at the side of their desks so that there was only very little space between them. In a chaste voice that also conveyed modest hesitance, she would then provide the details of illicit sexual activity with pubescent girls, and just as they lost the fight to regulate their breathing, she would reach over into their laps to cover their large hands with hers, pressing down while she looked earnestly into their eyes and asked them to contribute to the boarding school as generously as they could spare. The checks would be huge.

But it would take years for the dormitories to be built, and in the meantime there was a child upstairs who was about to become somebody's sexual slave. "Well, Mother Elizabeth, what about placing her with a spinster? Or a widow?"

Elizabeth did not care for the brash young American social worker, and tonight she liked her even less. "My child, be assured that we have thought of these options long before you came to us. Spinsters and widows don't have children, not small ones anyway, so the exchange of labor for lodging doesn't work. Spinsters and widows are old women who need money from a paying boarder. Iris's people don't have cash."

But Mary-Alice had still another idea. There was one community in Roseau that might offer Iris refuge. When she'd first arrived in Dominica, she had been startled to find a small but thriving band of Arabs in the middle of the Caribbean. She saw them first at mass, which they attended regularly, some even on a daily basis. She knew so little of the Middle East, envisioning it only in terms of being far away, picturing a scene from a cut-rate movie of sheeted Muslims on camels waging jihads. She could not imagine how this bunch ended up so far away from home, seemingly at ease in a Catholic church. "Maronite Christians," another sister whispered to her one day, noticing her interest. "From Lebanon." And following Mary-Alice's blank expression, "You *do* know of Lebanon's Christian history, yes?"

Mary-Alice kept studying them from a distance, fascinated by the way they held themselves away from the rest of the Dominicans. Just from watching their body language in church, she concluded that the Lebanese did not so much look down on the others as they only had eyes for one another. Everyone else, they looked straight through. More precisely, they looked beyond them. They walked into church, sat, stood, knelt, recited prayers, looked up at the body of Christ when the communion bell rang, and bowed their heads when the ringing stopped; they lined up for communion and received the body of Christ on their knees, walked back to their pews to kneel some more—all these things they did as if there were no other people in the church but themselves.

At first she did not see them anywhere else: not in the market buying food, not strolling the streets, not airing their babies in the botanical gardens, not taking riverbaths at the popular pools. Then one day she happened to glance into one of the dark dry-goods shops that lined the main street of town. And there they were, populating each and every shop. Standing behind their counters in front of bolts of cloth, the husbands and the wives and the sons and daughters. Speaking Arabic among themselves and broken English and French Creole to their customers. Here, in their dusty shops, measuring out cloth and taking money, they did not look through anybody.

Mary-Alice befriended some of the old women in order to learn their story. She questioned them while the overweight women with their heavy gray hair and intimidating eyebrows pounded kibbeh with heavy wooden pestles. Dragged the tens of thousands of miles from Lebanon to Dominica, the knee-high marble mortars they used to mix the bulgur wheat with the ground meat weighed as much as they did, which was saying a lot: they ate continuously, without limits. Mary-Alice interrogated them: Had they left because of religious persecution? They didn't understand the term. What led them to the Caribbean? Why not somewhere else? They laughed and waved their hands vaguely and said that Lebanese traveled all over the world. The members of the first generation did not speak enough English to explain, the conditions under which they left Lebanon and arrived in the Caribbean. They kept inviting her back, though, despite their inability to provide Mary-Alice with the answers she sought, happy to have the company of the white missionary from America. They fed her so much raw kibbeh, baked kibbeh, fried kibbeh, tabbouleh, stuffed grape leaves, *lamni,* and *shish barak* that the priest at her weekly confession suggested she should add the deadly sin of gluttony to the short list of wrongdoings she habitually confessed.

She gained weight but no information. She was only able to garner that they were all from the same village in Lebanon and were for the most part all closely related. She also learned that they had not only settled in Dominica, but in every other island in the Caribbean, starting with the French colonies of Guadeloupe and Martinique. But that was as far as her inquiries with the old people got her.

The second-generation Dominican-Lebanese spoke bad Arabic and excellent English, but they yielded even less information. They knew a few anecdotes about their parents being poor, had heard stories about oppression and hard times at the hands of Muslim officials of the Ottoman Empire. Their parents made reference to mountains and cedar trees and olive farming, to their long journey by ship via France, and inevitably they would describe how their parents started out with not so much as a roof to sleep under. And to her questions about their clannishness, their separation from the rest of society, they looked at her in astonishment, and they regaled her with words:

"But what else do people do?"

"Our parents come here, strangers. Outsiders. How else to make it except stick together, help each other, keep our own customs?"

"People must give up their ways because they're in a new place? But no! The more reason to keep them."

Some of the answers she got were not quite connected to her questions, and they told her more than she was expecting to hear:

"And you think those people wishing us well? We used to sleep on their dirt floors when night fall on us in the country, but now look what happen. Their floors—still dirt. Our houses have two stories."

"We came with nothing. We walk across ravines and rivers and we sell out of a suitcase on our heads and we work hard and look at how we prospering."

Mary-Alice felt sorry for them. They were oppressed people who had transplanted themselves among other oppressed people, but oppression has its own hierarchy. Those who had known enslavement would not forgive the Lebanese for being spared that kind of heritage. Mary-Alice could see that the blatant prosperity of these strangers, whose culture dictated that they would set themselves apart, did not bode well for them. One day soon to come, poor people would need a target, a burnable reason for their misery, something made of wood to catch fire and be reduced to ash. She would look at their street of shops above which they lived, and the words *sitting ducks* always came to mind.

In the end, this second generation didn't know or care about anything to do with the why and how of their parents' immigration. Their passion was consolidating and maintaining their new and vastly improved economic conditions in their new homeland, appreciating their new status at the top of the social food chain, and addressing the difficult question of finding Lebanese husbands and wives. Their fathers, those who had not come with a spouse, had traveled all the way back to Lebanon to find and bring back their true loves, all of whom started out in arranged marriages with dowries. But for their local-born offspring, a trip back to Lebanon had zero appeal. Lebanon was forgotten history. So this Caribbean-born set chose strictly from the slim pickings around them, often marrying their first and second cousins, as their foreparents had done before in Lebanon.

This closed culture that shut out everyone else was what Mary-Alice was hoping would save Iris: the fact that they only mated among themselves, for life.

The following day, without telling her mother superior, she went to the store of one of the more successful families and climbed the back stairs to their home. She spent the morning convincing Amelia Fadoul that she needed Iris to help her with her toddlers. Amelia really did not need her, served as she was by the standard army of local maids, nannies, cooks, washerwomen, ironing women, messengers, and man

Fridays, but it was a request from a woman of God, and Amelia had no choice but to agree.

Iris began her life in town as a schoolgirl boarder-servant in the Fadoul household. There, as Mary-Alice hoped, she was left alone by the menfolk and treated well by the women, for the Lebanese might have ignored the population at large, but their servants—provided they were loyal—were given honorary Lebanese status and were no different from family.

Mary-Alice turned her attention back to the unmarried pregnant country girls and the question of their prenatal care, full of self-congratulatory prayers of thanks for the deliverance of Iris. She had completely underestimated the power of lust or, as the same thing is often manifested, of love.

12

PENANCE

Teddy could see that she was anxious, hear it in her voice as she asked about the death penalty case he was following. "Doubt it," he said. His reminiscing about their college years was distracting, he was not engaging well and their conversation was off-kilter. "We probably won't get a stay. Come on, it's Texas for God's sake."

She was talking too quickly, rattling off the names of organizations that might be willing to join the last-ditch effort to save another Black man from the chair. She had good contacts with a network of grassroots Catholic groups, and she was urging him to pull them in on his death penalty work. She had suggested it before, but he could not, politically; working with the Catholics would get tricky when it came to just about anything else.

She had not stopped playing with her cuff links since she sat down, and his eyes were drawn to the nervous way her fingers circled the gold. He recognized them, the Adinkra cuff links that should have been his, but he had never begrudged her the withheld gift; it was one of her few indulgences. Lillian lived as if she were caught in a perpetual Lenten season, doing a lifetime of penance, as if trying to pay for a sin, in that Catholic way of hers.

He had only recently come to understand the extent of this feature of her life when, after the income from his book began to complicate her accounting, she'd used his accountant to file her taxes. "Not a penny saved," the accountant, Teddy's close friend, reported back. "No investments. Wires some to an account in Dominica, her mother, I think. Gives away every cent after food and rent. Starving children, Red Cross, church charities, homeless shelters, name it." After his initial surprise, Teddy saw that it made sense. It was a reflection of that sense of sacrifice in everything she did.

S he was still going on about Catholics being good on the death penalty. This was an example of her personality, how strange she could be. Faith, he believed, was what people had been taught by their parents or whoever was responsible for passing down fairy tales. Despite his cultural adherence to Jesus—Black people would never listen to somebody who did not claim to have a personal relationship with him—it was hard for Teddy to understand when educated people truly had no doubt. At first he was sure that Lillian was an atheist. She had an obvious aversion to churches, not even attending church weddings. But later, in grad school, when the philosophical discussions turned around religion, it became clear that she was not even agnostic—she had refused any debate: God is a given, was all she would say. She seemed willing to leave it at the level of blind faith.

She was still speaking, now having segued into liberation theology in Latin America—apparently trying to prove that the Church was not always reactionary. It was one of their running debates, but he was not in the mood for that, nodding occasionally while he gave himself over to an idle analysis of what she was wearing. Like her face, her style had not changed with time: completely classic. But then this accidental stylishness was offset by her refusal to capitalize on her body. Her clothes had always been *modest*. Modesty seemed somehow perfectly applicable to Lillian's persona, a persona that had drawn him in and kept them together even though, notwithstanding his clumsy teenage grope that one time, he knew that their relationship could never have been one of romance: the women he had pursued with something more in mind needed a pedigree other than what an immigrant could offer, and later on he had married true to type. Some might have said that he was color-struck, but color had nothing to do with it, it was all about where he had come from and where he wanted to go—it had been all about the climb.

13

TO HAVE AND TO HOLD, OR SLAVERY

Had Iris not been artificially inserted into the Lebanese community, where their sudden richesse had given rise to the indulging of their children—including her—as part of their new way of life; had she not been sent to the Convent School with their children, where her sense of elevated status, formed since infancy at the breasts of vying women, was given further shape and form; had she not sat with them at mass on Sundays, where she was taught how to hold herself above the rest, she might still have had a chance to be put in her place, to understand what was available to her and to know what was beyond her reach. She might have understood the rules that applied to love in a society that was still too near the time when one group of people owned another. When she caught the eye of John Baptiste escorting his mother to a wedding, she might have looked away, she might not have smiled at him.

She did not usually go to see weddings, that Thursday afternoon ritual of schoolchildren, old women, and the idle. She didn't care much for the pushing and shoving and the shouting outside the cathedral. She seldom got to see much. A schoolgirl like herself, barely into her teenage years, would almost never be allowed any of the coveted places at the front of the throng. Those were reserved for the professional wedding-watchers, self-appointed to keep up a running commentary on the apparel, hairstyle, and demeanor of the invited guests, the wedding party, and the bride, boisterously leading the laughter and mockery of the unfortunate ones who did not meet the high standards of the crowd.

She was a naturally kindly child who did not like to see the way the low would use the only thing they had to strike down the high. There was one woman in particular, a beautiful dark-skinned woman from a big island, popular in her circle, whom poor people despised for marrying too rich for her color. Her wedding clothes and hats were made according to the unfamiliar American haute couture standards of *Vogue,* and she always fared particularly badly when she stepped out of her car and prepared for the walk up the cathedral steps. The derision would increase in volume and intensity, the reactions turned overdramatic as the frontliners would hold on to each other for support as they screeched their laughter, raising their index fingers to point at the asymmetrical hem that should have been one length, the drape in the back that should have been in the front, the too-high turban, the one-shouldered bodice—that one, the dress with the missing sleeve, had put people prostrate on the street, rolling on mango skin and banana peel, screaming and squeezing their crotches as they nonetheless peed on themselves, the hot urine seeping through the spaces between their fingers, darkening the cotton of their skirts. And although the woman never lost her dignified carriage, never dropped her shoulders or lowered her head and always kept the same smile on her face as she mounted the steps with her husband's hand touching the small of her back, it still made Iris sad.

But the main reason she did not go regularly to see weddings was that she could never get a good look at the bride. She much preferred the visits to the brides' homes the afternoon before, straight from school and still in uniform, when she would escape the boredom of the cloistered lives lived by the Lebanese children, overfed and overprotected. She would hang back as their nursemaids came to pick them up and walk them the three blocks home, shading them with parasols. She would pretend to help the teachers sweep the class, straighten the desks, erase the blackboard. Then she would join a gang of girls for Wednesday afternoon prewedding visits.

On these visits, the other girls always headed straight for the bedroom, where they would spend up to a full hour with everyone else coming in from off the streets, scrutinizing the carefully labeled opened gifts displayed on the bed, and passing judgment on whether enough money had been spent, considering the giver's status. Some of the older women would go so far as to examine the manner in which the display beds were dressed, lifting up the coverlets to see if the sheets were of Irish linen and if they had been hand-embroidered.

Iris preferred to wander around the house, catching glimpses of how people in society lived, rather than hear talk of crystal and silver, bedding and curtains. The Lebanese people with whom she worked had come with their ways—the rough ways of poor farmers. They had not yet acquired breeding, and did not yet know the art of beautification, of grace. Their attitude of dominion was unsubtle and coarse, unlike the smooth aura of entitlement the Europeans had passed on to the most privileged of their slaves, those who shared their white blood. For Iris, straight from her village, it was all brand new and wondrous.

She would watch the mother of the bride, walking confident and straight-backed, gesturing to her servants absentmindedly, taking their presence for granted in a gracious sort of way, turning her head regally to accept the gleaming silver trays delivered in advance of the wedding by the maids of the invited guests. Iris especially liked to watch the mothers open the presents borne on those polished trays. Their big round gold *pomme-cannelle* earrings would swing like early wedding bells, their thick bracelets would jangle as they bent to pick up the teapot, the platter, the monogrammed bedsheets, holding them aloft for all to see before bearing them off to the bedroom for display.

The brides' mothers were omnipresent on those Wednesday afternoons, but if she stayed long enough, Iris would also get to see the real treat: the daughters. What struck Iris about these girls was that, without fail, they were distressed, pale, and trembling with the swollen-faced look of days of crying. On occasion they would even streak from one back room to another, tears visible, sobs audible. "Tears of joy," "Over-excitement," "Nerves," the family members would murmur for the benefit of the people off the street. The family servants, proud of the girl's virginity, or attempting to dispel rumors, might also use the opportunity to circulate in the gift-display bedroom, glee unconcealed: "She 'fraid what she going get tomorrow night!"

Iris believed those explanations. She was the only one who did not understand that, in the days before the wedding, these girls were finally forced to come to terms with the end of a life in which they had any control whatsoever over what they did, when they did it, and with whom they did it. They would relinquish their ownership over their own selves, and they would swear in front of God to obey their new lord and master until death. These society girls cried because they knew they were about to become a servant: worse, in fact, because servants were paid and could leave when they wanted. They were crying because they were about to become somebody's slave.

The women who had come in off the street were too familiar with slavery to contemplate doing such a thing to themselves. For the next century or more, these Caribbean women, with their disinterest in marrying their children's fathers, would generate a steady traffic in befuddled missionaries, curious sociologists, and excited anthropologists. Official terms would be coined. *Visiting unions.* That was what the scholars called the Caribbean way of making babies: the men would visit the various homes of their women and children; they did not live with them. And when that man stopped visiting for his union, the women would unite with another visitor to have his children. *Female-headed households* and *matrifocal societies*—these were the catchwords with which the pundits would discuss the phenomenon of Caribbean women raising children without the yoke of the men. Theories would be put forward as to why they did this, studies were undertaken, and the scholars would line up into two antagonistic camps. One set would say that it was all about handed-down African culture, and that the visiting unions phenomenon was essentially an adapted version of polygamy. The other group would blame the laws that had prevented slaves from marrying and from staying together as a family.

All the big-brained people with their theories, their arguments and counterarguments, should have just talked to the women to understand that the reason they did not marry was a simple matter. Descendants of slaves, of course, had a natural aversion to slavery.

Iris, foolish girl, would live for the afternoons before a society wedding when she could catch a glimpse of a quaking bride, fodder for her imagination and dreams of romantic love, of the man and the marriage and the happily ever after. Conceited child.

When she first set eyes on John Baptiste, it was a prewedding Wednesday and she was standing off to the side, staring at the little table in the salon where the groom's gifts to his bride and to her bridesmaids were displayed. The house was suffocating with the scent of fresh white roses. They were everywhere, twined along the banisters, arching each doorway and window frame. She looked up, saw his face, and felt the room flip, floor where ceiling used to be. The women around who brought the smelling salts and helped her to her feet blamed the heat in the overcrowded salon and the humidity and the overpowering perfume, but Iris knew that it was the face of the man.

He had walked over to the gift table with the groom to admire the seven tiny boxes, arranged in a circle around a much larger box, each containing identical gold earrings in the shape of an orchid, nested in cotton wool. But it was the bride's gift they nodded over, four times the size of the bridesmaids' and studded with tiny pearls at the tip of each delicate calyx. He stood opposite Iris, looking down, and did not even notice that she had fainted clean away.

Thursday afternoon found Iris in the front row of the wedding-watchers, braving the curses of the old women. This time, when John Baptiste approached her on his way up the cathedral's steps with his mother heavy on his arm, she stepped out of the crowd and stood by herself for a second before hands grabbed her and pulled her back to the unmarked barrier behind which she and her kind were obliged to stand.

It worked. The movement caught his attention. She smiled at him, the man she had fallen in love with on sight.

John Baptiste could not keep himself from looking back at the half-Carib servant girl with the gleaming skin. As he climbed the steps, he was already anticipating what he would do to her, the bold little slut who had openly propositioned him, who had stood in front of the whole of Roseau, in front of his mother, to put her hands on her hips and shove herself at him with that smile, a smile that no decent girl would have made in public. She would get what she was asking for.

J ohn Baptiste was a man who knew that he was blessed. He went to
church regularly, where he did not pray for anything, since he had it
all. Rather he gave thanks for what he was. He was not white, nor did he
want to be; it was not a good thing to be a white West Indian in the days
when slavery was long gone, when the white man's day was done. He
was not black, and that was certainly no misfortune, either, to be spared
the indelible badge of inferiority: one's very skin. He was that wonderful
hybrid, that special creation that dominated many of the Caribbean
islands, those where the French and the Spanish had exercised less self-
control with their slave women than the British and spawned a new
race of the privileged. He had money, he had land, he had no siblings to
fight over his inheritance. His father was dead, his mother getting old
and in the process of handing it all over to him. He had chosen his
future wife well, from a family that matched his in status, and Cecile
Richard was not an ugly girl. He had no idea what she would turn out to
be like in bed, and it didn't matter. On top of everything, he now had
Iris.

When he told Iris about the upcoming wedding, he did so not to be
cruel but to prepare her for the day when he would not come as regularly. She took it well, he thought, with acceptance and good humor; she
seemed to have expected it.

I t had been easy for him to find her. Easier for him to take her away
from the life of a pampered pseudo-servant when he discovered
what it meant to be worshiped. He lodged her in a one-room house on
the outer bank of the narrow Roseau River, where from her window she
had a clean view of the spot where her washerwomen neighbors stood

in the shallow river among the stones, slapping clothes against rocks for a living all day long.

Amelia Fadoul found her and tried to drag her back home. Iris used her nails and teeth, but Amelia's arms were strong from pounding kibbeh. She would have succeeded if not for the washerwomen, who were happy for the young girl. She had been chosen by a member of the Baptiste family for the honor of concubinage. All indications were good that the two would be together long enough to have at least one child: he was not content to fuck her behind a tree, on the wet grass, in the bush. He would not sneak her into his mother's house late at night, to have her on the bathroom floor, not daring to use the creaking bed. No, he was doing right by her: he had set her up in her own house for which he paid, and he came to her every evening and sometimes also at midday. And this was no old man, drinking *bwa bandé:* he was young and strong with the face of an angel. He was so yellow as to be almost white in complexion, but thanks to the redeeming thickness of his nose and mouth, he was beautiful, sensual—saved from the ghostly ugliness of his white ancestors.

The sounds of their lovemaking would carry through the neighborhood, the single compound of one-room houses in which lived women and children but no men. And the women would stop their ceaseless talking to listen to the keening and the trilling, the rumbling and the growling, the kinds of sounds they used to make but no longer could. They remembered the time before they had children, when there were still men in their lives, and the memory would inspire some of the women to take each other to bed to make *zami,* and others would try to be kinder to their children, remembering that once upon a time there was such love in their life: love that was there for no reason, love that had no conversation, love that had no logic, love that you would die for, love that made rooms turn upside down and put you flat on your back with your legs

wide open. Love distilled into instinct so that there was nothing to do
but to *make* love, that is, until you made babies, and then you had done
your part in the grand scheme of the turning world. After that you went
back to being a washerwoman washing clothes to feed your children.

And so they could not believe that Amelia Fadoul had the audacity
to try to take Iris away from all of that, not only from the love (worth all
the suffering that would come when it was inevitably over) but also
from what Iris's children might have—a future that offered more than
the beating of cloth against rock. They were outraged: the Lebanese
woman, who had everything she could want, whose children would only
suffer in life because they had been given too much, that woman would
try to spoil Iris's chances. They waded out of the river, their skirts tucked
into the strong elastic of their homemade panties, the fabric ballooning
at the tops of their thighs. From a distance, the nakedness of their legs
might have given the impression that they were a bevy of models showing off a new line of fashionable bathing costumes. But then they bent
down to pick up rocks from the riverbank with which they pelted Amelia, until she ran back across Roseau Bridge to her side of town, straight
to the convent to find Sister Mary-Alice.

L ong before Amelia reached the convent gates, word had already
reached the consecutive string of dry-goods stores that she was
running, apparently wounded, through the town. As bizarre and unlikely
as that was, none of those who received the news had any question
regarding whether the report was true or false: before the widespread
use of telephones, there was no such thing as unfounded rumor, and the
word from the street—in this case, that Amelia Fadoul was running
screaming and bleeding across the bridge in the direction of the convent—would be accurate down to the manner in which the blood was

flowing from her body. The Lebanese had adopted a successful survival strategy for coexisting in prosperity with their poor countrymen and -women: they were pacifists, nonconfrontational and accommodating. But if one of their women was publicly disgraced in the streets, they would at least have to make a proper show of wanting retaliatory bloodshed. They got their guns, kept in a drawer and never used, locked down their stores, ordered the women and children upstairs to remain indoors, and headed silently for the convent in a tight group.

The townspeople who had not yet heard about Amelia saw the locked stores and knew that something serious had happened. Until that morning, the Lebanese had only closed their shops for a death of their own kind, when they would lock down for days on end. But the silence told them that this was not the case: had it been death, the sound of the women's wailing would have brought out the entire town to marvel at the intensity with which the Lebanese mourned the passing of their beloved. For centuries the Black people of the Caribbean had grown accustomed to losing their family members, whether it was to the auction block or to early death, and even though they had never developed the ability to let them go without the trauma of the screaming and the wailing and the collapsing at the graveside, they still had a strong appreciation of death as relief, as a conduit to freedom, a passage back home. But not these Lebanese people, who believed in the afterlife but who were enjoying their newly acquired riches in the present too much to welcome it. They did not let death steal in and out quietly; they put up resistance, futile as it was, with the kind of protestation that impressed Black Dominicans, noise that started from the drawing of the last breath down to the bitter end, the grand finale of the burial. The quiet, then, told the latecomers that nobody had died, at least not yet, and they ran eastward, where they could see people hurrying toward the convent in the distance.

A crowd of hundreds found a bloody Amelia in the courtyard in front of Sister Mary-Alice telling what had happened, and she did it in the theatrical Arab way, with kneeling and striking of breast, calling on the patron Virgin of her parents' village. She gave Iris everything she gave to her own children, treated her like family, but it had not been enough, and now she was mortally afraid of the Divine Retribution that would come raining down on her head. "I try. I keep she in the house. Feed she good food. De best seamstress in Roseau sew she clothes. Don't give she no hard work to do. Pay school fees and send she to school every single day, Sister, every single day. On my mother's grave I swear she never get chance to go look no man."

Amelia's exertions showed that her wounds were superficial, and when the men realized who had inflicted the damage, they were collectively relieved for an instant. They would not need to wear the pretense of vengeance any longer, as it would be unseemly to threaten to kill a woman, much less an entire neighborhood of them. But then they got to the root of the trouble, and they fired off anticipatory shots into the air. They understood love in terms of arranged marriages, through faithfulness, a bickering, cantankerous partnership for life, and the building of their version of passion over a lifetime of trust and mutual dependency. For them there was no other interpretation of the situation: John Baptiste had kidnapped and desecrated an innocent child, a daughter, of their household. They knew who he was, son of a rich *boug*, their only serious competitor in the dry-goods arena, and they knew that preparations were well under way for his marriage to Cecile Richard: her mother had bought all the bridal fabric from them. Forcing him to marry Iris was therefore not an option. They would have to rescue her, and they held their guns high as they moved off to signal their intent. They were not killing people, but for this, John Baptiste would be a dead man if he intervened.

Mary-Alice stopped them. Just the day before, she had learned the details of Iris's whereabouts and what she was doing there from the pregnant daughter of one of the washerwomen. Her bag was already packed, and she was waiting for approval from her mother superior to undertake a fabricated mission in the north where Iris's mother lived. She knew that nothing would keep Iris away while she remained in Roseau, short of a bullet to her head, or to his. But the child's mother could come and take her back where she belonged.

Mary-Alice called a priest and, using the authority of the Church, sent them home to put away their guns and to leave the responsibility of Iris to her. After several days, during which she fasted and prayed, her mission was approved and she left Roseau to find Iris's mother.

14

OBSESSION

The silence in the sitting room had not yet grown to the level of discomfort, but Teddy felt something building. He wondered if it happened to women also—his nonsexual feelings, anticipation in particular, could translate so easily into an erection. He couldn't keep his eyes from straying back to his computer, his mind from second-guessing the two short sentences she had written. *I need to see you. I have a big favor to ask.* She'd probably ask him to use his next TV appearance to plug a never-before-heard-of cause—she never quite got it, that it wasn't possible for him to suddenly start talking about the fact that women in Africa didn't have the right to inherit when he was being interviewed about a police shooting in New York. Activists were notorious for that, for having no discretion, not understanding limits. For expecting the rest of the world to also feel general injustice as a personal attack.

He slid another look at her, trying to catch an unguarded expression, a clue. She had started off sitting back in the armchair, but now she had moved so that she was sitting at the edge of the cushion. Her eyes were hooded, as usual, her face held off to the side and down in that way she had of not looking at anything, the way she had of always seeming to be *listening* to something.

"I'm going home," she said. She brought her face up in a rush to look at him. "To Dominica. I wonder if you might like to come with me."

His response was spontaneous. There was no hesitation as he shook his head, not yet saying no, but not able to make sense of the request. "Wait a minute. Tell me something." The surprise of what she said was putting a tone in his voice that was coming through as aggression. "You've lived here, how many years now. Twenty? More. You've never been back to Dominica since you left. Not one single visit home. You think it wasn't obvious? My wedding in Antigua. You hadn't seen your family in ten-plus years, and you should have seen your face when I asked you why not just fly over for a visit. Would have taken you forty minutes to lay eyes on your mother again."

"Your point?"

"You *refused* to go. You refused to even talk about the place. No mention of family, mother, father, nothing. So now—boom—one day you show up, and it's, oh, let's go back home?" He stopped, too tempted to give himself away, to tell her that he knew there was more to the few facts she recited whenever he'd asked: her parents were ordinary, unremarkable people and there was nothing in particular to say about them; in her early teens she was sent to live with an aunt in New York for the sake of getting into college in the U.S., and that aunt had since gone back to Dominica.

He knew there was more because one day, toward the end of freshman year, he had given in to his curiosity about the kind of life she'd lived before she left Dominica by picking the lock of her room. It was something he hardly ever thought about.

He had found a shopping bag crammed with over three years' worth of unopened letters, post-stamped from the time she had left Dominica until that very week, all with the same return address, all with rain-forest-themed stamps, birds and mountains and waterfalls. He'd stolen a handful, reading them back in his apartment. He had been shaking as he opened the first one. They were all from the same person, saying essentially the same thing, and too overwrought to provide any real detail, but Teddy was still able to figure it out: Lillian was adopted, he concluded, something she didn't discover until she was a teenager. When she found out, she cut off her adoptive parents, and he guessed that the aunt she lived with in New York might have been a blood relation. It was, according to the letter, enough of a big deal for a psychiatrist to be involved.

Teddy's patched-together version of what was wrong with Lillian allowed him to let go of his curiosity—it wasn't unusual, he knew, for children to have strong reactions against their adoptive parents upon discovering the truth of their biology.

He still knew of one of the letters, the one that yielded the most information, by heart, his mental recitation faking a Dominican accent, and staying true to the deliberately colloquial grammar and syntax the schoolteacher had used:

Roseau, 1983

My darling Lillian,

   I have the last report from your doctor and he saying that everything is going very good with you, I so glad to learn that. I hear from your Aunt Margaret you take big exams for university and you pass high; that is my girl, I know you are capable of such things and plus you have a schoolteacher for a mother, me! (laugh)

   Dou-dou, why you wouldn't just come home for a little rest now. A ticket is there waiting at JFK for you, prepaid, if you ever want to come, you go and tell them your name and give them your passport and that is all. Your aunt planning to come back home in

*a year or two and soon that going to leave you in America you-one
and Jesus. And what kind of a place is New York for a young lady
alone with no family. And maybe you could just send me a little
note if you can but not to worry if you don't feel to write, maybe you
could even call collect but I'm not pressuring you. And sweetheart
I don't take it too bad that you wouldn't write me, because I know
that you know I love you like my own daughter.*

*I would get on a plane tomorrow just to see your face but only
if you tell me come. Anyway one day you will come back, that I
know in my heart.*

Your godmother sends her love and she is in good health.

With everlasting love,
your mother, Icilma

Reading the way Lillian was gathering herself, the way she reached
down to locate her purse on the floor, he shifted off the chair onto the
table, swinging his legs across the narrow stretch of polished teak,
opening up his knees and planting his feet on either side of her. He held
her forearms, looking down at the cuff links when his fingers touched
the coldness of the gold. "Left field, you know?" he said, lowering his
voice, trying for an apologetic approach, and wondering how he would
find a kind way to convey that she was asking too much of him, now
that his life was such that he had to consult his publicist before commit-
ting any tranche of his time. He needed a gentle way to say that their
friendship was about ten years past the time at which such a request
would have been even appropriate.

The ranting call his wife had made to Lillian after their honeymoon
had done it, had forced them to relinquish what they had, something
undefined yet close, leaving their exchanges purely professional. Since
his divorce, they had been seeing more of each other, but it was a rela-

tionship with clearly defined lines of demarcation; it would not include a trip to Dominica.

It was not something that Teddy had ever shared, that he and his bride had not consummated the marriage on their honeymoon. He did not blame Diane, he blamed Yasmin, her matron of honor. "We are natural-born enemies," Teddy joked to Diane, unable to explain what had caused their mutual dislike; it had been instant.

As they pulled away from the curb, finally leaving their drunken guests to continue throwing one another into the pool, tension had put him in a high state of arousal. It had been harrowing, a day that refused to end, so bad that the pressing sense of dread about the marriage—the sense of leftover foreboding one carries around after a nightmare—had been beaten back and replaced by the immediate torture of the ceremony. Even without a formal church service, it dragged on for two hours on a hot beach—Antigua kept its promise of no rain, but with that came, even at five in the afternoon, extreme heat. The men, all in suits, were sweating like horses. The women in their halter-backs were doing a little better in terms of the heat, but all the work with the curling irons had been in vain: their hair had reverted to its original texture in the seaside moisture.

There had been three long passages, one from the Bible—the sexual one about the gazelle—and two the musings of obscure Eastern philosophical prophet types. One of Diane's sorors read an original love poem, four pages long. Every friend or relative with a voice sang a solo; what was it with Black people and singing at weddings? All the renditions were fairly decent, but only the Ave Maria was top class, performed by his cousin, Colt. That had been the one point of true entertainment for Teddy, not his cousin's voice, but his cousin's wife. Colt had announced that he had begun training his voice under the guidance of a volunteer who used to visit him in prison, and who was now his wife. The fact that he had been to prison was bad enough for his bride's bougie Black relatives (he was not in a kind mood on his wedding day), but when Colt had his wife stand, and asked for applause on her behalf, that was when Teddy had laughed aloud at the expressions on the faces of Diane's relatives. His cousin-in-law was not only white—the only white person at the wedding—but she was obviously trailer trash, the kind of white person that headed up the Black bougie's most hated list.

When the ceremony was over, there was still more ritual to be suffered through. He had deliberately stayed out of the wedding planning, and found himself unprepared for the feeling that he was participating in a farce. Diane wanted to jump the broom, and though he willingly agreed, he felt ridiculous holding her hand and jumping barefoot over a broom decorated with satin bows. He felt even more embarrassed when he, in the name of wedding traditions, had to crawl under her skirt to snag a decorative elasticized garter belt from her thigh with his teeth, powdery, itchy sand filling the arms and legs of his suit. The men performed in the usual halfhearted way when he threw it, but he was astounded at the catfight quality of the bouquet-catching. That was when, looking at the women scramble for the bouquet, he realized that, although Lillian had traveled all the way to Antigua for his wedding, she had not attended the ceremony. She had come up to him then, her gift still in hand, and together they stood some distance from the fracas, looking at the tangle of legs and arms. "Why haven't the feminists stopped this?" he asked her, making her laugh. It was rare, a belly laugh from Lillian, and he could remember his sense of accomplishment, her thrown-back head, her perfect teeth.

Teddy made his speeches and listened to speeches and danced the first dance and many Electric Slides. He finally told Diane that enough was enough, and eventually she agreed to leave. Then Yasmin had come running up to the limousine, her bony face set, holding up the frothy skirt of her froufrou peach gown, as typically hideously shiny as any he'd seen, even though Diane had sworn to her eight girlfriends and cousins that she had picked the kind of dress they would definitely be able to "get more use out of."

Unlike the other guests, Yasmin was cold sober. She handed Diane a leather-covered photo album. "A little present for you," she said, leaning in through the window at an awkward angle to kiss her best friend on the cheek. "You were too busy to hang with us, but look, a picture diary of how the rest of us spent your last few days as a single woman." Yasmin turned her face briefly toward Teddy—a face he eventually decided he disliked due to its sharp angles and hard edges—her smile momentarily disappearing. She opened the album, flipping through a few pages of mounted photographs to show Diane the posed group shots at the various Antiguan tourist attractions, the candid ones of smaller groupings, individual portraits, and head shots of two- and threesomes. She spoke in a high-spirited, innocent voice. "I developed them this morning—can you believe? Antigua has one-hour processing. Small place, but all the amenities."

He'd tried to distract Diane on the drive to the dock; they were beginning their honeymoon, after all, and immediate foreplay was in order, but she insisted on looking through the album. She had known Yasmin all her life, there would be a message somewhere. "Friends don't bring friends bad news," Yasmin liked to say, "but they are duty bound to point them in the right direction."

It started out playfully, with Diane fending him off with her feet and bracing against the door as she turned the pages, but by the time they boarded the boat that ferried guests from the mainland to the famous Jumby Bay resort on a tiny island just off Antigua's coast, she was rigid, arms folded around the album, jaw clenched tight, her body fully turned away from his. The boatman pretended not to notice, but the hotel maids, gathered at the jetty to bride-watch, called softly to Teddy after Diane walked past them, several yards ahead of her husband. Most of what they said Teddy did not understand, but he made out a few sympathetic murmurs: "Me sorry for you tonight, brudder" and "No kind of key going unlock dat tonight." There was a lot of soft laughter.

There were white rose petals strewn on the king-size bed. Diane climbed onto it, sitting on her heels, keeping her back to Teddy. He noticed the line of dozens of satin-covered buttons and remembered thinking that by right, he should be unbuttoning them, although desire had gone, and it was an abstract thought. He also noticed the soles of her dirty feet, crusted thickly from dancing barefoot on the pool deck. The grains of white sand embedded in the black dirt made it seem like she was wearing a pair of sparkling sandals. It made him think of Cinderella.

She opened the album and tore out twenty or so of the hundred-plus photos. She laid them out along the length of the bed, on top of the petals. "Tell me what you see, Teddy." She got off the bed and went through French doors to stand on the balcony.

It was obvious. She had picked out all the candid shots in which he and Lillian appeared together. In each one, regardless of how many other people were in the picture, he was looking at Lillian, but it was not that he was looking at her, it was the expression on his face, the *way* he was looking her, the exact expression in every photograph.

Lilly." She was not speaking. "But why now?" Teddy wanted to deal with it, this *situation*, with tact—in a way that would allow her to walk away with her dignity in place. His refusal of her odd invitation—he thought of it as odd, as merely asking too much, because what else could it be?—could make things uncomfortable between them. He would need to proceed carefully. This time, he would have to say no. No, he could not turn on a dime and go to Dominica with her to help her bring the world's attention to yet another cause, attend still one more critical conference on—what this time? What right did women not yet enjoy in Dominica? Or would this be about the nearly extinct Carib population, or the nearly extinct leatherback sea turtle population? He'd be firm without coming across as uncaring. He would blame his schedule.

Teddy reached over toward her held-away face, his open palm upturned, and used his four fingers to raise her chin. But his setup was miscalculated. The gesture was an unexpectedly intimate one. She raised her eyelids and Teddy saw the particular color of her eyes—a color he had never seen on a white person, but that showed up every so often among Black people of a particular mixture. "They say," she said, "that my grandmother was a murderer."

And when she saw his darting eyes, reflecting the way his thoughts were running around in his head, searching in vain for the connections, she said, "Once, you wanted to know me. My story. You wanted to know so bad you broke into my room. Lifted up my mattress, took all the books off the shelves." She was not blinking, not giving him the chance to drop his eyes. She would not let him look away. One of the many things he thought in those moments was that her face was different, it was wide open. "You searched everywhere. You went through my under-wear drawer." She turned her head so that she spoke her next words into the palm of his hand, her mouth dragging against his skin. What she said was low-throated and muffled, but he could still hear. "I could smell your aftershave on my panties."

He felt it again, then. What he had always chosen to interpret as a curiosity about her, but in that moment it came back honestly: it came back as what it had always been, it came back to him as full-blown obsession.

He went for her, sprang at her, capsizing the heavy armchair. He found out then, on the floor, on the opium table, in his bed, that every rumor his fraternity brothers had spread about her was true.

15

MATRIMONY

After the washerwomen chased away Amelia, they took an even greater interest in Iris's well-being. To keep up her stamina for her daily marathons, they concocted special back-strengthening tonics and boiled daily porridges for her breakfast. Her body filled out, her skin glowed brighter, and she seemed to grow happier by the day. They did not converse with her, as she was a child to them, and part Carib at that, with her reserved nature; but she was pleasant and helpful and so lovely to look at. She sometimes sat among them doing simple tasks: braiding the girl children's hair, stirring a pot of coconut cheese. Usually they didn't allow her to do much else, not even to fan flies from the lips of a sleeping baby. They realized that she was so consumed by the physicality of her love that she could not be trusted to behave responsibly. In addition, they knew that she would need her energy to perform when John Baptiste arrived, because she spared no effort when it came to their loving. They knew it not just from the sounds they made, but also from what they saw. Sometimes, if he came when the sun was low enough, the rays would hit at just the right angle, piercing the curtains, projecting their silhouettes through the opposite window onto the exterior wall of the next-door house. And what they saw told them that Iris needed her rest.

The one thing of deep concern to them, though, was the sight of her cloths on the bleaching rocks every month. They checked the moon and counted off the days, sure that the next month would be the one when the cloths would not appear. But too many months were passing by, and still the girl was not pregnant. They analyzed the situation, agreed on the reasons why she had not yet conceived, and discussed what was to be done. There was still time before his wedding, which rumor dated at about a year away. Of course, she could always get pregnant after the wedding, but it would be more difficult for that child to be accepted by his wife. A bastard son, born before the marriage, could have some of the privileges of legitimate children: financial support, education, an inheritance of land and property. And if the resemblance to the father was strong enough, and if God was merciful with the color, even a girl child stood the chance, the good fortune, of being taken away from the mother and raised in the father's home; or, almost as good, she might be given to one of his spinster relatives, a sister, an aunt, to occupy a hybrid space in her household, to become something encompassing both servant and family.

They picked Angela, the youngest among them, for the job of counseling Iris. Angela was instructed to explain to Iris that it would be possible for her to get pregnant quickly with a child that would resemble the father if she did as they advised.

First, she would have to take it on her back. From the shadows on the wall they knew that she did it every which way but missionary, and it was common knowledge that the fastest way to get pregnant was to get on your back and to stay there after, allowing the man's seed to drain straight into the womb. Angela was also to explain to her that the acrobatics should be discontinued for another important reason. With all her bouncing, bracing, bending, clambering, and general contortions, the child would end up looking exactly like her. For the father's features to prevail, Iris would have to lie still and let the man do his work.

The second thing Angela had to explain to Iris was that she had to stop doing it all the time. She was weakening her own body, but more critically, diluting his sperm with their daily and twice-daily sessions. She should completely abstain for the week immediately following and immediately prior to menstruation, and for the two weeks in between, she should only make love every third day. To accommodate the excessive sex drive for which Caribs were known, they instructed Angela on the points of compromise should Iris be difficult about it.

Finally, they were ready to dispatch Angela. They chose Iris's time of the month, when John Baptiste would most likely not show up, and when there was a chance Iris might take her mind off sex long enough to listen. They waited for Angela to report back at the pool where they sometimes bathed in the late afternoon, a spot just upriver from the place where they washed clothes.

Years before, they had cut down the trees on the banks, allowing the sun to knock the chill off the water. At the same time, they had shifted some large boulders into a solid line across the full width of the narrow river to create the deepening effect of a small-scale dam. They then moved more rocks and boulders from the deepened riverbed and stacked them carefully in a large circle, building a submerged, porous wall through which the river flowed, creating an invisible outdoor bath within the river, the top not quite breaking the water's surface. It was deep enough for an adult to fully immerse herself for a proper wash while the small children sat on the wall to soap and rinse themselves safely. It was a place the children loved—and so did Iris, who after all was still a child—where they would walk for hours in a circle playing a game they called *Jesus Walks*, because from a distance, or even up close, they could create the illusion that they had the miraculous power of God, it appeared as if they were walking on water.

The women were still washing off when Angela returned—far too quickly, in their estimation. Only the heads were visible of the fifteen or twenty women clustered in the center of the river treading water. Their thirty or forty smaller children were still standing on the top of the bath wall surrounding their mothers, hovering on top of the water, looking down at them like guardian angels.

They had purposely only brought along the small ones that evening, those who did not yet have understanding, as they expected Angela's reporting to be for adult ears only. The serious business, the matter of Iris's conception, was, from the reporting standpoint, practically a non-issue. Angela would tell her what to do, Iris would be grateful for the information, since she naturally would have been getting worried that she hadn't yet conceived. However, they expected that the good-natured Angela, whose own rampant sexuality was evidenced by her six children with six different men in seven years, would have drawn Iris into a ribald conversation. They would exchange tidbits, they would talk size, technique, and position, they would discuss best-evers. It promised to be an entertaining evening of crude intimacies. But well before they could have made out the expression on Angela's face, the way she placed her feet as she trudged up the hill, the droop of her shoulders, let them know that her conversation had not gone well.

"Fille folle" was what Angela said to the group of naked women standing anxiously shivering on the riverbank surrounded by their children. They were not surprised at the description. People in love like that, they replied, *are* crazy. They can't think, their brain gets addled. The

blood can't go up to nourish their brain, the blood is always rushing down to the privates. They were laughing a little, hoping that the kind of evening they'd envisioned might still be possible. Then they saw the sadness in Angela's face, and they stopped their nasty talk about engorged sexual organs to listen.

She told them that all along Iris had been drinking bush tea so she would not get pregnant. A collective intake of breath sounded their disbelief, and they started raising their voices at Angela, who had clearly bungled the mission. "What you was thinking 'bout, Angela?" A voice from the back, from a middle-aged woman with wizened, oversuckled breasts that she kept aloft on top of her folded arms. "*Your* brain addle? Your mind must still be on the man that was making you bawl in your house last night. I think you misunderstanding what the girl saying. I think is you she was warning to take some tea. Because maybe number seven done cooking in there, after what I hear you carrying on with last night."

A tittering started to gain momentum, but it didn't catch. Angela was shaking her head and crying. Five of her six children were young enough to be present, and they edged out of the group, surrounding their mother protectively. The other women kept quiet while Angela brought her voice under control and spoke again. Iris, she said, believed with all her heart that John Baptiste was going to marry her within the year.

This time the women cried out and then covered their mouths with both hands, their ultimate expression of shock. "I telling her is not true, I telling her that," Angela said, "but she saying is his own mouth he take and tell her he marrying her in one year's time. That is why she drinking tea, so she wouldn't make no bastard child. Papa God. She waiting to get married first."

They were the kind of women who did not believe in squandering tears, who regularly counseled that cry-water should be saved and used only for the death of one's mother or, God forbid, one's child. But walking back home that evening, all of them wept for the poor mad girl.

B ut Iris was not crazy, not yet, not then. She simply did not have a frame of reference to understand the meaning of her skin in a society of people who defined themselves in an ascending rank according to the shades that led up to white. She did not understand the meaning of her poverty, nor her resulting place on the bottom rung of the social ladder. Later on, when she finally understood, she was still never able to determine which one of the three—color, class, or poverty—was responsible for the inescapability of her destiny. To her mind, when she still had it, each was an equal part of the same whole.

16

PRAYERS

Lillian approached her building slowly, exhaustion starting to overtake. Her legs were trembling, but not from the walk; the distance between Georgetown and Adams Morgan was easy for her, she ran every morning, four miles along the Potomac, across Key Bridge into Virginia, and back. She stopped when she could see her building, leaning against a wall to rest, and she appreciated the intimacy of the two tight rows of cars lining her narrow side street, enjoyed the steady wave of solid noise flowing up, unencumbered, from all the Adams Morgan bars and eating spots. She'd paid too much for her condo, overpriced because of its location near the quarter's busiest intersection, one rambunctious, famous restaurant per corner, but she liked the congestion, it gave her a feeling of security.

For many, the drawback of living in Adams Morgan was the decibel level, but it was the thing she liked best about her neighborhood, especially at that time, ten-thirty on a Friday night. With the noise came patterns, with which she was able to play her game: finding the arrangements within what at first appeared to be an unbroken set of sound waves riding so close on one another's tails that the uninitiated ear could hear only an undistinguishable drone. The first few minutes were hard, requiring concentration, but once she picked out that first, simple sequence, she could break off the infinite combinations of minute spacings.

She was good at it, pulling rhythms out of whatever noise she could find in the air, not because she had a natural ability but because she'd been doing it for so long, ever since she found herself in America under a psychiatrist's care. She had been doing it since she understood the story of Matilda, not just that her grandmother had killed so senselessly, not just that Matilda had made a man's heart beat loud like a drum, but all the other implications of Obeah and of evil—her own conception, it was said, had been mandated by a dead Matilda.

But it was not the psychiatrist who had helped her, because she had told him nothing. He hadn't stopped the flashbacks, or prevented her from descending into a place where she would not need to think about her past. She had saved herself by drowning out everything but thoughts of the human heart and what it might have sounded like. Was it like this—kang-*kang*-ka-tang-tang; or could it have been faster, more like—kang-ka-tang, kang-ka-tang? And then, once the drums had entered her head, she would add the shield of a prayer, an impenetrable layer of protective, chanted words, and Lillian prayed only to Mary, because common sense would tell anybody that a man had no choice but to obey his mother. With the drums and the Hail Mary and the Magnificat, Lillian had constructed a firewall, she had built a dam that she still used, every day—that she was using right then to save herself, even as she entered her apartment.

She put away her cuff links first. She took off her clothes, opened out a pashmina and wrapped it around her chest like a strapless tunic. She examined her body, everywhere covered with tiny red scratches from his dreads, especially her face. She could still see the imprint of his fingers around her arms, white against reddened skin. There had been bruises on his body, already purple by the time she left, and small beads of blood on his back from her fingernails. There had been bite marks, too, his eyes had opened wide when he looked at his shoulder. Before she left, she had applied antiseptic for him.

She sat in her window cove, her back to the street. It was a delicate thing, this game she played. Too much of the sound barrier and it took over, disallowing any thought, incapacitating her, immobilizing her. Not enough and it was nothing but flashbacks, like a slide show lighting up her mind. Either way, she had to keep the right balance. "A tense look" was something she was known for, and it was an enormous strain, what she had to do every waking moment in order to function.

A new CD she'd just bought for her percussion collection was playing loudly. That helped, listening to ready-made drumming, it allowed her to relax a bit more if she did not have to create the rhythms herself.

She was trying to take comfort from the familiarity of her space, small, spare, with flea-market furnishings, but pulled together with an unerring eye. Untidy enough to be comfortable. Bamboo shades. Small drums sitting atop her entertainment unit, her matching djembes wedged in corners, hosting plants. A wall of nothing but books. Anthropology textbooks, history books, everything Teddy had ever written, starting with his dissertation on the Underground Railroad. She owned several copies of *No Justice,* the signed one with the handwritten two-page thank-you dedication was sitting right there in front of her. It was the only object on her coffee table, an oversized drum from Uganda, its wide face flaring from its narrow base, the black-and-brown hair of the cowskin establishing the tone of the room, earthy.

When it was released, Teddy's editor had warned him against unrealistic expectations; books such as his were not big sellers. But the size of the royalty checks, which Teddy, under no legal obligation, shared equally with her, indicated otherwise. *No Justice* sold steadily from January through December, proving another theory about African-American behavior, that their reading choices were not reflected in any standard bestseller lists. Since December, however, once the convictions were overturned, the book had blown up; it was reviewed belatedly in both the *New York Times* and the *Washington Post*.

All of this, her role in where he found himself today, was because Teddy disliked writing almost as much as he disliked teaching, but he understood the importance of a tenured position with a reputable institution like Georgetown University to get him what he wanted—to become a Famous Black Figure, a celebrity talking head. He was so intent on running away from the specter of his parents' life that he had never stopped to properly consider what he should have been running toward.

Teddy analyzed contemporary racism in its modern-day manifestations, providing explanations—he put it all together and told his public why there was no justice for them, he helped them to interpret their crazy world. But after answering the *whys*—which was so easy—he had no interest in doing the real work: fighting the injustice he was so good at analyzing.

Now, the very thing for which she criticized Teddy was what she needed of him—she just wanted him to think on her behalf, to make sense out of something she could not understand. If anyone could help her to figure out what was now making her believe that her grandmother had been hanged for a crime she had not committed, it would be this man.

She couldn't let go of the notion that Matilda, like the boys, had made a false confession. From December through April she had been listening to Teddy. Like a groupie, she was tuning in to his every television appearance, every radio interview, to hear him say the same thing over and over:

"The power of a confession is such that judges and juries will take the word of the accused as gospel—even in the face of evidence that clearly proves that they are lying."

17

BIRD FLEW

Even without knowing exactly where Matilda lived—knowing only that it was somewhere in the mountains behind the fishing village of Colihaut—Mary-Alice knew that she would find her easily: she was a nun, decked in full habit, and her status as a handmaiden of God was taken seriously by Dominican Catholics. From the second she stepped off the launch that, in the absence of roads, would take her up the west coast from Roseau to Colihaut, she would be approached and escorted wherever she wanted to go. She would be fed and lodged by woman or man and she would rightfully have absolutely no fear for her safety.

She left at dawn, and during the three-hour trip counted herself very lucky that she traveled well by water. Around her, people hung over the sides of the boat, seasick from start to finish. On arrival in Colihaut, when she said that she was looking for Matilda, the old woman who had been posed the question put her hands on her hips and stared, but only for a moment before remembering her manners. Of the multitudes that had come to Colihaut in search of Matilda, not one was white, or even near-white. Much less a nun. She walked Mary-Alice to a place on the shore where sweating, shirtless men were bent over nets, untangling them. She went up to one, a tall, broad-backed man, his black skin glittering from the sun. The old woman tapped his back and said to him, "Matilda." He set off with Mary-Alice without glancing back, knowing that the other fishermen would automatically secure his boat and nets and would share their catch with him later. They would not take chances with retribution when it came to a handmaiden of God.

He walked with the kind of lightness that came from the ability to balance at the bow of a five-foot-long rowboat, riding up and down waves that were nine feet high on a normal day, fourteen when it got rough. He took her along a footpath that soon ended at a river, and he looked at the hem of her habit, which touched the ground. He spoke to her in English. "Is foot trail most people taking to reach there, *oui*, but is four hours that taking. Night catching us coming back. By river, one hour."

Mary-Alice replied in perfect Creole: "Then the river it is."

He smiled his appreciation, but then when he went down on one knee in front of her, she didn't understand. Perhaps he wanted to have confession. He had turned his body so that he was facing away from her—she wondered if he might be ashamed of the things he was going to confess. "I'm sorry," she said, "only a priest can hear confession."

He looked around at her, and she was surprised to see from his eyes that he was laughing, although he had kept the rest of his face under control. "Yes, Sister, I know. I just need to carry you. If you would please get on my back?" She did not move, and he understood her hesitation, as unfounded as it was. From where they were standing, the river looked shallow enough. "Once the river turns that corner," he said, "the water is up to your waist and the current will be too strong for you."

"You can carry me upriver against the current?"

"Not *in* the water." He pointed to the scattered rocks and boulders. The tops of some could barely hold a child's foot. "I jump," he said. "I do it all the time, take people to Matilda by river."

There was something about the way he said the name Matilda, something she had also heard when the old woman said it to him. "Is Matilda somebody…of particular importance?"

His face opened up in surprise, and he got to his feet. "But you are going to her."

"About her daughter."

"You don't know her? Know about her?"

"I don't know anything about Matilda."

"You must be the only person in Dominica who doesn't."

"So what is there to know?"

"They say many things about her, what she is. The one thing I can tell you for sure: if you are sick, and if God not ready for you yet, then Matilda can fix you."

The word *fix* was one that had many meanings in Dominica, Mary-Alice had discovered. She wondered if he was talking about Obeah, some kind of voodoolike occult Dominicans apparently practiced in secret, but it was not the kind of topic a nun should raise with a stranger. She asked him, "So where are we going? I thought she lived here. Or nearby."

He shook his head. "Those people don't live on the coast with us. You have to go inland, to the forest."

This was the thing Mary-Alice was finding about Dominicans. They did not tell you things directly, but if you listened to their tone and other small indicators, words slipped into a sentence, they would give a little something away, and it was up to you to figure out their parable. "Why did you call them 'those people'?"

He shook his head. "Pardon?"

Mary-Alice wanted to keep speaking to this man. She liked to hear Dominicans use their French Creole, speaking it with an ease and precision denied them in their official language. She understood it easily, unlike their mangled English, which labored under the yoke of a broad French accent, African syntax, and unconjugated verbs in general. She was asking questions mostly for the sake of hearing his voice, hearing the way he sang his language. "You called them 'those people'—like they are different from you."

He shook his head. "You misunderstood my meaning. We are all the same." He pointed straight up. "They just live high up. Up There. The trails are very difficult."

"Up where?"

"Up to the flats. The top of the mountain."

Mary-Alice kept looking up, stepping back, unable to see where the mountain stopped. "So we go up the river, and then when we get to the mountain, we climb it?" she asked.

"Not at all, Sister. Nobody ever goes all the way up there, the climb is too much."

"I don't understand, then. Matilda—"

"You will pardon me, Sister. Everybody knows, I thought you would also. This is how it works. Matilda and some others live Up There, but you can always find a few of them tending some crops at the foot of the mountain. One of them will make the climb and bring her back down to see you."

"But—what is your name?—why does she cut herself off like that?"

"You are new to this island, Sister. It's only these last years we are getting roads and bridges and those things. Many of our villages are like that, not easy to reach." He lowered his eyes as he gestured upward, indicating the height of the mountain. "That is normal for Dominica." He knelt again. "They call me Bird, and please, if you would be kind enough to just get on my back?"

Some people, those who are more skeptical in nature, would say that what happened next was only to be expected. If you put a young and healthy woman who thus far had disowned her sexuality on the back of a muscular young man, then certain of her body parts would press against his back, resulting in arousal. In her inexperience, she would mistake her physical awakening for the more ephemeral condition of true love.

But there are those who would believe Mary-Alice when she said that her falling in love was completely spiritual. She would explain in detail to anyone who asked the question. Not why she left the convent: that was understandable. But why, having left the convent, she didn't go back to her rich parents in Texas, to the family and friends she knew. Why would a university-educated white woman marry a poor, uneducated fisherman and live with his people, bring herself down to their level, confining herself to their limited life?

It was, she said, something about his spirit—it was unfettered. She had first seen it through his eyes, when he had laughed inside of them and looked up at her from his knees. And then she felt it when she was on his back, eyes closed, flying from rock to rock—not jumping, not leaping, she would insist. He flew. His feet may have landed on the boulders, but there was such a weightlessness to his spirit that it suffused her, wrapped her up and lifted her, and it was no different from flight. The unbelievers would challenge her, telling her that he was merely an athlete, one who was good at long jumping, one with good balance; nimble on his feet, the kind who would do well in a circus as a tightrope walker, a trapeze artist.

She would not contemplate that. "His soul," she would say, "picked mine up, and we flew." And to those who gave her a disbelieving look, she would insist. "Have you never touched somebody and *felt* them? Felt what was inside of their body?" Only a few would know what she was talking about. To the others, who still insisted that she was with the man only on account of various nerve endings pressing on the muscles of his back, on account of his hands holding her thighs, to those she threw down a challenge. "The next time you see someone who is very, very happy, or very, very sad, put your arms around them. Not too tight, but all the way touching you. And then stay still, just a few seconds is all you need." And anyone who took the challenge would understand.

They took a boat to Guadeloupe the next day, because they knew there would be no priest in Dominica willing to marry them, and Mary-Alice, though no longer a nun, was still a Catholic and would not consider otherwise. The night before she left, she sat at the kitchen table of Bird's mother's house and wrote to her mother superior in the dirty light of a kerosene lamp.

Colihaut, 1945
Dear Mother,

I humbly ask your forgiveness in advance of my words. I have fallen deeply in love with a good and decent man, and must hereby renounce my vows. I realize the effect this will have on my beloved Church and on the convent, and on the good work to which you and your good sisters have given your lives. I will not be coming back to Roseau, thereby hoping to lessen the embarrassment and damage my actions may cause you and the Church.

But I write this letter not to highlight my transgression. I write instead about something much more important, about Iris, whose situation is well known to you. I have unsuccessfully pleaded with her mother to come to Roseau, to take her daughter away from the influence of John Baptiste.

Regretfully, the woman people call Matilda, an Obeahwoman, has turned out to have no sense of morality. She is a woman of great vulgarity. She is shameless and depraved. She finds no fault with her fourteen-year-old child being kept by a man who could be her father.

Mother, I beg you to remove the child from her current life of abuse, which offers her no future. If you or one of the fathers would go to take her away, the neighbors would never interfere.

I will pay, from my personal family funds, for the child's boarding school education in Grenada, Barbados, or Trinidad, and for her full support until she reaches adulthood. I have already written to my parents, and the money will be credited to the convent's account on a monthly basis.

I close with great trepidation, wondering if my own actions may cause you to look with disfavor on my intercession on the child's behalf. But I also pray that your reputation for goodness and compassion will prevail. I know that you will look beyond my weaknesses and my sins, and you will see your way to rescuing the child.

Asking your forgiveness, I remain,

Mary-Alice

The unopened letter was torn up and thrown at the feet of Bird's grandmother, who had hand-delivered it to the convent. For the next five months Mary-Alice wrote pleading letter after letter, addressing them to different nuns, to each priest, sending different messengers hoping to trick someone into reading them. But a policy was in place, once that had served the Church well and would continue to do so. When faced with the unspeakable, they would not speak, and to keep such silence meant pretending that the unspeakable had not happened. Not one of the perhaps twenty, twenty-five letters was ever opened.

Mary-Alice realized she would have to retrieve Iris herself, despite the attention it would bring to her defection, despite the shame it would bring to the Church. She was already pregnant, her belly showing high and round, but she would risk retribution. She would put on her nun's habit, and the washerwomen would have no choice but to give her the child.

She took her habit from under her bed and laid it in the sun, knowing that her pregnancy would actually help, it would evoke the idea of Mary. The washerwomen would see her not just as the Mother of God but also as his Bride—and what power, what potency she would have at her disposal. It would not be scandalous at all to those women, who, like the people in the time of Mary, could easily ignore the question of paternity in order to focus fully on the miracle of motherhood.

At times she believed she had offended her God with her grandiose fantasies of herself as his Mother and his Bride, but since her God was not supposed to be a vengeful one, she preferred to blame the devil—it was the devil who would not be crossed by a pregnant nun. Other times Mary-Alice wondered if neither had been involved, and if it was just that Iris had her destiny to which she was steadily spinning. From that perspective, it was a little easier to bear, because in such a scenario it was not personal at all: fate threatened Mary-Alice's pregnancy, fate put her on her back with her legs higher than her heart until her child was born, and fate gave her a birthing in which she almost lost her life, such that it was months before she was able to stand.

By the time she was strong enough to begin making plans to travel to Roseau, some force—fate, the devil, God, or the collusion of all three—had already sent Iris home.

18

BURNT OFFERINGS

Lillian found herself kneeling in an empty, darkened church the night before she left for Dominica, praying for peace. It was the first time she had entered a church since she was seven years old, having stayed away for thirty years.

Once, she had filled out a questionnaire in Teddy's presence, and she had ticked off the box next to "Catholic."

"No you're not," he had said, laughing. "You don't believe that hocus-pocus—you aren't even religious."

"If you say you're not Black," she said to him, "does that mean you aren't?"

He did not understand, and she did not explain that to be a Catholic was not so much a religious denomination, it was more like an ethnicity. You could reject it, deny it, but it remained there forever, it was under your skin.

She walked into St. Augustine's, the one African-American Catholic church in D.C. She blessed herself with holy water, lit her candles, knelt in front of the statue of the Virgin, and asked for a favor. Her life so far, but for her early childhood, had been one of torment, and she was praying in the way she prayed, letting the words come as a solid wave of internal sound, a barrier of protection, and she was asking for peace.

She had, just over a week earlier, knelt in her apartment praying that Teddy would go with her—she knew she could not do it without him, she would not be able to get on the plane alone, nor would she be able to process the details of her past without the flashbacks interfering and shutting her down. That had been the first time in her life when she had prayed for anything except for the forgiveness of whatever terrible sins she had inherited, because it was there in scripture, that the sins of the father would be visited on the son, and hadn't she been marked by whatever her grandmother had done, whatever her grandmother had been?

And now, fearful that she was being greedy with her wishes, she had come here, on her knees again, daring to pray that all she knew about herself and her history was untrue, and she prayed that, at the end of it all, she would have peace.

She had contemplated also asking that love might last—she had briefly thought she might pray for that, but she stopped herself from asking for such a bold thing.

L illian did not go home for some time, sitting in a back pew, feeling protected. She remembered the significance church held when she was a small child. She recalled how much she loved everything about Sunday and its ceremonies, the day of the week around which all other days turned.

Early every Sunday morning, Icilma would change Lillian's everyday Miraculous Medal, replacing it with a long gold chain with the heavy gold cross. She dressed Lillian in her best white and blue and took her to church. Lillian wore clothes of no other colors until the day she was sent away to America, because she had been dedicated to the Blessed Virgin. Until that point she had assumed that, like the other girls who wore Mary's colors exclusively, she had been ill as an infant—close to death—and the dedication had been a bargain struck—an understanding of some kind—between her mother and the Mother of God.

There was the echo of the cathedral and the warmth of it, the faint dankness and the incense smell, the longing sound of the organ, the feeling of being part of something exclusive—the way everyone, including those as young as Lillian, knew when to stand and when to kneel and could join in the communal recitation of prayers, even when the words were beyond their understanding.

Then, immediately after the solemnity of the two-hour mass, things would turn absolutely festive when the cooking for Sunday lunch began, and in those days Icilma's Sunday table was full of relatives and friends, so many that the kitchen stove could not handle the many dishes that had to be prepared, and any number of small coal pots would be set out in the backyard to cook the less intricate dishes—for the simple boiling of ground provisions or rice or the heating up of a pot of callaloo.

Lillian remembered one particular Sunday afternoon, a proud moment for her—four years old, and able to memorize the words of a Creole song she had heard on the radio after hearing it only twice. It was a song that confirmed to the child that her mother was right; that drinking Coke was bad for one's health, and having understood the song, Lillian was ready to acquiesce and stop pleading for the bubbling black drink that made such a satisfying burn at the back of her throat.

The song told the story of a lady who enjoyed eating healthily. This lady, the song said, truly liked her cucumbers, her carrots, her bananas, even the long tubers of cassava, she had them all the time, daily and twice daily; she enjoyed them massively, and was in the fullness of health as a result. Then one day the same lady had a bottle of Coke and it nearly killed her.

Lillian stood in her backyard on a Sunday afternoon after church singing this song for Icilma, who had been checking the heat of the coals, her hand held above them. The child noticed that her mother was not reacting; she seemed unimpressed, she was looking at her in a strange way, as if she were not really seeing her. And so Lillian sang louder, harder, with feeling. She put her hands akimbo, she bent her knees and circled her hips, attempting to imitate the way the maids and cooks moved when they danced.

It was only after, when someone had smelled the stench of her step-mother's hand, after people came running outside and somebody clamped a hand over her mouth, did Lillian realize that Icilma's hand had dropped on top of the white-hot coals, and had stayed there, sending up smoke, all the time she had been singing.

19

BODY AND BLOOD

The precise point at which people said Iris lost her mind was subject to debate. Some thought it was already clearly gone when she stood at the bottom of the cathedral steps watching his wedding, just as she had watched him escorting his mother the day she announced herself to him. It was the impassivity, the rigidity with which she stood and stared, that made them think she had gone mad. Others saw nothing strange about it; they themselves had adopted that same stance in the same spot against their own rivals, standing immobile, planting their feet down solid like tree trunks with deep roots to show they were going nowhere, to mock the women who felt that climbing up the steps of the cathedral in white and signing a paper meant they had won.

Others said it was the birth of his twins within a year of the wedding that did it. But all agreed that by the time she did what she did to Cecile Richard Baptiste that Carnival Monday, just months after his wife had given birth, she was already a bona fide lunatic.

It was Masquerade Monday evening, still two nights and one day to go before Ash Wednesday. Under normal circumstances it would have been a fairly calm night with a few soirees, over early so people could save their energy for Mardi Gras. Instead, it was as if Masquerade had not yet started. In every district of Roseau, the *chantuelles* had called back their drummers and spent all night practicing a new set of *chanté mas* songs that told the story of what had happened that morning.

That Monday, the one that went down in history, John Baptiste's wife, the former Cecile Richard, had not returned to her own house, but stayed at the Richard family home with her sisters, female cousins, and family friends. Her infant twins and all the other children of the Richard clan had been sent to their estate house to stay with the country relatives until it was all over, until all the songs had been sung.

The women surrounded Cecile and raised their voices in indignation and anger to hide their shame, as the doctor in the upstairs bedroom eventually gave her mother an injection strong enough to keep her sleeping until Ash Wednesday. Along with the children, men, too, had been banished from the house. John and his entourage, including the Richard men, were gathered at the Baptiste house, where they sat in silence, drinking.

The women spent the night analyzing, agonizing over the details of what had happened, trying to figure out why no one had stopped it before it got to that stage. There had been so many points at which somebody could have done something. It was the masks, they lamented, the compulsory full-body coverage, that allowed people to get away with all kinds of badness in the band. Were people going to wait until somebody got killed before it would be acceptable to dance in the streets with faces uncovered?

Even if Iris managed to enter the band undetected, what about when she elbowed out Cecile's younger sister and latched onto John's left arm? Cecile had not seen the switch, but others should have noticed. None admitted that it was obvious to everyone in the band that John was "running *mas*" with both his wife and his keep-woman, because that would be confessing to the indulgences they permitted themselves and one another during the two days out of each year when they lived behind a mask. So they lied collectively: behind her mask, they said, they couldn't distinguish Iris from one of their own.

What about when she stepped out of the horizontal line that had been formed by the three sets of arms interlocked around the three waistlines, when she moved from his side, when she stepped in front of him and rubbed her backside around and around, against the front of his pants? Thirty years later, when Cecile's friends and relatives had their wish granted, when it was acceptable for women to jump in the streets without masks, almost without any clothes at all, that particular rotating move would evolve into a standard form of Carnival street dancing. But back then, when Carnival was still Masquerade, what Iris did to John was the most obscene public demonstration they had ever seen.

At that point, they agreed, someone should have grabbed her and pulled her out of the band, thrown her to the *bande mauvais* people for them to beat her and stone her. But, they decided in hindsight, they must have been in shock, immobilized by seeing what they had never witnessed before in bright sunlight, except as performed by domestic and farm animals—certainly what they imagined they looked like under deep cover of dark, between their sheets, was nothing like what Iris was doing. And so yes indeed, they said, it was the shock of her vulgarity that stopped them from intervening.

What about what came next? How could they have stood around hiding behind their masks when Iris walked up to their friend—no, someone corrected, Iris had not walked up to Cecile. She had gyrated up to her, she had shown Cecile what she did with her husband, demonstrated to her the act of fornication. She had writhed up to her, pelvis rocking back and forth, in and out, first one leg up, then the other, and with both her hands pulled off Cecile's mask and then easily ripped off the man's pajama suit Cecile was wearing. Tore the top off, brassiere and all, and then pulled off the bottoms by the elastic, panties and all, Cecile going down hard on the tarmac as they came off. John—wearing Cecile's white lace-and-voile nightgown, the one she had worn on their first honeymoon night—had beat Cecile to the ground. He had instantly fainted at the sight of his wife's swollen, milk-dripping breasts springing out from between Iris's hands.

By the time Cecile was lying naked and unmasked on the street at Iris's feet, there was silence in the band and nothing was moving. The *chantuelle* had stopped her lead when she realized that most of her band was not singing back the chorus. From her vantage point at the front of the band, dancing backward to gauge the mood of her revelers, choosing her song and directing her drummers accordingly, she could see that something was happening in the center of the band, and she signaled for her drummers to stop. Then she heard the refined voice of Cecile Richard shouting, "*Salop*, I will kill you." By the time the *chantuelle* pushed her way to the center, she found two naked women rolling around on the ground.

Then the silence was over, and the men began to cheer, because there is no sight more arousing to a man than that of two women together. Whether they are making love or doing battle against each other is of no consequence, since to an observer, in the absence of the context, there is no visible difference between the two.

It didn't even take Mrs. Richard a full week to enact her plan: two days to wake up, one day to rant and throw nonvaluable breakables around her house. Two days to make travel arrangements and put Cecile, her nursemaid, and the twin babies on the boat to Barbados for a long vacation. On the day before she went to find Iris, Mrs. Richard visited her confessor and was very careful to speak in nonspecific terms. She was not afraid that the priest would tell the police. He knew her well and probably would not. Even if he did, the police understood such matters and would think she had every right.

The motive for her preemptive confession was not particularly to seek advance forgiveness, although that would be fine. But vengeance is mine, saith the Lord, and she needed to buy herself some time. If her carefully worded confession were to be delivered to God through the filter of a sympathetic priest, she might just pull off her plan before the Almighty, in his omnipotence, found out what she had done. Then he could strike her down, and she would go to her damnation happily. But not before she paid her visit to Iris.

Six days after the disgrace of her daughter—of her entire family— Mrs. Richard went to find Iris in broad daylight, knowing that a lightning bolt might strike her down, but that there would be no earthly intervention, not even from the loyal neighbors. They would understand that a limit had been reached, a boundary crossed: there had been an abomination, after all. Those black washerwomen, diluted into brown and red and yellow as some were, who only practiced Africa's religions in a corrupted, secret way, would still quite expect that there would need to be some kind of purification to placate the gods of social order and the gods of class distinction and the gods that allowed a man to have as many women as he so pleased. There would need to be a bloodletting, a sacrifice. Mrs. Richard had chosen blood, and it was her prerogative.

The two assistants Mrs. Richard chose were her servants, the cook and the housekeeper of her estate house, whose great-grandmothers had been owned by hers. In fact, the three women shared the same great-grandfather—which the cook and the housekeeper advertised widely. She never even had to ask them, never had to tell them what they were going to do. When Mrs. Richard arrived at her estate in the early morning to look for them, she knew to go to the river. They spotted her first, walking high above them along a narrow ledge curving around the mountainside, careful in her town shoes on the slippery moss. They left the soap on their bodies, scrambling up the stony path to the ledge where she balanced, unaccustomed, with one hand holding the side of the mountain for support. They wanted to save her the indignity of having to seek them out, of appearing to need them. They stood in front of their mistress-cousin out of breath, white triangles of froth respectfully covering their private parts.

"Yes, madam, we ready," said one.

"Today," Mrs. Richard told them.

"Yes, madam, we ready," said the other.

Iris was waiting for them, sitting calmly on her dressed-up mattress, wearing white lace and an oversized pair of *pomme-cannelle* earrings that looked exactly like the fruit after which it was named, small balls clumped together into one large sphere. She had aired out the mattress the day before, taking out each piece of the old clothes with which it was stuffed, shaking them and sunning them to kill the mites and to remove the musty smell that always accumulated over time. The mattress did not have a frame: it sat on the floor, but it was elegantly made up with a hand-crocheted bedspread, the finest of the dozens that were neatly stacked in her tall armoire. She did not take money from John except what she needed for food. What she demanded from him was a regular supply of new bedspreads and linens, like those used on the gift beds in the homes of the brides-to-be. And she demanded gold *pomme-cannelle* earrings in every size and variation.

Iris had withheld sex from John once and only once. That was when his mother had died. "I want your mother's earrings. The ones Cecile wore for her wedding." John had refused. They were a family heirloom, and would go to Cecile for her to pass on to their first girl child. "I can copy them for you. I can make them bigger. Smaller. More modern." He offered her a trip to Martinique, where she could pick out any one she wanted. She laughed at that, because she went nowhere but to the river to wash her skin and her clothes and to pretend to walk on water with the children. She kept her legs shut tight. Within a week John had brought her the earrings, the same ones she was wearing that day as she waited for Cecile's family to come.

They used their bare hands and feet. The first thing they did was to tear the earrings out of her ears and hand them to Mrs. Richard. "These do not belong to you, little whore."

Iris took her beating as she had intended, like a Carib; she would have fought to her death if she had a chance of winning, but she would not give them the satisfaction of a futile struggle. She did not even raise a hand to protect her face when their knuckles had pulverized her flesh, tenderized it so that each new blow caused the spot upon which it fell to burst open, blood oozing or jettisoning out, streaming down to the wooden floor and collecting in small pools. Not the smallest sound forced its way out of her windpipe when the pain began in earnest, when the knuckles and the feet began targeting internal organs, the kidneys, the spleen. Not even when one of them jumped on her chest and sent a rib into her heart.

But when Mrs. Richard said, "Enough of that," and opened her handbag, when the beating stopped, that was when Iris began to scream, to fight against the two sets of hands that were now holding her limbs down. She had seen what came out of the purse, and she knew what it was for.

Mrs. Richard moved away from the wall, where she had stayed quietly watching the beating. She held the bottle by its narrow end, raised it high, and hit it against the wall, then against the corner of the tall armoire, then against the floor. The glass was too thick, the wood too soft, the bottle would not break. She stood in one spot in the small room, circling slowly, looking for something harder. Iris's screams had changed now, had become less and less piercing, until the sounds came from the back of her throat, a hoarse yelping.

Outside, the washerwomen had gathered waiting for it to be over, waiting to see if they would have to take Iris to the hospital or if she was so far gone that only her mother's medicine would help her. Even during the initial silence from Iris, they were not fooled regarding the severity of the beating: the girl was a Carib, she would take her blows in silence. From the steady dull thudding sounds, they could tell that they could not patch her up themselves.

The screaming so late into the beating confused them, started them muttering and inching closer to the house. But when they heard the animal sound that replaced the screaming, they went rigid. They began rubbing their arms, holding down the backs of their necks against their crawling flesh. They shuffled backward, fear on their faces. What kind of Obeah, their eyes asked one another, was being done in there? Because Iris now sounded exactly like she did when she and John were fucking.

In the one-room house, Mrs. Richard found what she needed, Iris's enamel chamber pot. It was a graceful movement, a single, fluid sweep of arm that came from high and went down low to break the bottle near the floor. Her whole body swung down, following her arm, and then she rose up in an easy pivot to align herself with the place where Iris lay on her bride's gift bed, knees pinned down to the sides of her chest. And then it stopped being graceful as Mrs. Richard planted the jagged end of the bottle as far up into Iris as her hand would go. And then again, and then again. Until finally her hand came out empty, covered with blood midway to her elbow.

They left Iris on her bed in the position her well-intentioned neighbors had once counseled her to assume. Advice she had never taken.

She was flat on her back with her legs wide open, and as her neighbors had also advised, she was not moving at all.

20

RECONCILIATION

His schedule had been reorganized: interviews canceled, meetings and appointments rescheduled; and if the trip took longer than the seven-day spring break, Teddy's classes would be covered by an adjunct. Just the previous Friday evening, he had waited for Lillian in his home two blocks away from where he now sat, alfresco, at a small table for two. Tomorrow he would travel to Dominica with her, but before that he had unfinished business that could not wait. He was meeting his ex-wife at the Georgetown waterfront. Diane had picked the venue; she would be having dinner with someone there later, she said.

Around him, the weekend scene was picking up. On his left, the open-air bars were filling with the trendy nymphet types. On his other side, forty-foot luxury boats were tying up to each other, having quickly run out of space to dock along the short boardwalk. The boats were four and five deep, stretching well out into the Potomac, steadily rocking from side to side thanks to the heavy foot traffic as people walked across them to access the bars. Many of the boat owners were, he saw, male, Black, and young (but not single, despite the absence of wives), and had he would guess—from the amount of shouting and pushing off, lowering of bumpers, and panic every time another one pulled up—minimal boating experience, certainly none beyond the Potomac. They had traveled the five minutes over flat river water from the nearby boatyards in vessels designed to handle open seas and ocean swells, only to sit there, be seen, and possibly pick up one or two or three of the sisters who came in small groups—safety in numbers—to stroll along the boardwalk, dressed to enhance the chance that they might be invited to sit on a boat, have a drink, and explore the other possibilities. It was, he supposed, a nautical version of what happened at Hanes Point with the parade of freshly waxed cars.

My people, my people, Teddy thought, shaking his head at the fleet of oversized boats bobbing on the narrow river, but he did not dwell too long on it. There were many other things on his mind: what he was going to say to Diane, as well as all the things Lillian had said to him, although, a week into the telling of her story and twelve hours before he would leave for Dominica, he still didn't have anything close to a full picture. They had made love every night since the first time (and in spite of its violent intensity, or because of it, Teddy could use no other words for what they did), but she told only small, often disconnected segments at a time, some nights not speaking at all, sometimes immediately falling into the exhausted sleep of a manual laborer, as if physically overwhelmed by fatigue. He remembered that about her, from the days when they would pull term-paper all-nighters—her hard, deep sleep, upper body flat out across the desk in the computer lab.

Lillian had long been obsessed with her grandmother's crime—her past, it had been about that—she was fixated on it. "Suppose," Lillian kept saying, "suppose she didn't do it? I don't think there was any other evidence, except her word. Suppose it was like the boys, the police interrogated her for hours and hours and eventually she surrendered like all the other people who give false confessions."

"Perhaps," he would say in response. "Could be." She was so distraught when she talked, he didn't want to push too hard. Asking too many questions disoriented her, but he understood, she had held so much in for so long. "Count me in," he told her, "I'm there." Fifty-three years after her grandmother was hanged for murder, he was going with Lillian to Dominica, where she hoped to sort out her past, to find at least some indication that her grandmother was innocent. There was little chance they could find anything concrete in one week, he was clear about that, but she obviously needed to go for closure. At the very least, she'd be able to reconcile with her stepmother, that alone would be worth the trip.

Not that it mattered to him what the purpose of the trip was. He would go because she asked him to go. Before he went, though, he wanted a word with his ex-wife. He was apprehensive: it was to be their first meeting without their lawyers since their divorce, when her interaction with him had deteriorated into a kind of venomous hissing over his refusal to return the wedding gift she'd given him, even though he had given her the house and all of its other contents. He was surprised she took that tack, because she was the one who initiated the divorce, and it hadn't been over any of his affairs—those he had kept from her using the successful male tool of categorical denial; but one day, a few weeks after joining some kind of reading group, she announced the marriage was over. His memory of the moment was one of acute relief on two fronts, that he was free to just walk, and that they'd delayed having children. Seeing her approach now, he felt the same relief again as he stood to draw her chair.

She moved casually, easily, as she sat, turning to hang her purse on the back of the chair. Her skirt was short; her hair grown too long for her age. She had lost class, Teddy thought, but acquired confidence. "I didn't think you'd come," he said.

"Curiosity got the better of me. So. What's this all about?" There was calculated amusement in her tone. "You nervous, Teddy? You're playing with your hair—oh, my manners. Congrats on the gang-rape business. Amazing, that I was married to a famous man. Thought of calling you in December, but I figured sleeping dogs should lie. No pun." She was reading him, could see the sincerity he was trying to project, and was thwarting it.

"I owe you an apology," he said.

"You owe me a Bearden." Her tone shifted to the one he remembered from the negotiations. "That painting was my grandfather's. He willed it to me—but you know, Teddy, that's fine. I let go of a lot of things, I'm past that—"

"Diane. Tell me something. Why did you give it to me?"

"Fucking asshole." Teddy flinched when she said that. It was the first time he had ever heard her curse, not even a *damn* had crossed her lips in the years he knew her. "Use the brains they say you have. How about, I gave it to you because I was in love with you. How about, I thought we'd get old together and die together and the painting would pass on to our kids—that ever cross your ignorant mind?" She was not quite shouting, but her body language—hands on hips, leaning forward from the waist, neck rolling—was drawing attention from the boaters. They recognized him, they were pointing.

Teddy let a few moments pass as she composed herself. "I'm sorry," he said. "I let you think the divorce was your fault, I never admitted—"

"You're insulting me. *You* said you weren't fucking them, but that doesn't mean *I* was stupid enough to deny my own intelligence. Please. Exactly what am I doing here? All this belated truth-telling, that's for you, to make yourself feel good. I don't appreciate being used for your catharsis."

"About Lillian," he said.

She was silent for a moment. She put her palms together, just under her chin, as if holding it up by her fingertips. Then she clasped her hands, rested them on her crossed knee. Her head remained at an unusual angle, as if she realized that her whole body had slumped, and this, the head held too high, was all she could do to compensate. "I knew it. I knew it. I knew it." She was almost whispering.

"No. No, it was just friendship, at least—Di, I swear, it wasn't like that back then, not an affair."

"But now?"

Teddy nodded. "Yes. Now, yes." It was easy to know when a woman was about to end her interaction with you, Teddy thought, the way she instinctively reaches for her purse. He spoke fast. "I lied about the affairs, but I just want you to know that I never lied to you about Lillian—because I didn't let myself accept it—wait a minute, wait, Diane, what I mean is that—"

"Now *you* tell me something. Why the fuck did you marry me in the first place?"

"I married you because I had a grip on our attraction, I could understand why we were together. For me, it was who you were, your social standing—you knew that—and for you it was my ambition. You always admitted that."

"For me it was falling in love with a man I worshiped."

"Okay, listen. Don't go, Diane, just listen, just one more minute. I'm not saying we didn't love each other. I'm saying I knew our feelings made sense, you know? The feelings came from somewhere. We had things, qualities, that the other wanted. I had rejected that idea of a soul mate—"

"Like Lillian?"

Teddy lowered his head. She was through listening to him anyway, and even if he could explain, it would sound so trite, even though it had felt like he had uncovered a universal truth. He had loved Lillian for twenty years but he had denied it.

Diane was already standing, waving at a man seated at a nearby table. Teddy reached under his chair for the package he had so carefully wrapped in plain brown paper, tied with simple string. "This belongs to you," he said, rising to give it to her. "It was small of me. I apologize."

21

CLASH

It was *j'ouvert,* the opening of the day, and it was still dark. The true start of Masquerade, Monday morning. One year less six days had passed since Iris was placed in the back of a pickup truck like a sack of onions, a bunch of bananas, a bag of limes, and taken to the waterfront, where she was loaded onto a tiny wooden boat and motored north out of Roseau to Colihaut.

A year less six days since Mary-Alice had behaved like the Lebanese women and gone down on her knees at the Colihaut wharf in front of the dying girl to cry out to the Blessed Virgin for mercy and for compassion and for pity. And a little more than a year since Matilda worked on her daughter, drawing out the infections from every crevice of her body, from her very blood; realigning joints that had been twisted out of their proper places, constructing complex traction devices with rope and stones for the limbs that had been broken, taking needle and catgut to sew back together the gashes. Matilda did not waste too much time on the vagina and uterus, knowing that those are designed for rapid healing, having to withstand the regular battering of sex and the periodic punishments of childbirth. It was the punctured heart that would have killed her daughter, and it was the resulting infection that Matilda fought as if it were a personal enemy, not only with medical science but with the fresh blood of white chickens spilled up and down her child's body, with oils and pig fat, with the lighting of black candles and the incantation of unintelligible words. And just when Matilda was going to send her daughter back to town, to turn to even the inferior medicine that was practiced in Roseau, the fever broke and one could say that Iris recovered, although her heart had been permanently damaged, and nothing could be done about what had happened to her soul.

Iris left her mother and her village not long after she regained her strength, just got up and walked away, using the footpaths through the mountains, back to Roseau, and she never saw mother or village again.

That dark *j'ouvert* morning, all the *bandes mauvais* were already out, early as usual, to taunt the police. In their houses, the people of Roseau could not yet see them, but their presence was violently announced by the sound of their feet hitting the road, the metal Coke bottle tops nailed to their high-platformed wooden shoes, the sound of thousands of tiny cymbals clashing at exactly the same time. For Roseau people, especially the children, if their yearlong anticipation of Masquerade could be compressed into a single sound, it would be that shattering predawn noise from another world that interrupted their dreams and told them it would soon be time to put on their masks and costumes, pick up their sticks, hold them high, and "find the road." The roads of Roseau would happily be their home for as much of the following two days as their stamina and the law would permit.

Six in the morning was the permitted time for the revelry to begin, and the rule was strictly obeyed by the other bands of masqueraders "running *mas.*" The variety of costume options, and their simplicity, ensured that anyone, so long as they could lay hands on a mask, could run. A man needed nothing more than his woman's nightgown or one of her traditional outfits, especially her *jupe*—its drawstring lace petticoat and madras overskirt could easily be adjusted to accommodate a man's larger frame, as would its wide-necked chemise. A woman could pull on a man's pajama or his long-jacketed, padded-shouldered, thin-ankled zoot suit, so long as she penciled in a mustache. They could go a little more elaborate, running in a band of Indians, cowboys, clowns, sailors, matadors. They could cover themselves head to foot with oil and soot to run with a band of darkies, or choose to do the same thing with red ocher mud.

But the *bandes mauvais* were out long before six. It was their raison d'être, to demonstrate that they were the highest authority. To have the police back away when they menaced, to have people run in fear when they approached. To command respect. To show they ruled the road in their fearsome *sensay* costumes, some covered with their thick mantles of dried banana leaves, some with their layers of frayed rope, some with their stripped cloth, their girth and stature magnified into threatening proportions, with their cow horns sitting up on their heads above their wire masks. Those few men and those fewer women who were allowed into the *bande mauvais*, who remained theoretically anonymous, had no idea why they did these things—why they beat up those who did not defer, why they faced down the police, why they stoned houses; no idea why, when circling the narrow streets of town, they would never give way if they came face-to-face with another band.

They did not know that thousands of miles across the Atlantic, there were a few men who, during the times of African festivals, during harvest celebrations, during religious and political and judicial ceremonies, initiations, births and deaths, would adorn themselves in exactly the same attire, wear their masks and horns, and for a time would become the embodiment of the gods of the savannas and the forests, representations of the spirits of the ancestors, wherein lay the highest authority.

The only thing these revelers on the other side of the Atlantic knew was that they were to be feared and respected, otherwise there would be retribution, and it was in that spirit that John Baptiste had applied to join the Newtown *bande mauvais*. He had tried to get in before and had been rejected, not being considered of *mauvais* enough temperament for what amounted to a secret society of drunken brawlers and bad-johns. But after what had happened the previous Masquerade, John had grown in the estimation of his townsmen. He had fainted, yes, but nobody remembered that, nobody had even noticed, given what had been going on with his wife and his mistress. Certainly he had to be some kind of a bad-john to have such things done in public on his account. And six days after that (although the fight would have been enough), his mother-in-law guaranteed a place for him, she had put the servant in her place.

By eight o'clock that morning, all the galleries of Roseau's residential homes were filled with spectators, many of them looking down specifically in search of him, straining to be the first to identify him, a veritable superstar in their eyes, although the real hero was in their midst—his mother-in-law, who made a point of leaning over her veranda railing, the better to be seen by all. She had persuaded Cecile to stay in town for Masquerade, promising that there would be few if any embarrassing *chanté mas* songs in the street to chronicle the previous year's episode. Mrs. Richard had gone personally to every single *chantuelle* and offered bribes in amounts that could not be resisted. So Cecile was there, too, though reluctantly, standing next to her mother, two fully vindicated women, acknowledging the people on the galleries who waved at them in solidarity and in victory.

The Newtown *bande mauvais* was coming up the street, and a roar went up from the veranda spectators up and down King George V Street.

They had spotted John running *mas* on top of the highest wooden shoes, which, as he had promised, were painted devil red to help his fans identify him. His cow horns were the tallest and fattest, his Coke-bottle covers slammed hardest on the asphalt, his rope *sensay* costume the thickest and the most meticulously made, the heavy rope bleached for weeks in kerosene and unraveled and then carefully combed to create just the right consistency, texture, and volume. His beard of frayed fiber reached all the way to the ground, adding still another layer to the many that had been sewn in overlapping horizontal panels to the base coat of the costume. John Baptiste now looked like a being from another realm, a thing one would come upon in a forest, should a forest be capable of generating a spirit representation of itself—something at once organic yet unearthly.

Cecile was standing next to her mother looking at the masked thing that was her husband, wondering how it was possible to hate someone as much as she hated him yet be obliged to stand up next to him in public and lie down under him in private, until parted by death. She turned her head, looking away, up the street to keep the smile from disintegrating off her face, and she was the first to see them round the corner and start their descent down the hill.

"Clash," she said to her mother, and the word ran from gallery to gallery the length of the street.

The people who were downstairs drinking ran upstairs for a better view of the upcoming fight. The Newtown band realized what was happening and they stopped advancing, holding ground. They had just been jumping frenetically and now the bandleader held his sticks high, and for a moment they were motionless, soundless. Then he brought the sticks together again, hit them together, but this time slowly, setting a new rhythm, and he picked up his feet and put them down deliberately. When the pace was that slow, so tightly executed, the sound was a menacing one, a sound that bore no resemblance to celebration, but rather one that embodied dread and inspired fear. They added a third layer to the hitting of the sticks and the crashing of the metal bottle caps under their boots. They began to exhale on the offbeat with a force that made a primal sound, a grunt coming up from deep inside their chests, wordless, foreboding, and full of threat. They held their place, and the other band kept coming down.

There were now no children left lining the sidewalks of King George V Street, and most women had also sought protection inside the houses, which were now crowded, not only with invited guests and family friends, but with anyone off the street who could squeeze inside—such was the protocol of a clash.

A pair of colonial administrators, invited by Mrs. Richard to view Masquerade from her gallery, were greatly enjoying her rum punch and crab backs, the *akara titiri* and callaloo. They were both newly arrived in Dominica; it was their first Masquerade. The older of the pair had made the rounds of Her Majesty's African colonies for most of his career, the younger having attended a short meeting once in Nairobi.

"Astonishing, wouldn't you say," observed the elder.

"Remarkable. Exactly, I mean exactly, like the Masai."

His colleague stopped chewing on the grundy of a crab, the sweetest flesh he had ever tasted. "Don't be silly. Nomadic pastoralists don't have a masking tradition."

"The sound they're making, I mean, not the costumes. I've heard the Masai do that sound when they dance."

The older man, one Mr. Alfred Drummond, waved his crab grundy at his younger counterpart. "East Africa." A dismissal. "Too many settlers there for you to know the Africa I'm talking about. The real thing. West Africa. I nearly died there." He said it with pride. "Malaria." He pointed down to the *bande mauvais*. They were holding place, they had not advanced at all. "Those, if you imagine wooden masks instead of the wire things—those are exactly like the West African masquerades. I'll show you my photographs sometime."

His colleague looked up the street, not particularly interested. The other band was getting closer. He squinted. "*Those* have wooden masks," he said.

The older man raised the binoculars hanging around his neck to his eyes, lowered them quickly. "Fascinating." He blinked fast and raised his eyebrows to emphasize his interest. "An incredible assortment—the thing is"—and he looked again through his binoculars—"thing is, they're wearing masks from all over the west coast. Nigeria, Sierra Leone, the Gold Coast, Liberia . . . If I'm not mistaken, there could be some Central African masking traditions in there as well." His face showed fond reminiscing. "I once was a guest of the Belgian king in the Congo. Now *that* was the heart of Africa!" He was becoming very excited, getting red in the face. "I should invite the British Anthropological Society down here. One look at this, they would have a full list of all the African tribes that ended up in Dominica."

His colleague shrugged. "Who would care, at this point?"

"You would be surprised how many British anthropologists would just love to know who went where—of course they can tell the large concentrations from linguistic evidence and so forth, but the slave ship records are terrible in terms of the tribal identity of the slaves. Generally the records just gave the name of the port where they were loaded, if that much." He drank his rum punch and smacked the flat of his tongue against the roof of his mouth. "Wonderful drink, all those fresh limes. But you know, you're right. It doesn't matter to these people, but anthropologists find that kind of thing rather interesting—ah, the Igbos were here for sure!"

"How can you possibly tell?" They were the only people speaking.

The spectators were waiting for the clash, and they stage-whispered at each other, not wanting to break the unwritten code that was now in operation.

Alfred Drummond handed over his binoculars. "All kinds of indicators. Take a look at the one in the front, to the left a bit? You see? That's a bird carved at the top of the mask—it's bending over. It's captured a serpent in its beak—see the serpent carved along the forehead? That's a common theme among the Igbo, the serpent and the bird."

"But how can the person under there see anything? The mask is carved from a solid block of wood—doesn't seem like the eyes have holes."

"It's a *helmet* mask. Sits on top of the head, makes them look taller, more fearsome. That stuff hanging down from the bottom of the mask—raffia—the fringe that looks like squiggly straw, that's what covers the face. They can see through it. Look at how the whole body is covered with the raffia."

The band with the wooden masks was in no hurry, but their advance was steady. Unlike the *bande mauvais,* they did not make their rhythm from sticks and stomps and grunts, they were coming down with their retinue of drummers in the rear. When it became easier to see them, the wooden masks did not come as a big surprise to the Dominicans: most of the older spectators remembered the time before the wire masks, when they all used to carve their Masquerade masks out of wood.

But excited fingers still pointed, eyes squinted and strained to see better, because these certainly seemed, even from a distance, to be more elaborate than what they remembered, more detailed. Certainly more grotesque.

Pinned between her mother and the older British man, Cecile put her hand into the pocket of her skirt and pulled out her rosary. At the sight of the masks in the distance, something had filled her stomach, then her chest, her heart. Something she later would describe as a premonition. She rolled bead after bead between thumb and forefinger, and found that she was not reciting the entire prayer, that she kept repeating only the very end: *Holy Mary, Mother of God, pray for us sinners, now and at the hour of our death.*

Directly below the town home of Mrs. Richard, in the street in front of it, her son-in-law was facing the first test of his bravery as a member of the Newtown *bande mauvais*. As a child, he had run away from fights, a reputation that had followed him into adulthood, and now that he had finally made it into the club of don't-care fighters, he could acknowledge that he was only proving a point. He would have much preferred to use the opportunity to be with one of the new women he'd found since Iris was gone, since the grudging machinations Cecile called sex would not satisfy a monk. Poor Iris, she did not deserve what she'd gotten, and he would always think of her with sad longing, although now he mostly just thought of his new women, and what sweet loving they gave him, the kind of crazed passion that happened in bed with a woman when there were no disappointments to turn her into a close-faced, close-legged bitch, the kind of pleasure that was possible when all the woman wanted from him was the same thing he wanted from her, just the simplest and greatest pleasure this short life had to offer.

He turned his head to look up, trying to spot Cecile on her mother's gallery, but there were too many people. Even to be with her today, that would have been preferable to being here in the suffocating costume, the thick and heavy rope *sensay* suit still smelling of kerosene, the wire-mesh mask chafing his skin, even with the cloth lining that had been sewn in to protect his face. He would have much preferred to be up there drinking some rum punch, a *ti ponche* with ice, made with just-picked Dominica limes and sweetened with brown sugar, getting drunk and talking old talk with the men. Instead, prevented by the mask from having a proper swig, he had to put a funnel into his mouth through a tiny circular opening and pour the warm rum down his throat. He reached into his costume for the flat bottle and funnel, secured in a pocket that was sewn in for that purpose. As he tilted back his head to pour, he finally caught sight of his wife. She looked transfixed, although her lips were moving purposefully. She was watching the other band coming down.

He looked in the direction of her stare, and now he could finally see them clearly. What he saw was enough to make his intestines instantly bubble and froth; and something warm dribbled down his legs, filled his boots. His first instinct was to run away screaming like a woman. But he could not run, he could not move. Transfixed, like his wife, he stood, man-sized sobs heaving his body, giant teardrops spilling from his eyes and mixing with the rolling sweat, although no one could see that. They thought he had stopped moving in anticipation of the fight, they thought he was frozen in one position to better conserve his energy to take on the band with the wooden masks.

Upstairs, the older British colonialist was now speaking to his hostess. "Not exactly what I would have expected for this kind of celebration," he said. Mrs. Richard had pushed her way back to the front line of her veranda after she secured her valuables following the influx of people from the street.

"Sorry?"

"Those masquerades."

She shrugged, not caring, not understanding, wondering why the other band was moving so slowly, wondering when the fight would begin and keeping her eye on her coward of a son-in-law, because if he did not prove himself today, act like a man this time, she would go down there and use her own hands to beat him, and then she would go to the bishop, to the pope if necessary, and get the marriage annulled. Fainting like a woman while her daughter had been defiled by his whore. He had better fight, fight good today.

"I'm puzzled," Alfred Drummond said, still trying to engage Mrs. Richard. "I'd have thought they'd be more of the entertainment genre, but there is definitely some kind of social control element happening here."

The annoying white man was still talking. She spoke to be polite. "They all look the same to me. Damned ugly, Mr. Drummer."

He tried to flirt a little with his hostess. "Drummond, madam. And thank you again for your kind invitation." He raised his *ti ponche* and bowed his head in genuine appreciation. This was why he enjoyed his postings to places his British friends and family would never dream of visiting, primitive places. The people were so open and welcoming, their culture so rich. He probably should have been an anthropologist instead of a representative of the Crown. He looked back up the street. "I imagine to the uninitiated eye they would indeed appear to be rather ugly. But I was saying, these are what would be called dangerous masquerades in Africa. Some of them seem to be war masks."

She shook her head. "We don't have anything like that here. War masks and so on. We here in the West Indies, we are not Africans, you know." She looked down at her bare arm to prove her point. "It's a long time since we could tell you anything about Africa. Those people"—she pointed up the street—"they carved some ugly masks like old-time people used to do. They're trying to bring back old-time things. That's all."

When Alfred Drummond looked again, they were close enough for him to see them in their entirety, for him to catch his breath from the full impact. Before, he had only been able to see them in detail in little round magnified sections, one mask at a time. Now he could see them as they were, a river of them. He remembered something he had read, that there were few African languages with words that accurately translated as "mask." He thought of some of the translations he knew. *Face of the Forest Spirit. Spirit of Death. Death Gathers In.*

Alfred Drummond had spent twenty years in West Africa and he knew what he was seeing. How much time did he have, he wondered, to warn the people below? How would he explain to them that they should not stand there making strange sounds and stamping, that they should use their feet to run away? Who would listen to him, in the few minutes that were left? Mrs. Richard was gone, insulted by his reference to Africa. His younger colleague had squeezed away from him, bored with an old man's stories of a place in which he had no interest. There was a young woman at his side, turned completely away from him, seemingly very interested in watching the oncoming band. He had to try. He shook her shoulder.

"Miss, I beg your pardon." When he bent down to speak near her ear, he saw that she was praying. It was a famous Catholic prayer, one he often heard Dominicans reciting, something about the hour of death.

"Those masquerades," he said, and then was not sure what else he could say, how to explain it to people who, although so obviously African, were yet and still not African at all. Perhaps it would be better if he did not try to speak in African terms. He would not try to explain that the people coming down the street had become transformed, that they were now possessed by the spirits represented by their masks and headdresses, their full-body covering of raffia. She might listen if he did not elaborate on the significance of the masks. He would not tell her that the front lines of the masqueraders were going to war, with their small, round eyes representing anger, and the sharp, straight noses showing that they would never retreat, and the block of bared teeth saying that their fury had no bounds. He would not point out the rusty-brown color of some masks, heavy patinas of sacrificial blood.

He would not point out to her the next group behind the warrior spirits, not show her that these were even more dangerous. There was one in particular he knew well, with the big round forehead from which grew antelope horns, the warthog tusks sprouting from crocodile jaws that jutted far out. It was a masquerade that only came out to direct strong magic against those who had broken the law, perpetrated a taboo. And he would not mention what was for him the most frightening part, the most telling part, the large group of funeral masquerades in the rear, some of them dancing on stilts, higher than the two-story town houses. Those, with their delicate, feminine-featured white masks, were more terrifying than all the others.

This young, cultured woman with her milk-and-coffee skin would not understand any of this. He thought of the servants downstairs in the kitchen, and knew that they would understand, but he did not speak Creole and they might not speak English. In any case, there was no time. So he said only this to Cecile: "Miss, I fear that there is about to be a great deal of trouble."

And she replied, "Yes, sir, I know."

Then it was too late. Though Alfred Drummond was the most pre-pared, he roared the loudest as the remaining spectators on the side-walk scattered, running down the side streets. Somehow unnoticed until that moment, leaping out from the middle of the band, the thing looked as if it would jump up into the very sky. It raged against the three sets of rope noosed around its head and torso, tethered to the street only by the effort of three struggling masked beings with whips.

The Newtown *bande mauvais,* the men with the wire masks, all turned and ran, all except for John Baptiste.

I n the end, there were fewer eyewitnesses than one might have expected. No one was left on the street, and the people on the galleries were panicked, and had mostly turned their backs as they tried to push their way back into the safety of the house. Those who did stay on the exposed galleries, who claimed that they saw everything, were already "very drunk" and were "unreliable witnesses." So said the police, who were faced with page after page of statements, most claiming that the masquerade had levitated, then had flown around John Baptiste. The statements, from well-educated members of the middle class, even doctors and lawyers, all said that the thing that broke free of the three sets of rope, the thing that flew three times around John Baptiste, was not a human being, because not only did it fly in a circle at the level of his head, it also clearly had no limbs, no arms, no legs. And it emitted a sound, the high pitch of which could never be made by a human voice. And, the statements all agreed, the thing never, ever touched him.

Alfred Drummond had stayed on the veranda with his eyes wide open, watching, and had gone down to the police station to give a statement, but the heavy smell of rum punch on his breath had been detected by the inspector, and he was turned away. He wanted to explain that he had seen such a thing before, when he was a very young junior colonial officer stationed in West Africa. Where exactly, he could not remember now, it was that long ago. Not on the Gold Coast, for sure, because the Twi speakers did not have masking traditions, so it would not have been in Asanteland. Most likely in Nigeria somewhere, maybe in Igboland or in Yorubaland. The memories of where he was and why he had been there had faded, but he remembered that he had accidentally walked into the middle of a feud between two clans of a large village, a land dispute gone out of control. There had been recent killings and counter-killings, and it was widely felt among the people that they were sense-less, unjustified, and were being instigated by one clan head for no other reason than greed.

Alfred had been standing in the middle of the village, in the open public space, when he saw women and children running as if for their lives. A man had grabbed him and locked him in a small hut crammed with cowering women and sobbing children. All had been warned not to look, not to move until it was all over, but he had been able to see through a large crack in the door.

It was the same dance of fury. The same drumming, relentless. The men with the rope and the whips keeping the men of the community at a safe enough distance. The tiny white-rimmed eyes on the mask, the bared teeth, nails and the rusted metal stuck into the face, the towering headdress adorned with feathers. "One of the chief's three masks," he had been told by the senior wife of the man who hid him. "This one has not been danced for more than twenty years." It was so strong, so dan-gerous, that women and children could not look upon it, so powerful that it came out only in times of deepest crisis.

Through the door crack he saw the man who had started the killing spree being dragged before the masquerade. And the young Alfred Drummond had seen it, seen the masquerade jump so high that it seemed to fly, around and around the man, while the drums urged it, enabled it, gave its movements greater and greater scope, until the man fell back onto the dust, and the masquerade danced back into the sacred forest from which it had emerged.

All of this he wanted to explain in his statement, to say that the masquerade on King George V Street had not really flown, that the pounding drums were designed to intoxicate, so that your head became light and what you were seeing became magical in quality; you thought the masquerade was flying when in fact it was only jumping and twirling. He wanted to say that it had indeed been a human under there, with hands and feet he'd seen with his own eyes, but the police were overburdened with nonsensical statements and did not want more fantastical stories from an old drunk white man talking about Africa.

He would later write of the incident in great detail in a letter to the British Anthropological Society outlining the survival of West and Central African masking traditions in the island of Dominica and urging further study. "But one variation, an adaptation of significant note," he wrote, "is the fact that here, unlike in Africa, women also perform masquerades, even the masks imbued with the most authority and power. In fact, I am convinced, by the sound of the ululation emitted from the masquerade in question, and also by the relatively small size of the hands and feet, and by the fact that I perceived the swell of large breasts under the raffia, that the so-called Flying Masquerade was a woman."

22

MAGIC, OR REALISM

It was only midnight, but Teddy found the things with which he normally made time pass—his detective stories, his television shows—impossible now. He was feeling like an adolescent, he admitted, consumed by the throes of a first love. And giving Diane back her Bearden had left him feeling light, giddy, and excited—like a child who had done good and was hoping for a big reward.

Lillian had not come that night; they would be meeting at the airport. He had finished packing days before, but there was no point in going to sleep, not with a flight leaving at seven from BWI. Between the hour-long ride out to Baltimore and the two-hour advance check-in, it would be easier to stay up, and sleep was not possible anyway; he was overcharged, actually breathless with anticipation—every few minutes he was forced to calm himself with exaggeratedly deep breaths—and he felt slightly foolish, self-consciously aware of this new state, of being in love.

He looked for ways to pass the time. He went online and searched *Dominica*. It was not, he knew, your typical island, not like Antigua, with its white-and-blue coast of consecutive isolated beach. He had liked it there, flat and cloudless and open and bright, there was a pretty-girl shallowness to it, a kind of candor: what you see is what you get. But Dominica would be all overwhelming mountain and greenness, daily rain and brown rocky rivers.

He looked at photographs—Emerald Pool seemed to be a popular spot; there were shots of ecstatic tourists bathing under a waterfall in a pool that seemed too perfect, too textbook a rain-forest setting to be real.

He came across an article on a place called Jacko's Flats, named after a Maroon leader, where runaway slaves had held off the Europeans for forty years. He thought that he would like to go there, if only as a sentimental ode to his Ph.D. He had once known everything there was to know about the Underground Railroad and American slaves who took flight for their freedom, and in that early academic period—when he was still a historian, in the phase where the dissertation would be squeezed until it was absolutely dry, pilfered of any germ of an idea that could be isolated and elaborated—he had done a comparative study of the freedom options available to American, Caribbean, and South American slaves. The primary option for the American slaves had, of course, been the Underground Railroad, but Florida's Black Seminoles had featured heavily in his study—one of the few known examples of Maroons in the United States.

He narrowed his search to *Maroons, Dominica* and read from his monitor for a while. The trails going to Jacko's Flats were not maintained, although there was funding earmarked to open them up as a tourist attraction:

> . . .KNOWN TO LOCALS BUT NOT YET TO TOURISTS, THESE
> TRAILS CAN STILL BE HIKED WITH AN EXPERIENCED GUIDE
> IF THE ADVENTURER IS FIT ENOUGH, HAS GOOD BALANCE,
> AND IS NOT AFRAID OF HEIGHTS OR THE POTENTIAL FOR
> DEATH BY MISSTEP.

He would not be visiting Jacko's Flats, after all; he was rather afraid of heights, but he continued reading, bookmarking other sites, one of which told an interesting story about a Maroon leader in the late 1700s who had abandoned the women and children of the camp when Jacko's Flats was attacked. In retaliation, it seemed, the women gave away information that allowed the man to be found, the fearless leader meeting his end as a result. Served the motherfucker right, Teddy thought. He should have taken them with him.

He checked his watch again. He'd only used up an hour; there were three more to go.

Teddy lay on his bed and gave up. He closed his eyes, dropped one hand to his crotch in a long-abandoned habit from his younger days. Women had become so plentiful in his life, even during his marriage—especially then—that it had become completely unnecessary. He unzipped his fly, and then found himself in an indelicate struggle—it was past the extricable half-turgid point: it would not bend and he would have to stand up and pull down his pants to get at it. Laughing sheepishly despite the fact that there were no witnesses to the undignified spectacle of him on his back throttling and yanking the neck of an uncooperative penis, he buttoned his pants and sat up.

He stayed sitting on the edge of his bed, concentrating on the only thing he could. Lillian had told him that there was a lot more to the story, but what he knew of it so far sounded like one of those novels the Latin Americans liked to write, *magical realism*, and he wondered to what extent those stories were distorted when they had been translated into song, to what extent Lillian had internalized some things that were closer to myth than truth.

The world she described was so different from his reality. His history, his parents' handed-down stories, contained some of the same elements as hers—there was no shortage of chanting crowds in his history, clashing and spawning murder, but they were not of Carnival and Masquerade and revelry gone awry.

There were Black crowds and there were white crowds in his parents' stories. Marching and rioting and burning buildings and looting and singing songs promising to overcome. And murdering and lynching, bombing churches and burning crosses, these crowds clashed, too, with dogs and fire hoses, handcuffs, beatings, Black Marias, and jail. But it was all factual and verifiable, some of it still watchable in black and white on television—the terrible things done in his history had really happened. Bullets to heads and bullet-ridden torsos, children blown apart by dynamite, bodies swinging from trees. Material things. His urban parents' stories did not speak of spirit representations and men dropping dead because of some voodoo, Obeah, some magical kind of African religion.

He thought of her Masquerade story, the clash of the bands. She told it as if she really thought it possible that the masked thing—Matilda—had flown and had killed the man without touching him. That story was connected to some strange idea she seemed to have about herself, that there was something *dark* about her, something—he hesitated at the word, it was not one he ever used seriously—something evil.

He went through what he knew, pulling out and setting aside the elements before organizing them: during Masquerade, her grandmother—dressed in masquerade costume—had killed a man who had jilted her daughter Iris—Lillian's mother. Before that, there had been that awful rape-by-Coke-bottle incident, the murder being retaliation for that. The grandmother, Matilda, hanged—apparently for the murder. Lillian's mother, who died before Lillian knew of her existence, had become a prostitute. Her father had been one of her customers. A schoolteacher had taken her away from her mother as a baby, raised her as her own. Lillian grew up thinking that her stepmother was her biological mother. She didn't seem to know who her father was.

It would of course have been rough on her, on any child—teenager—to discover that her stepmother had lied, but the things the stepmother had kept from her were, in fact, scandalous, and by now Lillian should have understood that the deception was in her own best interest. There *had* to be more to the story, he decided, something was obviously missing. This preoccupation, this obsession that had so stunted her, made her cut herself off from the life she knew, it could not only be on account of a grandmother killing a man; nor from having a prostitute for a mother. He would get her to tell him the rest of it on the plane.

Thinking about her, he found himself again in a state of arousal. He reached for the phone to call a cab to her apartment, but replaced the receiver without dialing. She would probably be sleeping, he should let her rest. His hand strayed to the button of his pants for a moment, and then he went on point of pride: he was not an adolescent, he would not while away the time that way; in any case, that would only take care of three, four minutes. Resolute, he put on a light jacket and left his house.

23

HARVEST DANCE

Cecile Richard Baptiste had not moved when the masquerade—the creature—began leaping around her husband, or had it been flying, as they said? She did not know. It was moving too fast, the drums beating too terribly, the inhuman sounds coming from the masquerades, all of them, had been too shrill. Her vision had blurred, her hearing had become muted, but all along, even when she saw her husband fall, she continued her prayer until she understood, only by her words, what was happening. *Pray for us sinners, now and at the hour of our death.*

"I can hear his heart beating! He's not dead!" her mother had shouted up at her, after the masquerades had all disappeared and people had rushed back to the street to surround him and strip off his costume and pick him up and carry him on their shoulders to the hospital.

Yet, Cecile thought. *Not dead yet.* And she never moved, stayed hanging over the railing, rolling her rosary beads, because the least she could do for the father of her children, and the most, really, was to pray for the sinner at the hour of his death.

☙❧

People gathered outside of John Baptiste's hospital ward because, it was said, the pounding sound was clearly audible to the naked ear. It wasn't morbid curiosity on their part, but in the way of small places, the unheard-of and the supernatural were one and the same, and who could pass on the chance to get a glimpse of, hear the sound of, those things that rightfully belong to the other side? Those who heard it, the older ones who could remember when *bois batailles* were still fought, said that it was like the sound of drums beating the rhythm to which the stick fighters battled; and when the story was chronicled into a song—a very famous one, "Hospital Masquerade"—the *chanté mas* would describe how Masquerade had only come to an early end for the family and friends of John Baptiste—who entirely made up Dominica's upper class. They, with the exception of his mother-in-law, who stood at his bedside cursing him, had shut themselves in their homes, afraid of something that was bigger than death.

For the rest of the Dominicans, the inconsequential masses, the song would say, the celebration had continued outside the hospital room, where they kept time to the beat of John Baptiste's heart, picking up their feet and putting them back down, hands in the air. And when, early the next morning, Mardi Gras, they knew he had died because they no longer had a beat on which to move, then they continued their last day of Masquerade in earnest, with the kind of fervor that kept them on the road through the night. There was something in the way the chanting crowds were giving the *chantuelle* back the chorus, the way her *la peau cabrit* drummers were hitting the goatskins of their drums—the words, the beat, the feet, the furious pace. Something about the fleet-footedness of their dancing, making round after round through the streets, told the police it was better to let them keep going than attempt to break it up, even though they normally took great pride in using brute force to make sure the fêting stopped before the start of Lent.

Eventually, when by sunrise it was clear that people would continue into an unheard-of Ash Wednesday morning jump-up, the police finally came out on their horses to whip them back home.

Find her. Hang her." Mrs. Richard was standing in front of her friend the next morning. "I going live to see Matilda swing. She going burn in hell."

The police inspector resisted. "You know John died of natural causes."

"Autopsy can't show no Obeah. Go up there. Get her. Is she kill him."

He went to look for Matilda strictly as a favor to his late drinking partner's wife. He took fifteen of his senior officers, heavily armed, only to impress her, to keep her quiet; she stood watching on the wharf as they boarded the launch and went up the leeward coast to the northern villages. Beyond this show, he was powerless to do anything else for her. They might be able to bring Matilda in for questioning, and then they would have to let her go, because the coroner's report was unequivocal. John Baptiste had suffered a massive heart attack, he had been frightened to death.

Not until they reached Colihaut did they realize that none among them knew exactly where Matilda lived, and not a single villager from Colihaut would assist the posse of police. "We know she live Up There. Everybody know that. Everybody know that is Colihaut people does take people to find her. Somebody go and call Matilda for me." The inspector was shouting in vain at the faces of people who had switched off their eyes.

"Matilda don't live here. She live Up There," and they pointed again and gave the inspector their backs.

When, hours later, they found their way to the bottom of the mountain, when they saw that there were only a dozen or two women and men tending crops there, the inspector was ready to turn right around and go back to town. The favor he was doing Mrs. Richard did not include climbing to the top of a mountain in Dominica's highest range. But then, with the exception of a few who had turned and walked away, the farmers began to perform a beautiful harvest dance. They held their hoes in both hands, bringing them up horizontally, up to their faces, and higher, above their heads, and they began twirling the sticks, moving them from hand to hand, while their legs, slow and graceful, began synchronized movements.

The police exchanged looks mocking the country people, so simple as to put on a spontaneous welcome performance at the sight of official uniforms. Under the smirks, though, they were enjoying a sense of importance, honored that they were being welcomed as dignitaries.

I t is good enough to know oneself to be superior, something else entirely when the inferior confirm the fact with a show of their adulation. Such acknowledgment of one's cemented place in the scheme of things must be an intoxicant. Nothing else could account for the failure of the police to properly interpret what was taking place.

Advancing. That was what the police should have realized from the start, that the farmers were advancing on them. They should have been able to discern something in the basic stance they had taken, in the way they crouched, their weight first above their flexed front legs, back legs stretched tight behind them; then a shifting back with a liquid motion of their torsos, the back knees bent now. Flexing, straightening, so went the legs, while the bodies glided over them on oiled hip joints, the feet making small, imperceptible forward movements.

And once the pattern was established, when they had moved themselves into a front, a solid, advancing line of crouching combatants, the other movements began with incredible speed—the sprinting and the leg sweeps and the jumping and the no-handed somersaults, the hoes no longer ornamental, hacking at heads, the feet snapping against necks as legs extended in the middle of flying leaps. Three policemen were dead, skulls neatly opened, bone cleanly sliced through to expose quivering brain, before the guns could be cocked and fired, before the whirling legs and slicing hoes all lay flat and still on the ground, the farmers' blood turned fertilizer, seeping into their soil, wetting down their crops.

24

REVELATIONS

For entertainment Teddy favored intimate dinners in undiscovered restaurants, where vintage champagne was his drink of choice, one more affordable luxury item of the many with which he was able to indulge his taste for fine things, thanks to the success of his book (Lillian's book, as he thought of it).

Although he could also be found regularly in the better jazz clubs, where he often knew the performers personally, he sometimes needed something more up-tempo, where people moved to a stronger beat. But he was past the stage of the regular clubs. From time to time he would hook up with a frat brother and brave the smoke and the bass and the overpacked bodies just to stay current with the music and the general vibe, but not very often: he did not like to appear out of place—a middle-aged man trying to cheat on his wife, or worse, come off as a faithful henpecked type, sneaking out to somewhere forbidden only for the thrill of it, looking delighted just to be there among all the young girls but obviously lacking the tooth-and-claw to do anything about it.

The Nile, pitch-black except for the lit-up dance floor, was where he went instead, the night before he left for Dominica. He stood in his usual spot against the wall with a drink, watching until he felt like danc-

ing, although he didn't exactly dance, just migrated from the wall to the
outskirts of the dance floor, where he kept time, moving easily and without self-consciousness and only occasionally breaking into something
more energetic, and there would be many more like him, men and
women, riding the beat, and they were not at all dancing alone, they
were participating in a communal event.

A Diasporic Experience, the radio ads said, and indeed it was. He
had no trouble telling the men apart, spotting the Africans—continent-
born—from the Caribbean brothers, maybe it was a carriage thing, and
they in turn were obviously not African-American, that might have been
on account of the haircuts. The women were harder, at least for him, an
Antiguan no different from a Ghanaian, a Jamaican indistinguishable
from a Nigerian or from the occasional Black American woman. Even
the Ethiopians, with their distinctive Arab-Africa look, could be mistaken for an India-Africa mixed-up Trinidadian Dougla, although the
henna hair tended to give the Ethiopians away.

For accurate differentiation, he analyzed the dance floor, because the
club had built its reputation on playing no more than three consecutive
numbers from one region. So the West Indians identified themselves
because none of the others could whine properly, could get the swivel of
the hip smooth enough. Africans dancing to *soca*, with their overarticu-
lated movements, gave themselves away with a jerkiness that somehow
did not look awkward when they did the same thing to *hilife*, and then
there were all the cross-continent anglophone-francophone subcatego-
ries of sound that Teddy could not always name: *zouk* from the French
islands—when that played, it was one of the few times where people
paired off and held on to dance the fast beat; the electric guitars of Con-
golese *soukous*; and then the newly popular *mbalax*, the instrumentation
reminiscent of the kora, with the tonal talking drums and the Islamic
influences obvious in the way the Wolof lyrics were sung, like an early-

morning call to prayer emitting from a minaret, and so polyrhythmic that it was braved only by the Senegalese, doing a strange, open-legged kind of staccato funky chicken on an in-between beat Teddy had tried in vain to find. And so he was happy when the Senegalese trooped off and the old-time reggae began, presenting none of the nationalistic dance-floor divides: this one belonged exclusively to nobody, not even to Black people, because Bob had made it international property, and all four walls were empty.

When the reggae was over, it was time for the Liberation music— always that sequence, reggae being its natural precursor—and that was when the man came toward Teddy, hand outstretched.

Aside from Teddy, there were a limited number of African-American regulars at the Nile, mostly those who had been part of the Struggle. There had only ever been one Struggle—and now, years after elections, long after there was any need to build shantytowns on university campuses or get arrested for the sake of divestment, now that South Africans no longer stomped their way through funerals and Nelson Mandela was not just free but had twice been president, had not just walked hand in hand with Winnie but had divorced her and married Graça; these members of the Struggle still came here every Friday night, because it had been more than something they did in their spare time, it had been their life, *their* Struggle—their culture, even, and sooner or later the DJ would acknowledge them and what they had done. The Struggle songs would start, always, with the high squeal of Hugh Masekela's introductory trumpeting, and they would flock from the bar and onto the floor, the underclass D.C. locals who had never set foot on African soil and most likely never would, but who carried the memory of their enslavement so close to their consciousness that they could still feel it as an injustice and not as a historical fact, who as a result had taken on the South African fight as no different from their own. And even though some said that the South Africans had negotiated away their country in exchange for the government, and that there was no justice in Truth and Reconciliation, they still danced their victory dance every Friday night in celebration of one of the few times in history when Black people had fought and come away, free and clear at least on this one level, the winners.

Teddy, although he had never been more than a peripheral part of the Struggle, had stayed near the floor, and he did not immediately recognize the man. "We met a long time ago," he shouted in Teddy's ear. "A conference in New York. But I see you on TV all the time."

The music was too loud to speak, but there was another reason for the way Teddy held the man's forearm and pushed through the crowd to the outside air. "I remember you well," said Teddy. "Reggie…Liverpool? Yes. New York office, L-San." The Lobby on South Africa and Namibia, he had been the president, and in apartheid's heyday had been moderately famous for his dignified speeches and quietly effective hunger strikes. "Lillian Baptiste introduced us. You're originally from Dominica." He tried to appear more interested in savoring his scotch than in any conversation he might make. "In fact Lillian and I are going to Dominica tomorrow." Quick sip, and then, "Vacation."

What were the chances? Teddy was wondering. He allowed a digression into a reflection on the true nature of a coincidence—starting with Lillian's perspective, a habit he now had, of appending any thought to something that would connect it to her. This coincidental meeting, for her, would be a part of her superstitious concept of religion: the unfolding of life's sundry events as a function of battling forces, good or evil, God or the devil, at work specifically on your behalf or against you. He held that up against the way he saw it: a shit-happens approach that might or might not be attributable to a God who might or might not really be there, but to whom he occasionally prayed, just in case.

And then it occurred to him, and he felt genuine surprise, that he had not acted on just any undirected impulse in leaving his house to lean on a wall and drink and dance: he had, as deliberately as if the thought had been a conscious one, gone to the one place in Washington, D.C., where there was any chance of finding a Dominican.

"Oh."

Teddy heard it, the start of a word, the beginning of a sentence, taken back and replaced with the nonresponse. He had also seen how the man, with his gentleman's comportment and an intellectual's quiet aura, had quickly covered his look of surprise, relaxing his face into the same expression for which Teddy was striving, bland disinterest. Another look, in addition to the surprise, had also flashed, something to do with the nature of people who come from the same small place, a protectiveness. Teddy let the "Oh" remain, unsubstantiated and without response, forcing Reggie Liverpool to speak again.

"I didn't realize you two were together."

"A recent development." He brought his glass to his lips, found that he could no longer use it for special effect, it was empty. He would go fishing now for the rest of the story, he had no choice, even if it meant betraying her confidence. "Not easy for her, you know, going back. After all that," Teddy tried.

"Yes."

Teddy saw the blink behind the thick glasses, knew that this was not a man to stand around gossiping about his countrywoman with some new boyfriend. It was of no consequence that Lillian was only a professional acquaintance, someone with whom the man was no longer even in touch. Small-island code was in effect. "Her grandmother," said Teddy, "you know, that whole history." He needed another word, one that would make Reggie Liverpool think that he had Lillian's full confidence, that he knew everything there was to know, and that in continuing a discussion, nothing would be given away. "The whole *trauma*."

Teddy had chosen well. Reggie Liverpool nodded, let down his guard a bit. "Would have been hard for anybody, if they didn't know it all along, just to find out one day, would have sent anybody over the edge."

"Over the edge." Teddy nodded, waited for more, but Reggie Liverpool had seen how Teddy leaned forward, how he repeated the words with too much nonchalance, the nodding now obviously overplayed without the interspersed sipping, and he went on guard again, saying nothing.

"The hanging," said Teddy, "it was hard for her to deal with that."

Reggie Liverpool relaxed. "Yes. But I would say it was the multiple killings—you know, that was the really bad part. Make anybody crazy. And then, of course, when she came to understand who exactly her father was—Winston Baptiste—that was really what sent her . . ." He stopped at the look on Teddy's face.

"Sorry. Sorry, you said 'multiple' . . ." he stumbled, abandoning any sense of posturing. Lillian had only spoken about a man, a single man, killed during a Carnival celebration.

Reggie Liverpool shook his head, looked away. "You know, that kind of thing, is best she to tell you all that." Discomfort had reverted his accent and syntax to the way he spoke before he emigrated. "And a lot of it is hearsay anyway." He tried to walk away, to go back into the club, but Teddy blocked him, actually jumped in front of him and stood against the door.

"That wouldn't be hearsay," Teddy said. "That would be fact, if she was convicted." It was the right move, barring the door; Reggie Liverpool was not the sort who could tolerate a scene, two men struggling outside a club. "If I could just explain ... She asked me to go back with her—she asked me to help her, find out if maybe her grandmother was innocent—she thinks maybe it was a false confession. But she didn't give me the whole story."

Reggie Liverpool kept silent, looked down at Teddy's hand holding the doorknob.

"Please," Teddy said. He let his hand fall from the knob. "She's very ... *troubled.*"

After a few moments, Reggie Liverpool said, "Tell you what. I will tell you what is historical. What you might find yourself if you do a little archival research. Things that anybody you stop on any street in Dominica will say freely—about the grandmother, that is. The rest, that kind of thing is best for you to get that from Lillian. If she choose to tell you."

Teddy nodded. "I appreciate it."

"Facts. Lillian Baptiste's grandmother on her mother's side was a woman named Matilda. She confessed to killing a dozen or so men and women. Bodies were found—skeletons, actually. I don't remember the exact figure. I don't think they ever said much more about it—I think they may have been poisoned. Forensics in those days was not that precise. She was hanged for those murders. Those are the facts. But all of this is well documented."

"When." Teddy cleared his throat. When he spoke again, his voice had hoarsened. "When did this happen?"

"Long before Lillian was born. In the 1940s it started, with her mother and all that business, then the grandmother was hanged in '50, I believe. Iris—that's her mother—was a very young girl at the time."

"But what about the man? The Flying Masquerade, that story?"

"I think of that more as folklore. I mean, oral tradition says *something* happened in the band—he died for sure—but you really think a masquerade levitated and flew around him and killed him with Obeah? Apparently it was a heart attack—natural causes, anyway."

Teddy focused on normalizing his voice. "So no motive? No defense?"

"She offered no defense. There was no motive. She was an Obeah-woman, they said, so she would have had access to sick people, weak people, and that might have allowed her to indulge an appetite for killing. But that's just my opinion, not fact."

"Angel of Death," said Teddy.

"Pardon me?"

"Do you read detective novels?"

"No."

"Angels of Death, that's one of the categories of female serial killers." Teddy stepped away from the door, someone was trying to get out. His voice was now unabashedly pleading. "Is there anything else you could tell me?"

Reggie Liverpool shook his head, anxious to go, but then reconsidered, as if feeling sudden sympathy. "A lot of people believe the killings had to do with Obeah, you know, devil business. But that's not fact." He began to edge past Teddy. "Good night, Dr. Morgan." He did not extend his hand. "I came with someone, she must think I've run out on her."

"Lillian's mother. What about her mother?"

"I saw Lillian's mother one time only. I was a small boy. She was the most beautiful woman I'd ever seen." He did not say that he had been part of a large crowd that had gathered just to get a glimpse of her, that he had been standing outside the jail, which, in the absence of a mental institution, also served as the crazy house. He extended his hand this time, trying to bring finality to their encounter. "I can tell you that her life was a hard one, an unfortunate one." He had to pull his hand free from Teddy's grip. "That's all I can tell you about Lillian Baptiste's mother. Anything else would fall into the realm of gossip . . ."

Reggie Liverpool was walking through the door when Teddy realized that he had said something else, right after the part about the serial killer, something that had been muted by the shock.

Teddy concentrated, replaying it, focusing in on the image of Reggie Liverpool's face in his mind. "Her father!" he called to Reggie Liverpool's back. "Winston Baptiste—you said something about her father." But he was gone, through the second door where the bouncers stood checking the stamps on patrons' hands with ultraviolet light. By the time Teddy got past them, Reggie Liverpool had vanished. Teddy searched along the black walls of the Nile but could not find him there, neither was he on the dance floor, where people born on the continent were moving to their music, something clearly African, but unfamiliar to Teddy, something he could not name.

25

WHAT SENT WINSTON

Lillian's stepmother, Icilma, had loved Winston since she was a teenager, ever since she first set eyes on him, fresh back in the island after completing boarding school in Barbados. She was determined to marry him, despite the fact that his mother did not approve of the match: the Baptistes were still who they were, and notwithstanding all that had gone on in their family, their consistent high color still vindicated them, left them high up on their pedestal.

Icilma's family, on the other hand, with the exception of her almost-white mother, barely made it across the color boundary. Though Icilma came in a respectable shade of shiny copper-brown, her family's gene pool was unreliable and had a reputation for sudden throwbacks. The main thing working against Icilma's bid to marry Winston was her brother, christened Jonas but called Midnight, a name taken from the infamous exclamation of the shocked midwife at the emergence of a coal-black baby from between his mother's milky thighs: *"Bon Dieu! C'est minuit même!"*

She set her mind on marrying him, even though her own mother was also against it. The intervening years had done nothing to soften the edge of all that had plagued the boy's family since the Masquerade

twenty years earlier, when his mother ended up unmasked and naked
on the ground; and after that, all the Obeah village business and the
killing and the hanging—"What you bringing on you head, girl?" her
mother warned. "What you want with that?"

And Icilma's mother did not approve of the match for another reason: Winston was known to be a sweet-man; a man with a quality that
called to women and made them follow him, entice him. Some sweet-
men were pretty, and it was the prettiness that caused the trouble. Others
were very ugly, and it could have been this very ugliness that gave rise to
the signals they apparently sent out unwittingly. There were sweet-men
known for the hefty bulge of their pants, but just having a thick stick
was common enough and there would need to be something else to
transform the man from just another donkey-dick—perhaps it was the
way he adjusted or stroked it absently—that made him so alluring.
Sometimes it was something as abstract as a drawn-out smile or eyes
that blinked slowly. There was no way to predict what would do it.

Although sweet-men did not chase women the way the wild-men
did, they were the worst kind of man to love and inevitably caused
heartbreak. Sweet-men did nothing; it was the women who presented
themselves, and there is no mortal man capable of turning down the
magnet pull of a woman in heat. A sweet-man might try, he might want
to be faithful, he might shoo away the majority of them, but one day, an
unexpected ordinary day, he will turn around and find it right there. He
will smell her, he will see the sweat above her lip, he will sense the liquid
pooling between her legs, swirling through the places that curl and fold,
that swell and darken and pulse, and he will have no choice but to run
behind the thing, which will be bucking and leaping and dragging him
unwillingly along. He will be completely mindless until his flesh-
turned-missile meets its target and sinks down or rams up into it.
Unluckily for Icilma, she loved sweet-man Winston, who, rumor had it,

had already fathered several children in various villages around the island.

And even though Icilma knew that his mother had turned into a shadow of a woman who never left her home, she also knew that a mother's hold on her son can never be broken. To better her chances, Icilma had talked to the maid, who was only a few years older than she: "Cynthia, how to tie a man?" Cynthia by all means wanted to take Icilma to her Obeahman, but knew that word would make it back to both their mothers. People living next door to any Obeah practitioner were inevitably gossipmongers of the highest order, and there was no way a girl like Icilma could get away with such a visit undetected. Cynthia, of course, could go freely, in fact her mother had taken her there for one reason or another since she was a baby. The repercussions she would face for taking Icilma, though, were clear: her own mother would beat her and Icilma's mother would fire her, so they had to move down to the next best thing for tying a man.

In the end, Icilma had to cook the rice twice. The first time, she prepared it on the kitchen stove and, having collected a small amount of menstrual fluid in the bathroom, added it to the boiling water. Cynthia threw it away, amazed at Icilma's stupidity. "Useless. How you going cook it on a stove? That have to cook on coal pot, because you have to stand over it for your blood to mix in good, straight from inside your body." It took Icilma three months to steel herself for that, and to arrange a time when no one from her household or from the neighbors' yard was around. Everyone knew the story of the man who found his woman squatting over the coal pot, and how he held her down in the boiling rice water, and how she died from the burns. Winston ate his food with relish, and would have laughed in their face if anyone had suggested that it would ever have crossed Icilma's mind to *kacoa* him.

The rice did not work, not really. He married her with not too much prodding as soon as she became pregnant. And once married, he never acknowledged the children of his other liaisons or their mothers—with the exception, later on, of Lillian—and, as was expected of a good middle-class married man, never provided a penny of support for his outside children. But the *kacoa* failed in that he continued to believe that there was nothing he could do about the women when they presented themselves; and moreover he believed that they and the resulting children were simply the privilege as well as the burden of his maleness. Over the course of the years, quite apart from Lillian, Icilma came across children whose faces also told her that they were made by her husband.

I cilma had a reputation for being practical and fair-minded. When Winston confirmed what she had heard about the child in Iris's house, admitted that he had known about it for nearly two years already, admitted that it was his baby because she was the image of him, Icilma first gave her body time to absorb the blow. When she was sure she could walk without falling, she went to the kitchen and contemplated what he had said, holding on to the sink for support and breathing slowly and deeply.

She was the kind of Catholic who genuflected and crossed herself each time she passed the photograph of the pope hung on the wall of her salon. She knew the inevitability of suffering, that you might be offered a fool's paradise on earth for some time, but that you could not escape yours, neither should you try: how would you appreciate your heaven without your hell on earth? She had been watching and waiting for the honor of her cross to bear, and now she realized that she had been given a sign of what its nature was to be.

She remembered her pregnancy, when she had been in such good health, so fit and bursting with life, so happy that Winston had married her, had not left her to shame her family with a bastard, that she had not bothered to go back to the doctor after the first visit. She had not gone to the doctor, but one day the doctor had to come to her, the day the thing came early, the thing that looked like a bunch of grapes.

By that time, 1960, Masquerade in Dominica was being transformed into Carnival: the *chantuelles* and their masked lyrics and their scalding satire and their African call-and-response singing and chanting and drumming were in decline, giving way to male calypsonians, queen-shows, elaborate costumes, and the ponderous steel bands from Trinidad. But still, a bona fide *chanté mas* had been written about that portentous event: "Something Take Icilma Baby," the people sang, because they had seen her swell, her nose spread, and her ankles thicken. There had been milk in her breasts after it had been delivered, and never mind what name the obstetrician gave it, didn't matter that he called it a hydatiform mole and said that it happened in such and such a percentage of pregnancies, that it was the fertilization of an empty egg that had caused it. She and every other Dominican knew that it was a token, and now she understood fully what it had signified.

Icilma was able to instantly recognize her cross when it was placed so obviously before her. She was ready to embrace it and to shoulder it, take it all the way to kingdom come. But when she let its weight settle, she staggered, if only for a few seconds, her feet dragging useless on the floor, held up only by her elbows, caught in the deep sink. The news of an outside child—another one—would have been small-time, something she would have batted away like a cobweb, not even worthy of being called a trial or a tribulation. But this one? *This* one? She was in her Gethsemane and she prayed, *Let it not be, not this, take it away.*

That lasted only a moment. Then she searched for her heaviest pot. She broke her husband's jaw with it first, opened the left side of his head next, and then drove to his sister's house.

She stood close to her sister-in-law as she spoke, to catch her when she fell. It was natural that Margaret would take it harder, much harder, than she had. "Girl. Come, les' go. Your brother have a child with Iris."

"Iris who?"

She spoke softly. "How many Iris you know about?"

Still Margaret refused to process the information. Such a thing could not be possible, and her expression was one of genuine puzzlement. Icilma went all the way up to her and held her by the arms, knowing that Iris's name would soon break through the flimsy barrier that Margaret's subconscious had flung up.

Margaret was built like a Baptiste woman, all of them tall and solid, and Icilma was thin; she would not be able to hold her up. She tried to edge her toward a soft landing. She repeated herself, this time raising her voice. "I telling you, Winston make a child with Iris."

When they went down, they missed the sofa. By the time they hit the uncarpeted parquet floor, Margaret was moaning and thrashing, arms and legs flailing weakly, as if knowing the fight was futile. She was spinning herself in a slow, untidy circle on the polished wood, and Icilma pushed the nearby furniture away, giving her space, and went in the kitchen to make a strong cup of sugar water, good for shock.

The two women drove the forty minutes around the coast mostly in silence, but in complete understanding of what had to be done. Once, Margaret spoke. "Obeah. You know that. Is only that could send Winston to make this child."

Icilma made her voice hard, for Margaret's sake. She had to force the words out of her schoolteacher's mouth. "Your brother went and fuck an old whore. Nothing *Obeah* about that." She made herself continue.

"Winston and his worthless ways. That's the only thing that made the child."

Margaret made ugly rasping sounds as she started crying. "Winston? Pay for a woman? That is joke. And is not *any* whore. Papa-God have mercy."

"That was a long time ago, Margaret. Twenty years. Nobody remember that old story." She could hear the untruthfulness in her voice as a physical thing, as if something were taking her words and tightening the timbre. That story came up at every gathering where people sat down to talk old talk. It was history now, but not forgotten: well documented, remembered and passed on through the *chanté mas* songs that had chronicled the scandals, the upheavals. And now, with this, it was all going to start up again. "That is a forgotten story. Today, when people talk about Iris, they only say that what she have between her legs make big men bawl like children. That is what sent Winston—"

She broke off, realizing that she was talking about her own husband. So she tried to console herself while pretending to speak to Margaret. "It was before we got married. You know how men get before the wedding. Is las' lap, they go wild." She stopped talking for the rest of the drive, thinking. Whatever had sent Winston to that woman had nothing to do with what was between Iris's legs, that much Icilma did know.

I t had been after his stag party, he had told her, crying like a little girl. The car was full of drunk men, and somebody started singing the songs. "Naked as They Born," they had been singing, a song that detailed how his mother had been stripped naked by Iris, and vice versa; a song in which the first verse described how one woman was spread-eagle on top of the other, pummeling her, the second verse detailed how they had locked legs and arms and bit each other in the face while they rolled. The third verse said that they had tried to twist off each other's breasts, and referred to his mother as a cow on account of the amount of milk that had wet down Iris by the end of the fight.

This was what Winston and his friends were singing about the night before he married Icilma, and somewhere along the way Winston told his wife, in the middle of all the singing about what his mother and his father's lover had done to each other, the car approached the turn to Iris's house. It was a dare, he told her, sobbing like a woman. They had all stood around and they had cheered him on, and—this part an obvious lie—he could not even remember what it had been like, he had been that drunk.

S he had not broken Winston's jaw for the simple sin of having an outside child. That happened before they were married and such things had to be understood, especially if it had happened the night before the wedding, when illicit sex was practically compulsory for a man. Winston already had had other children with village women, and if she were to be realistic, he would have others in the future. Normally she would never meet these children or their mothers, whose world did not intersect with hers, and they should have caused her no concern, because Winston had settled down at his own social level with her and would treat her right—not by being faithful to her, that was a little joke recited to the priest—but he was a decent man and would give her discretion, the one and only thing she was entitled to as a wife.

She had not broken his jaw because of who Iris was, either. Winston could have blamed it on a carful of drunken men, Winston could explain it anyway he liked, but there would have been a greater force involved.

There was badness, there was the will of a devil-dealing dead woman determined to give her daughter what was hers. But for him to know about this child, and for him to leave his *girl child* to be raised in the house of an unholy prostitute—for that, Papa-God, she should have done him more damage. Because in Icilma's world of middle-class Caribbean society, a whore was a whore, but a man's child was ever his child.

Icilma and Margaret walked into the house. Icilma took one look and fell in love with her cross. She had no choice: there was Winston's face looking at her. It was true what they said about the children of Baptiste men. Every child they made came out identical. It didn't matter what the mother looked like. Color in general—of the hair, eyes, skin— might fluctuate somewhat, and as far as the hair texture, well, that was flexible, as hair could always go either way and even disappoint and turn back after the baby got older, but the strong Baptiste features would always be the same. This one was a Baptiste all right, but with her mother's hair and unusual goldish eyes. Icilma picked up Winston's child and looked at Iris, who sat like a statue in the chair by the window facing the mountains, her head turned away from the door, unblinking, unspeaking.

"Is her father house we carrying her at." The two women and the little girl went down the narrow stone path to the car, the thorns of low-growing bushes scratching their legs, not able to see that Iris had gotten up, taken the blank stare off her face, and was smiling.

For twelve years Icilma guarded Lillian, protecting her from knowing who she was, letting her out of her sight only to attend school, where she knew the nuns would keep as close a watch as she did. She could have loved Lillian no less were she her own, and this love blinded her to the inevitable certainty that Lillian would one day discover her history.

And that day did indeed come when, with the assistance of Lillian's godmother, Icilma picked up the phone and placed a long-distance call. Winston's twin sister, Margaret, had long gone to America. She had married for a green card and was now a naturalized American citizen. "Margaret, Lillian coming up."

It had been discussed before, but Margaret was taken by surprise. "Girl, I not ready for that. We said it would be for college. Still what, another year at least. She not even fifteen."

"Time for her to leave this place."

"What you mean? Don't talk parables, Icilma, tell me what you saying."

Icilma became agitated. "Girl, is you and me walk in that house together! You know what kind of history that child carrying. What more you need to know? Some things not for telephone. I tell you she coming next week, you hear? Next week self."

"But she first need a green card." Margaret believed she had an out: she knew immigration law. It would take years for applications for a niece to be processed. "You think is like before? This is 1980, *oui.* They not letting people just walk in they country again, nuh—they turning you around right at the airport. And if she lucky and get in, illegal people can't get benefit and so. Is a mouth to feed, I go need food stamp. Icilma, tomorrow self I go file for she—"

"Is me you talking to, girl! You know better than me how we do it down here. I already set up all the adoption papers for you, I mail them already, registered. Lillian coming in on a touris' visa, and you get your lawyer to fix it up—the same Haitian man you tell me is a boss when it come to immigration story can do Lillian same way he organize you. When she reach, you look in she valise, I putting a letter in there for you."

"Wait here, is what all dis hide-and-seek business? You hiding letter in suitcase?"

"She might go tear it up if I give she. Plus she not speaking."

"*Bon Dieu.* Is pregnant she pregnant? You sending me trouble, Icilma?"

"Pregnant is nothing. I talking big trouble, Margaret, but I not sending you the trouble—the trouble is down here and it going stay here, you following me? This child must cross ocean and is your own blood she be. I sending her up next week."

Margaret started to bawl. Icilma could imagine her standing in a high-rise in the Bronx, unable to follow her instinct to run outside—she lived on the eleventh floor. She'd be acting like she was stamping in the swept-bare dirt of a Roseau backyard, hand to her head pulling at her hair. Women always went outdoors to wail in the Caribbean, the easier for their lamentation to sail up and catch the ear of a busy God. Also, they reasoned, he wouldn't need to trouble himself too much, he could just glance down without effort and see their physical exertions and take pity. Icilma pictured her sister-in-law first bending over, the hand not occupied with the phone would be holding her underbelly. Then she would be arching back, the same arm now reaching out and upward in supplication, crying a stream of words in a long, loud shout.

She was wailing away in Icilma's ear. "*Jésu, Marie, Joseph!* I know nothing good can come out of that child! Is evil make she, what I tell you? Anything natural could make my brother go lie down with the same crazy woman his father dead for?" She standardized her language for effect. "Icilma, I tell you, Matilda is more powerful dead than when she was alive—"

Icilma held the phone well away from her ear, having heard various versions of this many times over the years, from well-wishing family on both sides, from her friends, from complete strangers. And after Lillian's First Communion, after the child refused to go near a church, she heard it from the priests and nuns who showed how seriously they took the Lillian situation by taking the trouble to visit her home to pray. They never specified what they were praying for, but she knew why they came so regularly, unrequested. Devout as she was, she would rather they'd prayed for her from a distance as they did for the other faithful.

She didn't mind that they came with holy water which they sprinkled in all the rooms of the house. The problem was that the honor of their visits required getting dressed in good clothes, preparing a special meal, and suspending all normal activity around the house while they were in attendance for fear of accidentally sinning in their presence and thereby magnifying the sin a thousandfold. The priests and nuns working in the island were mostly Belgians, and thanks to the language difference and the even more insurmountable barrier of culture, they probably were not aware that their flock held them in greater esteem and awe than the Lord himself. After all, the villagers and townspeople only *believed* that God was a white man, but their very eyes assured them that his messengers were genuine real-life white people.

Icilma acknowledged that something that was not of this world was at play, but God himself would have struck her down had she left her husband's own flesh and blood to be raised by a madwoman prostitute.

Eventually she knew from the change in background noise that Margaret had found an open window from which to launch her tirade, from which she would also be stretching her open hand toward heaven. "Margaret! I hear in America the neighbors calling police anytime they hear bawling. Shut your rass before police reach. Listen. Everything you need to know, I putting in the letter. And walk with warm clothes to JFK, you know I can't find no winter coat and sweater down here. And another thing. You find the best psychiatrist New York have. Lillian going need that."

Margaret started wailing afresh.

26

BOILING LAKE

It would be nearly four hours from D.C. to San Juan, fifty minutes from there to Antigua, and thirty-five minutes from Antigua to Dominica. Lillian was two seats behind Teddy for the first leg. The flight had been oversold and he, hair and clothes smelling of cigarette smoke, had arrived too late for them to be seated together.

It was better that way. Side by side, she would have had to speak, to explain, and she was using all her effort to control her thoughts, to block out the images and the memories. Her firewall was on standby at the edges, ready to slam down and shut out the things she did not want to recall, but this time she used only her rosary—not really praying, just rolling the beads and allowing the familiar words to become a barrier— so that she could dwell on him instead.

He had walked straight up to her at the check-in counter that morning and took her by the shoulders in front of a long line of passengers. "What about the skeletons, Lillian? What about all those people Matilda killed?" He had seemed angry at first, his eyes red from no sleep and smoke. "Who was your father? Why the cat-and-mouse?" But then he had pulled her close and spoken softly. "Tell me." She could still feel his fingers on her scalp, grasping her hair, holding her head back, forcing her to look at him. "Don't turn away. Tell me."

She wanted to explain how she could barely process it all at once for herself, let alone share it with someone else. Her recollections of her life were like a fire gone out of control, she could say. *I'm there behind the wall that's holding it back, I'm bracing the wall, but my hands are burning and I'm going to have to let go. Then the wall will give way. It's only a matter of time before I burn.*

What she said to him was different: "I meant to get to that part," and he seemed to understand, the way he always got it, that there was more to her than what she presented to the world.

She had only allowed herself to think of him as her best friend, her only friend now that those few others from her college days had gone off to their separate lives. More than once she had been told by her fellow activists that they'd had enough. "You're just so *unresponsive*," a woman had said. "I give up," another had shouted, with anger that Lillian could not interpret, not even having been aware that they had been trying. Except for Teddy, who, with all his flaws, had always been there.

She thought of what her life in America was like before she met him, when the world of African-Americans was as foreign to Lillian as that of white people. In fact they represented more of an unknown, as she had at least seen a few Caucasian ecotourists here and there in Dominica, most of them oddly determined to hike up to the Boiling Lake for no good reason. These white people had left the wonderful privileges of America and Europe behind, including comfortable beds and well-constructed homes. They would fly to a hard-to-reach island, one so densely covered with steep mountains that there was absolutely no approach with enough flat land for a jet to land. But the determined tourists would not be deterred, changing planes several times, with the last leg on a small craft that felt each and every shift and sheer of the wind. They would then drive on narrow roads so full of hairpin turns and steep ascents and sudden, wheeling descents that carsickness was a guarantee. They would check into a hotel, only to leave those lesser comforts also. Pay good money for them but then abandon them to walk in sun and rain and mud under life-threatening conditions including bottomless precipices for three hours in order to pass through the well-named Valley of Desolation, stinking and sulfurous, arriving at the steaming crater at the top of a mountain. They would then turn around and walk three more hours back to the unfamiliar mattress of their hotel.

True enough, the water in this crater did boil and bubble, but Lillian and her fellow Dominicans did not think it necessary to see it for themselves. What for? It was there; it had nothing to do with them at that point in time: but one day, it might just start doing more than boiling; it might explode and erupt, spit ash and vomit its poisonous guts, and then they would get to see, hear, smell, and taste what the Boiling Lake was all about.

Not quite thirty miles south, Martinique's volcano had done such a thing, following on the heels of St. Vincent's one May day in 1902. There were still a score or more of Dominica's famed centenarians alive who remembered when it rained ash, that day when Morne Pelée turned mass murderer; and those not yet born at the time had all been told the story and knew details of the burning cloud, the fire in the sky, and the thirty thousand dead in the city they used to call the Paris of the Antilles.

So Dominicans mostly chose to save any long kind of hiking they might end up doing for something with a purpose, like running for their lives. They didn't understand what motivated the tourists. They had great appreciation for things like the beds for their backs at night, the roof over their head, and the happy fact that their land was fertile and their children well fed.

Strange as these white people were, Lillian felt she had some familiarity with them and their ways. But Black Americans were scarce in Dominica, and Lillian steered clear of them in America at first, the urban East Coasters with their loudness and swaggering, their shoulder-chip and posturing, and their undecipherable English. On arriving in New York, February 17, 1980, she had been told straightaway by her aunt that West Indians had nothing in common with American Blacks, not even the experience of slavery.

"You see," her aunt Margaret had explained, "we colored West Indians were always in the majority. Very few white people actually lived in the West Indies. Especially the small islands. It was just a handful of big plantations, you see, and the owners were sensible enough to stay back in England. You just had a few overseers. And we independent now. We West Indians running our own things. So we don't suffer this inferiority complex you see these Negroes here suffering." Margaret, like many West Indians of a certain age, had no idea that American Blacks had long stopped calling themselves Negro—except between and among themselves, where they affectionately or otherwise could refer to each other not only as Negro but as nigger, niggah, dog, bitch, ho, and the like.

"We don't know about this minority business," Margaret would tell Lillian, preparing her to understand the Black American psyche. "That's why they can't catch themselves yet from slavery. That's why they can't get ahead. Wouldn't look for work, just living like they still slaves. Sitting down on they backside talking 'bout slavery, slavery. Everything for them is slavery and white man fault. Blaming slavery when is they own laziness causing they problems, with they no-ambition selves. Still taking what massa give them and calling it welfare."

Margaret didn't hide her scorn for African-Americans, especially not from the one she had married for the green card, and he was happy to escape her once the financial arrangements were completed.

L illian listened, but rejected her aunt's analysis. She was intelligent enough to have scored high enough on the SATs to enter an Ivy League college without ever having attended an American high school, and she was able to see immediately that her aunt had, in effect, set up a dichotomy in which she claimed superiority over African-Americans based on a competition over who had the better slavery experience.

She jumped down from her aunt's imagined pedestal and she tried with all her heart for a new beginning, there in America with people who did not look at her the way they did in Dominica, with people who would give her a ready smile, would try to begin a conversation. But she found herself in the same position as before, unable to do what it took to interact.

It was hardest with the women, who interpreted her awkwardness, her lack of response, as snobbery. Men would put more effort into it, but many of the young African-American men who approached her would simply compliment her hair, her eyes, even express appreciation for her skin color. And then, inevitably, the conversation would follow the same script: "I love your accent. You from the Islands?"

"From Dominica."

"Yeah, the Dominican Republic, man, I knew you was a Hispanic."

"No, not the Dominican Republic. I don't speak Spanish. Doh-mee-nee-kah."

"Where's that at?"

"Near Guadeloupe."

Blank stare, or frown.

"Near Antigua. Heard of it?"

"Yeah! Yeah! Antigo Bay, man, my cuzin been there for Reggae Sunsplash."

And there would be nowhere else for them to go with their conversation after that except to the bedroom, where Lillian discovered that opening her legs was much easier than opening her mind, and that rough, hard sex was an easy language to speak.

Teddy, though, had heard of Dominica. He knew that Antigua was not a Jamaican resort, and he had found a way to make spoken conversation with her, to make her laugh at the things he said. Some twenty years ago, he had taken her in, even after she refused his advances. He had been, he thought, her friend, when in fact he had always been her entire world.

Inside her head there was a tightening sensation, and she braced herself against the onslaught of the drums, which sometimes came with enough force to make her lose her balance, but then she realized that this feeling was something physical, that the plane was beginning its descent. She began to pray her rosary in earnest.

27

HOMECOMING

Icilma had reached that liberated point in a woman's life, that point a decade or so past the half-century mark when middle age is over, but before she becomes unequivocally old—still vital, still able to enjoy her sensuality, to take advantage of it if she so wished, but old enough to enjoy the freedom of letting herself go or, more accurately, of no longer giving a damn.

Grown fat and comfortable, she sat on her oversized gallery embroidering linen hand towels, using mostly satin stitch to fill in the outline of the designs that she first pencil-sketched onto the fabric: the coconut trees, the seascapes, the farmers using their hoes, doubled over their crops, the sunsets, and her favorite, the cross being carried to Calvary by a broken Jesus, his back bent with humanness. She used thread so thick and a stitch so closely spaced that the final result was almost three-dimensional. She gave them away no sooner than she'd finished a set of three—to schoolchildren passing to take for their mothers, to her house help, to the few nuns who were left.

She had started embroidering over twenty years earlier to keep her hands busy, to prevent them from writing letters to Lillian, not one of which had ever been answered. She embroidered to prevent her hands from going to the telephone to make long-distance calls to America. In the early years, Margaret used to force Lillian to take the phone, holding the receiver to her ear, but Lillian had never uttered a word.

Then came university, and Icilma learned that it was possible to feel true hatred for an inanimate object, the thing called an answering machine. "I'm sorry," the voice of a robot told her twice a day, three times a night. "No one is available to take your call."

The embroidering could not prevent her from writing her letters of love to her daughter, nor could it keep her away from the phone, but it helped some, in those years, it kept Icilma from giving in to the despair that might have come with the guilt of having been unable to carry her cross.

She had never blamed Lillian, not at all, because she had kept Lillian's rightful mother from reaching her—what a terrible day it had been, when Iris had come for her child, and they had fought for Lillian, like the women in the Bible, Icilma holding the child's arms and legs on the right side of her body, Iris holding the limbs on Lillian's left side— like that they had fought—and Icilma knew she would have cut the child in two and taken away her half before she would have given Lillian back to Iris. That was sin for sure, to deny a child her own mother; it was one more sin on Icilma's long list, but that sin could not compare with what happened to Iris, because of Icilma's doing. She had called the police to throw her daughter's mother in jail, where she had died that same night.

Eventually Icilma had been able to cut back the embroidering, until she only needed to go occasionally to her sewing basket to pick out the six-stranded thread, to seek a few hours' worth of respite from a heart that, in over twenty long years, refused to stop breaking.

Now, though, Icilma had started again in earnest, working all day long and at night until she fell asleep. She was waiting for her daughter to come home, and when Lillian appeared in front of her, when she looked up from a particularly detailed section of her linen to find her big-woman daughter standing only a few feet away, standing like she was not breathing, like she was a marionette whose strings had just been removed, she spoke as if Lillian had been gone a mere month: "Eh-eh, *dou-dou*, I here waiting for you," and she removed her reading glasses, letting them sit on her slack unbridled chest, and she smiled, continuing to work her needle in and out, although her eyes never left Lillian's face.

A blessed face, even though the rest of the island looked at her and saw something conceived by unnatural and craven appetites, conceived by the power of a dead woman still avenging her daughter, showing her might, proving that in death she was even more powerful, because as a living woman she could only kill, but dead she could make life.

People looked at her beautiful baby girl and they saw something evil; Lillian's own father had looked at her and seen it, as eventually had the child herself. Not Icilma. God himself had chosen her, replacing the decoy in her womb with the gift of Lillian, the blessed child who had been *delivered from* evil, straight to her, and she had been happy to answer, in the words he had taught in his prayer. Amen, so be it.

Icilma loved her accordingly.

28

CONFIRMATION

Lillian had wondered what she would do, how she would tell the woman who'd spent her life protecting her that she was sorry, that she had blamed her only because there was no one else to blame. She had not been able to imagine her homecoming, and even at that moment when she knew the full force of her stepmother's love was streaming straight at her, she experienced it as if through a filter of sensory white noise, feeling it with a muting distortion. The only clue Lillian could find to her own emotional state was the sensation that her internal organs were trembling, that she was shaking from the inside, radiating out. But when she looked down at her hands, they were steady.

I should throw myself at her feet, Lillian thought. I should wrap my arms around her legs and stay flat on the ground in front of her. But she stood where she was, and nothing came out of her mouth.

"Is dream I dream you," Icilma said to Lillian's frozen form. "I dreaming you every night since last Sunday." Icilma aimed her face sideways to send her voice into the house, but her eyes stayed on her daughter. "Allie! Out here. She reach."

Her godmother. Nen Allie, the former Sister Mary-Alice. Lillian closed her eyes, she felt herself sway. She heard Teddy's footsteps start toward her, then pause as she steadied herself, placing her feet wider apart. He went back to his position half hidden by the potted bougainvillea Icilma kept at the gate of the gallery, at the top of the steps.

L illian had been fourteen years old the last time she had seen her godmother. "I know the songs," she had shouted at Mary-Alice then. "I know 'Matilda Swinging.' I know 'Bottle of Coke.' I know 'Naked as They Born.' I know what they mean." And Mary-Alice had no choice but to confirm the translations of the camouflaged words, the double entendres, the allegories that had been used to document her history. To confirm that Matilda was her grandmother and that Iris was her biological mother. That her grandfather had been her mother's lover and had lost his life over her. That her father was the son of that man— and all the rest of it, Matilda and the murders.

Then her godmother confirmed that it was Icilma who arranged to have Iris put in the crazy-people part of the jail when she came drunk, staggering into town to take back her five-year-old daughter. And it was there that Iris had died, the same night she was locked away. "It was her heart, Lilly. It was damaged. It had done take so much blows."

Lillian had run away then, from her godmother, not found until the next day, sleeping in her mother's grave, still alive only because the edge of the shovel she used on her wrist had not been sharp enough. Within weeks of digging up her mother's grave and attempting suicide, Lillian was put on a plane to America.

A llie!" Icilma called again, but Mary-Alice was already moving from the back of the house, falling over furniture and tripping over her dreadlocks yet still managing to keep her balance while every movable object in her path was knocked aside or broken by her flying hair as she avalanched through the living room's sliding doors to throw herself upon her godchild, the two of them keeling over, their fall partially broken by Teddy's muscled brown arms, which had come out of the bougainvillea to usher them to the floor.

Mary-Alice, at seventy-nine, still went every day except Sunday to work her land, to tend and harvest the food crops with which she fed her family of children, grandchildren, and great-grandchildren. She was bony in old age, with long muscles stretching tight and very visible right beneath her crinkled skin. When the Rastafarian movement hit Dominica in the late 1960s, she had converted, mostly because of the religion's rejection of materialism and its health-oriented lifestyle; and she would be the first to admit that it was a partial conversion at best, choosing to keep her version of God and disliking the lethargic effect of the required marijuana-smoking.

Now, having not combed or cut her hair for thirty-plus years, she had yards of dreadlocks, which the very last vestiges of vanity would not allow her to become clumped into the unaesthetic but more convenient uni-dread the older Rastafarians favored. So there were hundreds of them, silver gray and gleaming, although the last couple feet were dirty-blond, the color her hair had been when she began to lock. To prevent them from going the frayed, ratty way of white dreads, hers were meticulously waxed and twisted, palm-rolled several times a week by her grands and her great-grands, and they were a massive cascade of neatly matted cords. She had learned not to let them down in public, which she had to do regularly to ease the pressure on her neck: when, vinelike, they fell in front of her face, covering her entire body, back and front, and hiding her arms and legs all the way to the ground, villagers who came upon her unexpectedly would run away screaming.

Mary-Alice had promised Icilma that she would not carry on, that she would stay calm and in control, but she clawed her way out from under her dreadlocks, knocked away Teddy's arms, and got up onto her knees next to Iris's daughter to make the same kind of noise she had made in front of the broken-bodied Iris on the Colihaut wharf some sixty years earlier.

29

MIRACLES: HOW WHITE TURNED BLACK

Icilma and Mary-Alice had met thirty years before Lillian came back home to them, in the immediate aftermath of Lillian's First Communion abomination, after Icilma realized that serious measures were needed. She decided what had to be done after careful consideration of Catholic doctrine.

In hindsight, it was all very obvious, and Icilma blamed herself for not seeing it was inevitable. She had—as is allowed in accordance with Church regulation—baptized Lillian herself, in a nearby river, just minutes after she and Margaret had taken her away from Iris, in case the mother decided to come after them for her child.

Icilma had not forgotten that the child should have been properly baptized once the emergency was over, but it would have become too complicated. Lillian had never been formally adopted—that would have required the involvement of Iris—and was therefore officially a bastard. Lillian could not, for example, be properly baptized with legitimate children during mass, she would have to be part of the inferior ceremony afterward for the bastards, all children of maids and market women and such people. Then, too, the bastard status might have precluded her from attending Catholic school later. And so Icilma had faked a baptismal certificate.

Perhaps on another child, a child stained with everyday original sin, she could have gotten away with it. But Icilma had enough common sense to have known that her secular baptism would have done nothing to wash away the original sin of this child when the devil himself had a hand in her conception. Lillian, God bless and have mercy upon her innocent heart, needed the hand of God's anointed upon her, and, Icilma had to admit, to fight fire with fire, she would also need some Obeah on top of it. But Icilma could not turn to any of the ordained priests, or to the nuns or brothers. They would inevitably refuse the inclusion of the Obeah protection.

Icilma knew about the Rastawoman nun who married a fisherman, and who had somehow been deeply involved with Iris and Matilda years before, who had testified against Matilda at her trial. The white woman stayed away from Roseau and town people, but it was said that she had wisdom, that country people in the Colihaut area went to her with their problems. They said she had understanding of ordinary Black people and their ways. Immediately after Lillian's failed First Communion, Icilma went to Colihaut to find Mary-Alice.

Mary-Alice, thirty years before Icilma came looking for her, had almost gone back home to Texas. She had almost lost Bird, after she testified against Matilda.

It had started when Bird had taken her to bring Matilda the news of her daughter. After Matilda had come down the mountain to meet them, Bird had left the two women to speak in privacy, but a short time into the discussion, Mary-Alice had asked to be excused and had gone looking for him. She found him in the shade of a tree, speaking in soft Creole with a few men. "She doesn't understand me," she said to the man she would marry within a few days, asking him to come with her to translate. Her distress was obvious, but he refused her. "Your patois is flawless," he said, and when after some time she returned again, in tears, he had consoled her with words he would have occasion to use again, when, a few years later, she would be called to give testimony against Matilda. He said, putting her on his back to take her to his home, "You are the one who do not understand her."

She had defied him, when Matilda was put on trial. He had been so angry, even though he could offer her no proof, he could tell her no more than that Matilda had to be a good woman, she could not have been a murderess; even though the remains of all those murdered people had been found, even though he himself had never been Up There to where she and the other people lived. Even though she, Mary-Alice, had stood in front of Matilda and discovered that the woman's very soul was corrupted.

Bird, after she testified, had turned to another woman.

And she had succumbed to that pull, the double obsession women develop under such conditions: a heightened sexual attraction for the cheating mate, and the fascination with the other woman. Mary-Alice had followed her, had walked behind her for what reason, she did not know, trailing behind the woman as she did her farming, as she went to the market. She would peep at her as she bathed naked in the river in the mornings, sometimes just sit on a rock in the river, out in the open, watching her wash clothes. And nobody said anything to Mary-Alice, they didn't even seem to find it strange, as obvious as she was, Bird's slight white wife walking behind his buxom black woman.

Later Mary-Alice discovered that her behavior was not particularly unusual, and that people were expecting her to do the typical thing. They thought she was just choosing her moment carefully, waiting until they were in a public place with many witnesses—often it would be the market—to establish their relationship of rivalry with loud and graphic cursing, with a set of standard obscene gestures that involved turning around and bending over with a hoisting of skirts, and the baring and shaking of bosoms. Often a cutlass would be pulled out from under clothing for effect, and one or the other woman might even offer a chop or two, although it was rare that the wounds would be more than superficial—unlike the chops that were given by men who felt their women were cheating: they did not go after the other men, their cutlass encounters were with their women, done in private, indoors, and those cutlass strokes generally killed.

Mary-Alice, without the socialization that would have told her what to do, simply went along with the instinct that made her follow the woman around, until, to her surprise, she found herself beginning to like her, a strong-bodied hard worker who was always stopping to talk with the people she passed on the road, always ready with a joke to make them laugh. When both their bellies began to grow at the same rate, Mary-Alice finally went up to the woman and pointed to her stomach. "If you and me have two children, and those children are sister and brother, then you and me must be some kind of family, too, not true?" she asked the woman in Creole. The astonished woman, after considering the question, agreed.

Bird, as soon as he became aware of the alliance of the two women, stayed away from both of them.

Over the next five months they became good friends, establishing themselves as something along the lines of family, and they decided that they would live side by side, so that their children would be raised as true siblings.

One day, as they sat together on stools in the shade of a tree with their enormous bellies, they were deep into the logistical preparations for their upcoming house-moving—both houses were to be relocated to a choice piece of land that was near enough to both their farming grounds. They had already secured enough of the round logs on which the men would push the houses. Mary-Alice had seen it before, and she was looking forward to the *coup d'main,* she wanted to hear the special songs the men would sing as they pushed, and she was making sure there would be enough food for when they arrived at the new site. And rum, especially; she wanted to make sure they did not run out of rum.

Without warning, Mary-Alice stopped calculating how many pounds of eddo and green fig and pig tail would be needed for the number of people who would come out to give a hand, how much rum it would take to quench their thirst.

And she told her friend that she did not come from a culture that prepared her for the open sharing of men. "Bird," she said, "is my man. I want no other. You now, from what I see, you are just passing time with him." She got up and went inside for her cutlass. "I swear," she said, holding up the cutlass to testify, "I will put your child to my breast and give him my milk if he is hungry, but I will slice you open like a melon if you only so touch Bird again."

That was how Bird and Mary-Alice came to be together for life, and when Icilma found Mary-Alice, the former nun was approaching fifty, and pregnant, something that no one, including Icilma, seemed to find strange.

30

FLASHBACKS

In the kitchen they were all drinking bush tea brewed by Mary-Alice from an assortment of nerve strengtheners she had just foraged in Icilma's backyard. Teddy had not been formally introduced, his presence accepted and dismissed in one vague acknowledgment, the way women who have lived long enough tend to do with young men. They accorded him no status, nor had they any expectation of him: the points of intersection between their world and his were too few. Right then, their orbit was taking them deep into purely female territory, and the two old women ignored Teddy with benign condescension.

"You don't have to feel bad," Icilma was saying. "The psychiatrist done explain everything to us." She opened the spiral-bound report in front of her, the leaves of each page fat from years of damp Dominica air. She moved her reading glasses from her chest to her nose, licking her middle finger and turning pages. "Here. *Lillian's refusal to have any contact with you is only one element of the many behavioral strategies she has adopted to cope. We refer to this as an avoidance symptom, and it includes severing her ties to you in her effort to evade activities, places, or people that are reminders of the trauma.*"

"And the school. Columbia University." Mary-Alice ran her hand up and down Lillian's arm. "The counseling people, they used to phone us, tell us how you were doing."

Lillian made as if to speak, stopped. Then she rushed the words. "I remember everything."

Icilma and Mary-Alice looked at each other, blinking a message, and then Icilma carefully touched the report. "But he told us you don't remember that night."

"I lied." How could she have explained to a young man raised in Wisconsin, recently relocated to New York, who had never heard of Dominica, who wasn't quite sure where in the world one would find "the Islands," as he called them, or what sort of "natives" could be found there, as he once asked; who had never before held conversation with any kind of Black person, much less a West Indian, who sat down to dinner every night with his family eating ice cream for dessert, a man who had not yet cheated on his wife—what would that man fathom of a place so small that one woman could orchestrate an islandwide conspiracy of love to preserve a child's innocence. How to start to tell the man, as they sat in his office in the middle of winter, artificial hot air hissing at them from a ticking radiator, a man descended from people who had stepped fully clothed off their boat, a man who sat in church most Sundays and sang bright and cheery hymns in major keys—how to tell that kind of person her story, one in which history was recorded in *chanté-mas* songs, a history centered around a village on a mountaintop where unburied bones were found in a forest; a history that included Flying Masquerades and a man who suddenly dropped dead; about a violent rape and a middle-aged crazy woman making a baby with her dead lover's young son.

Lillian knew much better than to do that. The nice white man with his neat life would not understand how logical it had been for her to want to see her mother's face, a face that was so beautiful an entire song had been composed to describe it. Lillian was smart enough to have avoided the damnation of a New York psychiatric hospital by claiming no recollection of that last conversation with Mary-Alice about the songs, no recollection of digging up her mother's grave, and no recollection whatsoever of using the edge of the shovel to slash open her own wrist.

The round wooden kitchen table was big enough to hold the four of them, but Teddy stood apart, leaning against the Formica counter. To sit with them would interrupt the way words were moving among the three generations. Sometimes one or the other would throw out a major revelation: Lillian's father had suffered a stroke, had been abandoned by the host of women with whom he had consorted since his departure, and ignored by his multitude of children, was being taken care of by Icilma, who visited him daily to feed him blended food from a spoon.

Teddy's eyes were on Lillian's watch. She had returned the thin-strapped one he'd given her, exchanged it for this. He struggled against the urge to unclasp the catch, to see what the scar looked like, touch it. I have known this woman for twenty years, he was thinking, and I have never seen the inside of her left wrist, not even in that last week. He warned himself to say nothing, to just wait. One of them would soon react to Lillian's statement about lying to the psychiatrist.

It appeared, though, that no one else needed further information. Finally he took the risk and spoke, his first words since they had arrived over an hour earlier. He tried to imitate them, their loose phrasing, not quite finishing the thought, leaving the end open to interpretation. "So how could he have treated you, then, if..."

Nobody answered, although, after a long pause, Icilma scraped the fourth chair away from the table, and he eased into it, carefully placing his folded arms on the table with the understanding that his physical form could damage whatever was in the air. He sat across from Lillian, an old woman on one side, an older one on the other. He had come across such scenarios all his life, only now gleaning what really transpired when women sat around a kitchen table, hands around cups of hot liquid, eyes focused downward, divining something from the steam, the bits of conversation secondary to what was transmitting through the silence. He did not fool himself—Icilma's invitation did not include him at the level of participant, but at least he could now watch what went on in that underworld. The cooking of food was just a decoy.

But with all his understanding of this, he was still a man. He had a question, he needed the answer. He rephrased, direct now: "What was the diagnosis?"

Lillian looked up from her tea, her face blotched from the heat, damp with condensation, but it was Icilma who answered. "Post-traumatic stress disorder," she said, and with a clinking of teacups on saucers and chairs being moved, sitting patterns reconfigured, the ritual was over. The old women pulled away to become spectators, conceding that they were now excluded. Mary-Alice and Icilma watched as orbits changed direction, pulling Teddy and Lillian into the ritual of woman and man.

"I should have known," Teddy said, recalling years of emotional numbness, detachment, what he used to call zoning out. That classic mark of someone damaged from a traumatic experience. He tried to recall the other symptoms—suicidal tendencies were one—and then he remembered. "Flashbacks," he said, leaning in on his folded arms, making the table rock. "You get flashbacks. I know when you get them. When it's like you're listening to something." He angled his head, half closed his eyes. "When you do that."

She shook her head. "That's what keeps them out. It's what I do to stop them. A kind of wall."

"But you're hearing something."

"Prayers. Sometimes it's all I can hear. And there are drums, too. Rhythm patterns. Like what the heart might have sounded like."

Teddy was unable to connect her reference to the heart until Icilma spoke. "My mother heard it, you know. She was in the crowd outside his hospital ward. She put her hand up to heaven and swear to me that she heard it loud like a drum. She knew the beat and all. Same beat stickfighters used to fight to when she was a child."

Teddy could sense Lillian slipping away back to where he could not access her thoughts. Submerged into women's territory or, deeper still, back to the drums in her head. He unfolded his arms, stretching them across the table, touching her forearms with the tip of his fingers, sending a message to the old women, that he was claiming her.

"But the flashbacks," he pressed. Lillian had never been treated, and he could now see the extent to which it had affected her. She was not well. He was thinking ahead, he needed information for the call he would make later to the head of psychiatry at Howard. A fraternity brother. He would take her back home, arrange her treatment. "So when you get the flashbacks," he said, "they are of—" He found it hard to form the words. "The night in the grave? That was the trauma?"

"The grave," Lillian said, "and everything else."

"By the time she went to the grave, that was already the first stage *after* the trauma." Icilma reached for the report again, flipping pages. "What they call 'impact stage.'" She read: *"Disorganized, stunned, confused reactions."* Now she was not reading from the report. "Her whole life was the trauma." She looked directly at Teddy as she spoke. "But you couldn't understand. An American like you."

"I could," he said, and he got up and walked around the table to stand behind Lillian, to lean down and say into her hair so only she could hear: "If you tell me, I will understand."

She stood, turned to him. What he wanted to do then was to take her hand, unclasp her watch, look at her wrist, put it to his mouth, but knew he could not; it would appear superficial here in the presence of women who had been through life and come away believing in the dispensability of men once their purpose had been served. He kept his hands to himself and waited for her to speak.

"Words couldn't tell you anything," she said. "If you don't have the…" She made a gesture with her right hand in the direction of an open kitchen window, a window that was nothing but a simple opening in the wall through which it was possible for her sweep of hand to encompass the night outside. "If you don't have the frame of reference."

Lillian walked away from him and reached out into the night, pulling in the two sides of the wooden shutters and closing up the hole with a diagonally turned bar. She said to her mother and her godmother, "I came home to face it."

Now it was Icilma who made the noise, who stood up and spun the window bar, pounded the shutters open again to throw the psychiatric report out into the night, who pulled off her kerchief so she could put her hands down into the roots of her hair as she put twenty years of volume into her voice. "Face what again! You come so far now, look at you, a big somebody in America. Leave all that story! You face it already, you dig up a whole grave and you done face it," and Icilma, in an impulsive act for which she immediately began months of self-imposed penance, went to her wall, pulled down her Sacred Heart, and threw it after the report she had no need for, having memorized each word over twenty long years. And she set no store by its jargon, in any case, its talk of this syndrome and that syndrome. She did not need technical language to tell her that Lillian had inherited some part of Iris's madness.

Lillian walked up to her and used her T-shirt to dry her stepmother's eyes. "I already faced Iris. I understand her, what happened to her. But

Matilda—I just have this feeling. People go to jail all the time for crimes they never committed. Innocent people spend a lifetime behind bars for being at the wrong place at the wrong time. Maybe Matilda was one of those people." Now she turned her back to her mother to look at her godmother. "You testified against her. I need to know what you said. Why you said it."

Mary-Alice was tying her dreads on top of her head, getting ready to wrap them for sleep. "Tomorrow. God willing. Time enough for that whole story, tomorrow."

31

BAPTISM

Mary-Alice knew who the woman standing before her was even before Icilma stated her case. The news of what happened in the cathedral the previous Sunday was big enough to make it to Colihaut the same day. As often happened since she'd heard about Iris's baby, she had been overcome by a feeling, a combination of guilt and love and, above all, regret that she had failed so badly when she tried to help Iris. She resisted the temptation to go to Roseau in search of the child Lillian, just as she had forced herself to stay away from Iris's funeral two years earlier, although she had wept for weeks over the wasted life. And now here was this woman in front of her, with her honest face and her pleading eyes and her strange request.

Icilma wanted her to put on the clothing of a nun, white habit and black wimple and large brown wooden rosary around her neck, and she wanted her to baptize Lillian in a clandestine ceremony in the cathedral in Roseau, a ceremony that would also include—"in just a small way"— the participation of an Obeahman. Mary-Alice understood perfectly why Icilma needed the Obeah, why she would ask for her involvement—and she also understood why she would need to dress the part—it was not a matter of trying to fool God with fancy dress; but the rituals of the Church were never performed without all the trappings of the ceremony. The more important the event, the more elaborate the costume. Of course God could not care less what she wore, or who baptized the child. But God was not Catholic; Icilma was. The baptism would have to be done in full regalia.

She had no illusions: her status as a former nun carried no weight against Matilda and whatever she was able to do from her grave, neither did any kind of so-called Obeah, but she quickly put her fears aside. So much of any religious belief was just a matter of faith, and Icilma had faith in great abundance. Icilma had knelt at her feet and had reached up to reverently touch her belly, drawing some biblical significance from the late-in-life pregnancy. Who was she, Mary-Alice, to turn away from this woman of faith, to take away her hope that her God would come through for her, for the child?

She agreed to the ceremony. Mary-Alice also agreed to arrange for her close friend, a Colihaut Obeahman, to be there. She had chosen her friend because she knew him to be a harmless charlatan. She could tell he had a good heart, and long ago she had sought his friendship because his obligatory Obeahman scowl seemed to be no more than a theatrical stance, unlike the authentically sinister looks of the other Obeah practitioners in the area—and he was clean, fresh-smelling, without the rankness that enveloped the others.

He had, as their friendship deepened, admitted to her that when he supposedly extracted objects from people's bodies, nails and bones and rusty razor blades and such, it was nothing more than sleight of hand. Mary-Alice had also questioned him closely about the use of the mirror, given the stories she had heard about it, so critical to any Obeah experience that people simply said that they "went to *gadé*"—to look. All he did, he said, was to hold up a mirror and then the people's minds did the rest. "But suppose they look and see nothing?" she had insisted. "They always see," he told her. "They always see what they want to see."

On occasion he might use a little bush medicine, he said. For example there was a man in the village who was beating his woman excessively, and so he gave her a little something to put in the man's food after each beating. It made him vomit ceaselessly for a few days. It was not long before the man came to associate the vomiting with the beating, and he stopped.

And there had been the policeman rapist whose victims were all very young girls, who had never been brought to justice because he was the law. The Obeahman gave one of the victims' fathers a little acid to be used in a judicious manner, and that was the end of all the raping. Such was the Obeah practiced by Mary-Alice's friend, and she had instructed him well regarding what was to happen in the church. Nothing elaborate, she told him, he should just recite some gibberish, and give them the usual ball of chalky mud and sticks and hair to bury outside their house for protection. Under no condition should he pretend to withdraw any substance from the child's body, she said, but he could give her something to drink, something harmless that didn't taste too bad.

Icilma was terrified as she dressed Lillian in the early-morning dark, conscious of what was wrapped so carefully in soft toilet paper at the bottom of her purse. Mary-Alice's Obeahman had insisted on it, that she should steal them for their ceremony: one to give the child after the baptism, and the rest would be his payment—he had no use for the papery round white circles in his work, but he could sell them for big money to the serious Obeah people. Icilma had argued with him—the consecrated hosts left over from mass were heavily guarded in the sacristy because it was one of the most coveted items in the practice of

Obeah—but to no avail. And she had done it the day before, pretended to be deep in adoration on her knees while waiting for the moment when the ever-present sexton, whose main function, apart from ringing the church bell, was to prevent exactly such theft, went to relieve himself outside. She had stolen the very body of Christ, opened the tabernacle and thrust her hand into the ciborium, grabbing a handful and stuffing them down her bra, breaking a few in the process, and it was no question a mortal sin she had committed, one for which there would be no forgiveness, as she could never confess such a thing. But she willingly, deliberately sacrificed her eternity for her daughter.

And Lillian did not believe Icilma when she said that they were going to a special novena mass, because the novenas she knew about took place over the nine days before Christmas. Christmas novenas did mean going to church in the early hours of the morning, just as they were doing now, but that was something joyous, and Icilma was not happy, Lillian could see the fright shining from Icilma's big smile, and she could also smell it, a strong animal smell she knew was fear.

Mary-Alice and Matilda did not blame the sexton for what happened; they blamed the Obeahman, because even though he had been told not to bring his mirror, he had come with it, oversized and heavy from the ornately carved wooden frame, and making a scraping noise as he dragged it up the center aisle. "People must *gadé*," he whispered to Mary-Alice, so that Icilma could not hear. "Otherwise they wouldn't think is real Obeah we working."

They were setting up for what was to have been a brief and innocuous ceremony. Mary-Alice had gone to the back of the cathedral to scoop some holy water from its stone basin for the baptism. She was walking slowly due to the constriction of her habit, which was not designed to accommodate a middle-aged, pregnant woman's body, and she was now beginning to feel differently about what she was doing. She had too long been absent from all that went along with this kind of worship of God. She only occasionally attended any one of the country chapels in Colihaut and the nearby villages, small wooden rooms undecorated save for a locally fashioned wooden cross, an occasional crude painting of Jesus or Mary, rendered in thickly applied housepaint. After twenty years, the cathedral had lost its sense of sacredness for her; it felt overdone and foreign. She felt like she had broken into a rich person's house and was about to get caught.

She tugged at the front of her habit, which kept riding up over her belly, and she was mildly embarrassed; she felt like she was dressed up in costume in a comedy of some sort, especially when she considered her friend, who had come to play his role in earnest, with some kind of white pigment smeared on his face for effect, and a ridiculous cape onto which he had stitched feathers and small squares of animal skin.

As she rocked from side to side down the center aisle, walking in that stiff, open-legged, pregnant way, holding an empty chalice she had found on the altar, she was not successful in keeping back the soft chuckles of amusement at her participation in what was now feeling like a charade. The only thing keeping her from laughing aloud was the knowledge that for Icilma, and also for Iris's little girl, this was no joke, it was good against evil, it was life and death.

The other adults were also occupied: Icilma had been lighting the candles at the foot of the statues of the Blessed Virgin, and now with the cathedral suffused in the gentle glow, she was looking down into her bag to extract the delicate cocoon of toilet paper in which the hosts lay. At the marble-and-brass altar, the Obeahman was removing his accoutrements from his knapsack: the bottle of liquid the child was to drink, rusty nails, a wooden basin, and the ball of mud he had fashioned with feathers and sticks. A naturally artistic man, he arranged his props carefully.

Unattended for just the few seconds, Lillian went up to the mirror, which was propped up against the front pew, and she looked.

"Mummy," she said without removing her eyes from the mirror. "Why is that woman swinging by her neck?"

Icilma screamed just once.

32

SMALL DEVILS

Lillian drove Icilma's car from her house to the cottage they had rented. She was completely comfortable maneuvering around Dominica's mountain roads, even though she had never driven in her country before. Teddy, sitting beside her, was not at ease. Quite apart from the foreignness of the two old women, he was in awe of the island. From the small plane's approach to the island, when the indigo sea stayed dark and high all the way up to the mountains that took the place of a shoreline, he felt its intensity. The pilot had pointed out the spouting just off the coast. Coastal water deep enough for whales—water the same depth as the height of the mountains that rose more than a mile straight up out of the sea.

The drive into town from the airport had been, it seemed to Teddy, ninety minutes' worth of one ascending or descending hairpin turn after the other, and it made him carsick. He kept his eyes closed most of the way, even though it made the nausea worse. But he couldn't bear to look at the narrow roads cutting into the edges of mountainsides with only the occasional safety rail. Should a wheel end up a foot or so off its intended track, there would be a plunge straight down that would not allow for survivors.

Once, the taxi driver stopped to fill recycled water bottles from a spring just off the road, offering them to Teddy and Lillian as his welcome-to-Dominica gift. "Straight from the source. Full of minerals," he said. Teddy looked at Lillian on the chilly mountainside, backdropped against green, the surrounding mountains so high that only the smallest circle of sky was visible directly above them, and he understood why so many immigrants, approaching old age, return home after having built their entire life in another country. He had thought it was something sentimental about being buried in the soil of one's homeland, but now he realized that it was because at home, in the place where they learned how to walk and to speak, they no longer had to strain.

That was how Lillian was feeling, being back in Dominica. The initial, immobilizing lurch of terror she felt as she stopped at the door of the small aircraft had retreated, and even though there had been an instant increase in the intensity of the sounds in her head, she felt like something had fallen away, her physical being was now synchronized with her physical surroundings. The possibility of peace, she thought, was now real.

Their cottage sat on the elevated bank of one of Dominica's few large rivers. It flowed more silently than the multitude of low-running rock-studded ones for which the island was famous, but the sound was thicker, denser, interrupted by groupings of boulders. After they had unpacked, Teddy stood on the balcony, designed to suspend him over the water, uncomfortable in the dark. Above them, Morne Diablotin loomed, and Teddy did not appreciate being in the shadow of such a mountain, Dominica's highest.

"What wickedness did this mountain do," he asked the housekeeper when they first arrived, "to get named after the devil?" And she had laughed hard and said that Diablotin was not the *diable,* it was a nocturnal black seabird that used to nest in abundant colonies on the cliffs of the mountain. It was said, she explained, that they were now extinct, and some white people from overseas had come looking for signs of them and had gone away without finding any. But they were around, she told Teddy, not many, but they flew along the coast near the cliffs at night, from time to time she had heard their devilish call.

It was late night now, Dominica river water was rushing underneath him as he talked fast and soft into a cordless phone. "I thought it would be just something she was doing to get a little closure, you know? See her stepmother again, reconcile. Talk to some old-timers about the grandmother—like people would say, 'Oh, your grandmother was a good woman, she wasn't capable of murder,' that kind of thing. So she could feel better about it. I didn't think she was really expecting solid proof that the grandmother was innocent, I mean, that's one hell of a long shot. She's convinced herself that the grandmother made a false confession. And—this is the part, it's just coming out now, she can't even talk about it—she attempted suicide, for God's sake—"

His anxiety transmitted well to his friend, who used his psychiatrist's modulated voice and a cache of soothing words: "It'll be fine. Bring her back. We'll see her. No problem."

Lillian walked out and shook her head at him as she trusted the balcony rail with her weight, forcing him to end his long-distance call. In spite of his lowered voice, she had been able to hear much of his conversation, and she wondered if she was expecting the impossible from a man who came from such a different place. His urban African-American life had been so secular in nature, he was so dissociated from his roots, ungrounded in his faith. He, and people like him, channeled their concept of a spirit world through a wholesome yet superficial obligation to a God based on a benevolent Jesus; religion as entertainment by massive choirs and the roaring crescendos of preachers' sermons. The casting out of demons was something they laughed at, done on television by charlatan born-agains. For them, the words "spirit possession" would first bring to mind something they smiled indulgently at when the older church ladies performed their jubilant and short-lived quickstepping, or their straight-up-and-down jumping. Teddy had even told her about the time, as a child at an Easter vigil, he had drawn attention and a measure of parochial fame when he authentically spoke in tongues, having deconstructed and reproduced the particular rearrangement of syllable that was, he explained to her, not all that different from pig Latin.

She looked at him, slightly turned away from her as he kept the same low, urgent tone, saying goodbye to the psychiatrist on the phone. His discomfort in her natural surroundings was so clear, his inability to relate to her kind of people, who might be well aware of the scientific explanation of their illness but who still believed that, at its root, someone—a jilted lover, a business competitor, a rival in love, an enemy— had worked Obeah on them.

Here in Dominica, the leftovers of African religion, the form without the substance, were inserted into the ritualistic framework of Catholicism, already full of preoccupation with evil—and Lillian wondered if she could trust his level of understanding, because in his American world, the conditions of her life would be but grist for the tabloids and the talk shows. Her mother had been the lover of an older man, and later she had a child by his son. That would be the extent of it. Her grandmother was a murderer who claimed mystical powers. Nothing else to it. Teddy would not be able to feel the specific nature of things that made her kind of people afraid when they were alone, when they turned out their lights in their houses, when the night air descended.

"I'm not going back," she said to him when he hung up.

"To D.C.?"

He registered her slight hesitation before she explained. "Not going back to any kind of institution."

"No institution. You'd see a good psychiatrist couple times a week for a while."

"That can't help me." She pulled him so that the waist-high wooden railing was now supporting the weight of two bodies. There, high above rocks and swirling water, they fed their clothes to the black and invisible river. Standing against the flimsy rail, they allowed themselves love of the most physical kind—the only kind of love of which Lillian was capable— with indelicate noises: grunting and loud panting; sucking kisses that turned into bites, slaps that left marks all over each other's bodies.

A s they drank their coffee the next morning, Teddy tried to resume the conversation he'd attempted the previous night. Lillian had played a clever mind game, his psychiatrist friend had said, she had found a way to stop the flashbacks by filling up her mind with sounds, but the most debilitating part of the disorder remained—the emotional shutdown, the maintenance of a protective wall, her mind's overly successful attempt to ensure that such trauma could not happen again. "Wallace says there's a Jamaican woman on his staff. She could relate. She'd understand the cultural—"

Lillian cut him off. He didn't understand that this was not about psychiatry. "Just me and you, Teddy."

He looked down at her watch and took it off, as he had the night before. The scar was, he thought, a thing of beauty. It had healed into a single, solid rectangular keloid, raised high and smooth, the edges neatly defined. He ran his fingers over it.

"Me and you," he agreed.

33

SACRILEGE

All kinds of rumors circulated in Roseau about the sexton who answered to the name of Pope. One story said he had been castrated as a young man by a jealous lover with a sharp cutlass, another that he was born with a birth defect—testicles but no penis. These stories were invented in speculation: Dominicans could believe that white men might give up having women and making children for some white-people reason to which they were not privy, but they would not accept that a Black man who was clearly not a *maco* (he lacked the affectations and the tight-bottomed walk) would freely deny himself the very things for which God put him on earth.

They were wrong about his sexual organs; Pope was in possession of all components of his manhood, but Dominicans were right, that he was not a homosexual—he was just a truly devout man who had received his calling a quarter century too early. The concept of transforming an illiterate Black West Indian boy into a priest could not yet be carried through. Knowing that, he hid behind the life of a caretaker and bell ringer, but he had taken his own private vows, studying the habits and the comportment of the missionaries, surpassing them in piety and devotion, and saying daily mass alone, in secret. When the parishioners began to call him Pope, it had come naturally off their lips, with only a small degree of mockery; it was a name to which he answered with confident humility.

Pope used to have a home—a back room in the house of a Roseau carpenter to whom he had been apprenticed since he was a child. He had, in the days when Mary-Alice was still a nun, gone back to the carpenter's house to sleep at midnight, returning at four-thirty in good time to ring the sunrise Angelus and prepare the altar for mass at six. But in the last few years, unknown to most people except to the priests, Pope lived in the stairwell directly beneath the bell tower—a space which might have been cramped to others, but which was more than adequate for a man who needed nothing but a place to kneel and pray, a place to quietly keep guard, protecting the most holy of holy.

There had been too many cases of sacrilege in the hours between midnight and four-thirty, and since he had been sleeping in the stairwell, he had chased off so many young vagabond boys, who were paid to enter the sacred space in the small hours of the morning by others who could not risk being caught in the act of stealing the body of Christ for Obeah.

The scraping, screeching sound of the mirror being dragged entered into Pope's dream, disturbing and warping it into one of his nightmares, all of which involved a depiction of hell. It was several minutes after it stopped before he woke, sweating, sure that he now knew what kinds of torturous sounds the sinners would be forced to hear for all eternity.

But, he realized, he could also hear the stealthy sound of a theft in progress, and he was not alarmed; all he had to do was show himself before the little boys would scamper off. But when he looked through the peephole he had chiseled in the wood of his wall, his hands went to stifle a scream. It was not some little *kawat* stealing a host for his mother to use against her rival—this could not even be called Obeah, this was real devil business.

A grinning apparition was slowly moving down the center aisle of his cathedral toward him. Something that could only have been called up from hell. A ghost in the guise of a nun—and this could not be something good, it could not be the spirit of a peacefully departed sister come to spend time in her favorite earthly place, because the nun—the ghost—a white woman with a nest of snakes for hair, well past childbearing age from the wrinkles on her face as she bared her teeth in an evil smile—was big with child.

And then he heard the single sharp sound, so abrupt that he did not immediately recognize it as a scream, and he looked beyond the apparition in time to see Icilma fall to the ground. He saw the hosts strewn all across the floor, he saw the Obeahman running down from where he had been busy defiling the altar. He saw the child, staring into the mirror, and he understood what was happening, recognizing the schoolteacher and her stepdaughter—the grandchild of Matilda. He had been there the previous Sunday when the host rejected entrance into the child's body. Icilma was trying to fix the child using Obeah, but that small-time Obeahman was no match for Matilda, who had sent the apparition.

He threw on his bishop's robe and miter, stolen so long ago, heretofore worn only when saying his secret mass. He knew that his moment had come. He would now prove that even though the white people thought God had no use for illiterate Black men who wanted to serve him, he, Pope, had as much power as they did, or more. He would cast out whatever demon was in the child, and he would take on the preg-

nant evil spirit. And as he ran up the center aisle with his bottle of holy
water in one hand and his crucifix in the other, he felt, for the first time
in his life, powerful.

But Mary-Alice and the Obeahman ignored him at first, having recognized and dismissed him initially. They were pouring holy water on
Icilma's face, trying to revive her. They needed to get out of the cathedral
quickly, before people heard the commotion and came to see what was
going on.

Pope looked at Lillian, who was still enthralled by the mirror, and he
tried to remember whether Christ had cast out demons, and if so, what
words he had used. The child finally took her eyes off the mirror. She
looked at him as he elevated the crucifix high above her head. As he
splashed her with holy water again and again, he noticed her catlike
eyes, how trusting they were. And knowing she was counting on him,
he used his imagination as he attempted his first exorcism. He had run
out of holy water and he dropped the small bottle, transferring the large
crucifix to his left hand. With his right hand he protected himself from
what was within her by making the sign of the cross, continuously. He
kept his voice low and spoke directly to the evil, and he spelled out for
Lillian what she had begun to suspect; he said, "You, child, were conceived and born by the hand of evil. I command the evil that dwells in
your soul to get out."

Mary-Alice hit him with the heavy chalice she had been trying to fill
with holy water for the baptism Lillian would never receive.

The story of what the two women had tried to do never got out,
because when Pope told the story, he had gone to the priests
dressed in his bishop's robes, and he had prefaced the story by admit-

ting that he had been a priest for a long time, and that he would, from then on, perform his priestly duties in the open.

He began to walk the streets dressed as a bishop, his miter sitting tall on his head, always carrying his crucifix and his bottle of holy water, and people continued to call him Pope, although now they laughed and pointed and did not try to hide their mockery.

34

CONFESSION

Mary-Alice was ready to speak. She would take her time. Lillian had grown into such a beautiful woman, but hers was a tormented face—it was in the eyes, when you could catch a glimpse into them—and she, Mary-Alice, had played no small role, been an unwitting cause of much of that torment.

Lillian deserved the details, and Mary-Alice would get them right, even the part she had left out of her testimony, the part she had refused to recall, which had caused too much shame even to have been recounted to Bird.

"I was a character witness," she said. "I was asked to give my opinion of whether she was a decent person or not." She dropped her cloudy eyes, and Lillian looked at Teddy. He understood what she was asking him to do: this was her godmother, she could not disrespect her with difficult questions.

"So, Nen Allie," he said. He tried out the term for godmother Lillian used, and was relieved when it did not sound pretentious. "You based your opinion of her on what—I mean, how did you know her?"

Mary-Alice untied her turban, shook down her dreads, brought some forward to cover her knees; a mantle. She stroked her hair. It was a meditational act. It would be harder than she thought, and she needed all the help she could get to delve fifty-eight years into her memory, to do her best to give an honest accounting of the role she had played in helping to bring about a woman's death, to describe what had made her feel in the pit of her stomach that Matilda was capable of what she herself admitted to doing. "My opinion was based on the time I met her."

Teddy said, too quickly. "'*The* time'? You mean, one time? You met her just once?"

"Child..." Mary-Alice looked away, and for the first time since Teddy's arrival, he could see all her years on her face. "I don't say it was fair. It was the late forties. I was a white woman, a former nun." She spoke as if she were no longer white, but after sixty years, perhaps she was not.

"So what you're saying," Teddy asked, more softly now, "is that they convicted her on that one conversation you had with her?"

Mary-Alice straightened her back. The day before, she had heard the hope in her godchild's voice, and she did not want to take it away, but in the lifetime she had lived since that day she met Matilda, she had remained fully convinced of the woman's guilt. It had cost her dearly, it had almost cost her true love, but not even for Bird had she been able to deny what she felt. "They convicted Matilda because *she* said she did it." She looked at Lillian. "You understand, *dou-dou*? Matilda confessed to killing the people. I never said she killed nobody. What I did was give my impression of her character. It was an honest impression, I was true to myself. I want you to understand that. What I said," said Mary-Alice, speaking carefully with her eyes closed, her head back, "what I said was that I found her to be morally corrupt."

35

NO EARS TO HEAR

When Matilda climbed down the mountain to meet Mary-Alice, she had at first greeted with anger the news that her daughter was no longer attending school, but on learning that a man of close to thirty years old was having daily sex with her fourteen-year-old child, that he had shown up at the home of the family where she lived and literally abducted her, taken her by the arm and dragged her off, housing her in a community of semiprostitutes—this information had been met with ... Mary-Alice searched for the word that would best translate her memories of Matilda's reaction. Acceptance, perhaps, that was there, but it was something more. *Approval.* That was the thing that set off the alarm bells, that had caused her gut to go into spasms: when Matilda learned the details of John Baptiste and Iris, she approved of what he was doing to her child.

"Iris is fourteen years old," Mary-Alice said, raising her voice.

Matilda for no reason was speaking to her with insolence. "I would know her age." And then she said, "It's earlier than usual. But when it happens, very little we can do about such things." Matilda had said something else right after that, and Mary-Alice struggled to remember: "She is like her father's people. I always knew that for her, love would be that way."

This Mary-Alice understood clearly, something commonly said

about Caribs, that they were *chaud*—hot, high-natured, oversexed. "Madam," she had said to Matilda, "the man is so much older than your daughter." And Matilda had said, "The better for her."

"He will marry another woman in just a few months," she'd said. "Do you understand that?"

"I understand that very well," Matilda said, and then spoke some of the most disgusting words Mary-Alice had ever heard: "Perhaps her temperament is best suited to that arrangement."

And after declaring her child better suited to be a grown man's illiterate concubine than to be a schoolgirl, Matilda only asked questions regarding the wealth and status of John Baptiste. Did his family have influence? Did he have land? Had he given her a house of her own? And Matilda wanted to know what John Baptiste had sent for her.

This last question Mary-Alice had not understood. She asked for clarification, and Matilda had been very clear. She expected gold, cloth, alcohol, and livestock from John Baptiste in exchange for her daughter.

That was when Mary-Alice had begun to shout at the big black woman who had climbed down a mountainside to meet her, who had not even done her the courtesy of inviting her back up to her home when Mary-Alice had come so far to bring word of her daughter. The unsmiling woman had come in everyday farming clothes to meet her—knowing that a sister of God was waiting to see her, had not extended her the respect of dressing appropriately, the way any other rural Dominican would have attired herself in traditional *douillet,* draping a section of her skirt over an arm as she approached so she would see that the woman had worn her best hand-embroidered cutwork cotton petticoats underneath in her honor, the lace eyelets threaded with red ribbon. But Matilda came with dirt under her nails and her head uncovered, sweat shining through the rows of her Congoed hair.

And unlike every other Dominican Mary-Alice had ever met, Matilda had looked at her with indifference, without deference, with no regard for her nun's habit—although by that time she was only technically still a nun. Matilda had treated her worse than one would have treated a donkey, she had not even offered her a drink of water, nor moved her out of the hot sun into the shade of a tree.

Mary-Alice had shouted at Matilda, screamed in her face. "So she is for sale? He is about to get married to a woman from his own class! Iris is *nothing* to him! I've seen how they treat them! He will abandon her! Use her to kick around—"

"That never happens." The calm of Matilda's voice had stopped her, although it might have been the authority of how she spoke, especially when she repeated herself. "Does that ever happen?" And then Matilda answered her own question because the truth was that Mary-Alice had no idea. "If a man is going to abandon a woman, he will do it for other reasons. He will not abandon her because he gets married."

Mary-Alice had tried to compose herself, and she made her final effort, but now she was sobbing. "But she is not a woman. She is a child."

Matilda did not reply; she was glancing down, beginning to adjust her dress, which was really only a length of fabric wrapped around her body, under her arms.

"Do I miss something, madam?" Mary-Alice asked. She was pleading. "Do I miss the reason you think it such a good thing for your child to be left with this man?" And then her breath stuck in her throat.

Matilda had pulled at the end of fabric that was tucked under her left arm, so that the whole panel came loose, and she held the ends, one in each hand, extending her arms slightly with elbows kept bent, repositioning the panel correctly under her arms. Mary-Alice had never seen an uncovered pair of black breasts before; all her work with the pregnant women took place long before they got to the point where they were naked and bawling on their backs; now she stared at the things that swung at her. She had never imagined that black could be so black—the powdery soot-black of the skin, the wide coal-black halos of prickled aureole, the thick rough pitch-black crowns of nipples, black on deeper black on denser black, each section impossibly darker than the one from which it arose.

Mary-Alice had not been able to articulate it into a thought, but Matilda's breasts in their infinite blackness—a black that was too far beyond beautiful to be categorized as merely black, a black that needed to be taken out of the category of color, shifted up into the category of feelings—had threatened her, had deeply stirred her to fear. She wanted to step away but could not.

When Matilda heard the gasp, she had been about to execute the quick alternating movement of arms crossing the front of the body which would have closed her *pagne.* She had just made the final instinctive shimmy that allowed the circulation of air between and under the breasts before they became strapped back down. An ordinary movement performed many times a day the world over by people whose clothes are not held together with stitches. Instead, she smiled, let the rectangle of cloth fall onto the dirt, and stepped in to stand close to her, high above her. With a quick, deliberate movement, Matilda jerked her upper body so that her breasts hit against Mary-Alice's cheek, first slapping the right side of her face, and then, another fast twist, another hard slap on the left side.

Matilda stepped back and made a speech for Mary-Alice, at least that was how Mary-Alice remembered it, a full-blown speech in which the mountain woman used a kind of Creole that one did not hear normally, the complex Creole of someone who never spoke English, a rich Creole that did not call on support from thrown-in English words but was nonetheless completely comprehensible.

Matilda said, with her black nipples like fingers pointing down at Mary-Alice, who was now sitting on her heels in the dirt with her shaking hands covering her cheeks: "You would never understand, even if I explain it to you. But Iris will come home, come back to us, when she wants to. If she needs to. How do you describe this? You say she is in love? We could just call it a kind of madness. It may run its course soon, it may not. But there is nothing you or I can do about it."

Then Matilda bent down to pick up her *pagne,* to wrap it around her and tighten it with a strong tuck under her arm, and as she walked away she said something prophetic. "You could break every bone in her body," she said, "and still she would find a way back to the man in the end."

36

FORGIVENESS

On their third morning in Dominica, Teddy and Lillian gave Mary-Alice a ride back to her own house, a ten-minute drive to a residential area that, even so close to the capital, still had a rural feel. She had been staying with Icilma from a week before their arrival when Icilma had her dream of Lillian's return, but now her crops needed tending.

The previous night she had come to the end of what she knew about Matilda—which, in the end, was not very much. Nobody, she had said, knew for sure what exactly had happened up there when the police went to get Matilda. There had been some kind of cover-up, it was suspected. The official report said that only a few people lived with Matilda, less than twenty in all, but a persistent story told it differently—it was said that when the police arrived, an entire village of hundreds had attacked them on sight; certainly a number of police had lost their lives violently. Villagers also had been killed, the story went, but the numbers ranged too drastically—from a few to a few hundred—for anyone to know for sure whether there had been a massacre. The story of how exactly the police had come upon the unburied skeletons in the forest was also never told; only that Matilda had admitted to having killed them over an unspecified number of years.

What people did know for sure was that the police spent that night
in Colihaut—the nearest coastal village to where Matilda lived—with
five of their own dead, and a handcuffed, beat-up Matilda. And they also
knew that the next day reinforcements came from Roseau, including a
contingent of Her Majesty's Royal Navy. They tried to go back up to
conduct further investigations, to make additional arrests, but they
could not: they could only stand at the bottom of the mountain and
watch the top burn. Who set the fire, why they set it, and whether people
died in the fire, these things remained untold.

"The transcripts," Teddy said. "The court records of Matilda's trial.
Newspaper accounts. There'd be details there."

They left Mary-Alice to her hoeing and drove back into town. Lillian
wanted to go to the market, and she asked Teddy to visit the Roseau
archives without her. She had asked Icilma about a girl—now a market
woman—by the name of Myrtle, and Icilma had shaken her head. "Why
would you want to go look for that wicked girl?" she asked.

"Because I never thanked her," Lillian said, but she was really hoping for forgiveness.

37

SINGING HISTORY

Six or seven of the older girls in Lillian's class had gone off by themselves. Some of them were so dull that they were three years older than her, having repeated more than once. Others had stayed down because of their intelligence—sheer boredom had caused them to ignore what was being taught on the blackboard. But disparate intelligence levels did not matter in such groupings, united as they were by knowledge of another kind, of which the younger girls were still only vaguely aware.

Two of the Big Girls had already disappeared from the class earlier that term—one briefly, sent to another island from where she returned pale and thin; the other without the means for her mother to give her a second chance. The rest of the class now saw this unfortunate girl on Saturdays when they went to market with their mothers, sitting behind her piles of eddos and dasheen and tania, the same place she would sit for the next twenty or so years, the same swollen belly and breasts repeated year after year until her body would eventually show mercy and refuse to reproduce anymore.

But the rest of Lillian's third-form class had, so far, escaped such a fate, and they were all enjoying a class picnic. It was Sister's Feast Day, and she had given her girls a holiday from school and had taken them by bus to celebrate with her at her favorite place for a riverbath. It was high in the mountains and close to the source, the icy water immensely refreshing and bracing. In one place, hot water gushed out from between the rocks and the younger girls were fighting for their turn to warm up under the miniature waterfall. They were having a great time, oblivious to what the Big Girls were doing that day, because they also had their own intrigue. They were giggling, preparing for the thrill of seeing Sister in her bathing suit, a rare chance to be amazed that someone's body could be such a color, especially the top part of the legs, the soft part where the luminous white flesh seemed to be transparent, so much so that they could even clearly see the network of veins—not the black-and-blue, old-people kind that bunched up and bulged, dark and ugly near the surface—Sister was young enough. But they could see the deep ones with their intricate pattern, as if Sister had somehow managed to put on a pair of green fishnet stockings under her skin.

Lillian was uninterested. She had been seeing all parts of her white godmother's body from the time she was seven years old, because Icilma and Mary-Alice had become best friends after they had tried to baptize her. What drew Lillian that morning was the sound of the Big Girls' voices singing, just close enough up the river to be within earshot of their teacher, but far enough for the lyrics of the songs to be indistinct. Lillian knew that something was off: there was the particular laughter, the screeching, in between the choruses; and also, more telling, there was a holding back to the singing when it should have been an open-throated rendition.

Lillian began to inch away from the other girls, who were splashing water on their good-natured teacher, some of them daring to tease her about the color of her thighs, the latticework of veins buried in them. She was listening hard to the snatches of song that were coming down-river, and she could catch enough of the melodies and bits of lyric to know which ones they were singing. She knew that the limited extent of her understanding prevented her from interpreting the songs. She knew that the song about the two milk-producing cows fighting over a bull—that song was not about any farmyard animal brawl; and she knew that when they sang about Matilda who could cross any river by swinging on a vine, that really meant something else; and above all she knew that "Bottle of Coke" could not be about fruit and vegetables and the corrosive effect of cola on the lining of the stomach—Icilma's burned hand had always attested to that. Lillian continued moving away from Sister, up the river toward the sound of singing.

They were in the middle of "Matilda Swinging" when Lillian rounded the bend in the river and stood in front of them. And when understanding came to her, it was neither because of the way a few of them exchanged looks and grinned and raised their voices as high as they dared, nor the way some of the others closed their mouths and lowered their eyes.

Lillian received understanding when she recalled what she had seen seven years earlier in the mirror, when her frightened mother had dressed her in her blue-and-white church clothes one dark foreday morning and walked her through back alleys and slipped into the cathedral with her. With the girls singing the *lavway*, the two simple words, *Matilda swinging, aye, Matilda swinging*, again and again, it all came together for her, and in the few moments when innocence is still in the process of being lost, before the weight of the new knowledge is fully absorbed, Lillian wondered why she had never put it together before, why she had never connected the song to what she had seen—the woman, swinging indeed, from a rope.

"Who is Matilda?" Lillian thought she had only raised her voice to be heard over their singing. But the scream would be heard downriver, where Sister and the young ones paused for a moment, believing that an animal was being slaughtered in the distance.

With only one exception, all the Big Girls slipped silently off the boulder on which they were sitting and crouched forward in the waist-high water, allowing the fast current to take them away as quickly as possible, back to the safety of Sister and the younger girls. Only Myrtle stayed, the oldest of them, who had doubled in three different classes due to genuine stupidity, and who by seventeen, aware of all the things that would never be hers on account of her limited mind, had decided that, at least, she could gain respect by being afraid of nothing.

"Who is Matilda?" Lillian asked her, calmly and quietly this time. "What is she to me?"

"She is your murdering Obeahwoman grandmother."

There would have been hundreds of other old *chanté mas* songs Lillian could have asked about, but now she knew exactly which ones belonged to her: because those were the ones that, like "Matilda Swinging," had never been deliberately sung in her presence, the ones that caused Icilma to immediately turn off the radio.

She could hear sounds of splashing coming up the river, she could identify them, the frantic leading stomp of Sister's heavy legs, the background swishing of the rest of the class following behind her. Even though she knew the water was about to deepen, forcing them to move more slowly against the current, she only had three or four minutes. She flung her questions at Myrtle, demanding interpretation of every song that told her story. And in four minutes and a few seconds, Lillian got a précis of her history, with names and dates and as much detail as time allowed.

As she turned to leave—she would go to Mary-Alice for the rest of it—she saw Sister coming around the bend, fighting the current with her arms, her legs magnified, big and blue-green under the water. Lillian wanted to stay, to defend Myrtle, who alone had the courage to tell her what she had been waiting to hear her entire life, but she could not wait.

By the time Sister put the print of her four fingers across Myrtle's face, Lillian could hear the sound of the slap and Myrtle's high yelp on the impact, but she did not see it, she had already started running toward the main road, in her bathing suit, to catch a ride to her godmother's house.

38

SIGN OF THE CROSS

Lillian could sit in her stepmother's house without difficulty, but it was something else altogether when she walked through the streets of Roseau, made even more narrow by the overhanging galleries on most of the houses.

The entire town had a feeling of not belonging to the present. Twenty years ago, the surrounding islands built concrete hotels and duty-free shopping centers during their tourism boom. But Dominica stayed as it was, and other islanders looked down on the farming people. Now the backwardness had turned profitable, it was now called authentic and untouched. Some of the town residents had moved out to the areas surrounding Roseau, but many still lived there, sitting on their second-floor galleries holding conversations with passersby down on the street.

She was heading straight down King George V Street, and she now knew the exact place where Iris had lived with the Fadoul family; the same dry-goods shop was there, members of the same Lebanese family standing behind the glass counter, standing in front of the bolts of cloth as they had sixty years before. She knew exactly in the center of which intersection Iris would have fought with her lover's wife. She now knew the house where the same wife would have, the next year, looked down at the clash of the bands, where her grandmother Matilda would have killed her grandfather, John Baptiste.

She walked quickly, wearing dark sunglasses, hearing the quiet that came over the small clusters of people on the sidewalks as she passed, the old ladies sitting behind their trays, with their madras head ties and their bright yellow gold earrings, the cataracts in their eyes not preventing them from seeing her, from knowing who she was. She heard the buzz that began when they assumed she was out of earshot. Many of them were people she would know, if she were to look; her stepmother's friends and acquaintances, who had been telephoning the house night and day to make their inquiries and offer their well-wishes for what they all called the return of Icilma's prodigal daughter.

By rights she should stop and smile, greet them, allow them to put their arms around her and make their exclamations. They would say, *"Mon Dieu,* is Icilma's big-woman daughter finally reach home. But child, you looking good, eh, you have flesh; come let me pinch you, you not *maigre* and bony like those foolish girls in America," but she could not make herself do it. She would see the way they had always looked at her, and she would not be able to take that. She would see fear, or she would see pity, or both; she knew she could never look into the eyes of any Dominican and find an ordinary look of recognition or of welcome; they knew too much about her for that. She kept her head straight and her stride brisk until the street widened at the bottom of Roseau, approaching the waterfront. On her left was the produce market, open-air and not very crowded in the middle of the week, but Icilma had said that Myrtle was not just a Saturday-morning huckster, that she was there all the time.

Myrtle had changed drastically, she had more than doubled in size, but Lillian still recognized her. She was positioned in the universal market-woman way, her backside one with the low stool on which she sat, the stool effectively hidden by splayed thighs so that she seemed to be suspended in a permanent low squat, her legs apart so that the fabric of her skirt could fall in between to create the work space in which some cash could be kept, the rest of the money secreted down in the deep bosom. She was surrounded by children of all ages, girls and boys, dressed so raggedly that it was not possible to tell the gender of the younger ones. All of them carried Myrtle's mark, the vacant-eyed expression of a slow mind, and they swarmed and darted around their mother in such abundance that Lillian could not get an immediate head count. Lillian suddenly remembered that Myrtle was only called Myrtle by her teachers; schoolchildren used to call her "Fish-Head" on account of the flat dead eyes, and the odd habit she had of speaking to herself silently, her lips opening and closing as she mouthed her simple thoughts.

To offer her thanks to Myrtle, and also her apology for having run away and left her to bear the brunt of Sister's wrath, Lillian had brought a small gift, a silk scarf, but she had no idea how she should execute the reunion. It should be done boldly, she knew, she should rush up to Myrtle and make big enthusiastic sounds of excitement, the way regular people behaved. She opened her purse and took out the gift, wrapped in festive paper, with a bow and a thank-you card. She held it out toward Myrtle, quickening her pace.

But when Myrtle turned her head and spotted Lillian through all the children, she made a violent sign of the cross with her right hand, kept making it, again and again; and with her left hand she picked up a sugar apple from the ground in front of her and threw it at Lillian with force. It landed right in front of her, at her feet, and Lillian stopped walking, although the hand holding the gift was still extended. "Don't come no further, I warning you," Myrtle shouted, with her old woman's haggard face and her destroyed belly hanging down in folds between her open legs. "Don't bring none of your…"

Lillian didn't hear any more of what Myrtle was saying to her. Like the last time she had seen her, she was again running, this time across the bay front to the archives, where she found Teddy. He sat with her outside under a tree until she stopped shaking.

The judge's notes are what you mean," the middle-aged white-looking woman behind the counter told them twenty minutes later. She had been drinking from a cup at her desk when they first walked in, and as soon as she saw them, the cup fell from her hands, spilling tea all over her documents.

The woman approached them after wiping the tea from her papers into a small trash bin. She tried to look steadily at Teddy—he was the one asking the questions—but she was not always successful, her eyes kept making short darts in Lillian's direction. "You want the judge's notes," she said to Teddy's request. "Those days we didn't have stenographers."

"Okay. The judge's notes, then."

The woman turned away, started walking toward the wall of cardboard binders, and then stopped, turning her head to Teddy. "That was 1947?"

The sound of typing on a manual typewriter had not stopped since they entered the room. The archivist's assistant was so skilled, so fast, she created the kind of background noise that went unnoticed, and it was only when she spoke that they looked across and saw her in the far diagonal corner, almost hidden by a stack of loose papers. "Forty-eight," called out the typist, without breaking the rhythm or looking up from the handwritten pages she was transcribing. "That's gone."

The archivist walked back up to the counter. "Sorry. Everything from forty-five to fifty-two," she shook her head. "David took all that."

Teddy stared at her. "So … have him bring them back." There were a few seconds of disconnect, the woman looking directly at Lillian for the first time as if to check the sanity of her friend. Over in the diagonal corner, they heard the typist make small sounds, three consecutive exhalations, suppressing her laughter.

"Category five," Lillian said to Teddy. "Seventy-nine," and it still took him several seconds to realize that she was talking about Dominica's most devastating hurricane since 1834, one that had caught the island completely by surprise, suddenly veering course away from Barbados. After six hours of 150-mile-per-hour winds, nearly the entire population was homeless, not a banana tree still standing—the entire agriculture-based economy destroyed, set back a solid ten years. Still, Dominicans had gotten off easily, if human life is to count for something: David killed maybe fifty people in Dominica, but had headed north to take over a thousand souls in the Dominican Republic.

"Police records," said Teddy. "They would have filed reports. Let's see those. And newspaper articles."

"You don't understand," the woman said. "We file documents by year. Every piece of paper for those years—blown away. Or destroyed by the rain." She pointed to the ceiling. "The roof went. A hundred-and-fifty-mile winds. You can imagine."

Teddy saw Lillian's look drop off at the news that there would be nothing in any archive to help them. There was not much else to go on apart from the little Mary-Alice could tell them about her testimony: the judge had ordered the trial closed after the initial day. Thousands of people had come close to stampeding, rioting outside the courthouse when they were unable to get inside to hear the proceedings.

"Should still be some people alive," Teddy said. "We could talk to them. Jurors, lawyers, court clerks, those types. Some of the police?"

In the corner, the young typist returned the carriage with a sharp zipping sound and hit two returns, spacing up her work. With the steady clacking gone, the room fell quiet.

"More than fifty years ago," said the woman behind the counter. "Those people would have been what, in their thirties? Older, most of them. The youngest would be eighty-something now." As they turned to leave she made a clucking sound in the back of her throat, a sound intended to convey sympathy. "Sorry. We have a lot of centenarians in Dominica, but to my knowledge nobody from that trial is alive today."

39

SCARS

Lillian had not left the house since her exchange with Myrtle two days earlier, and Teddy encouraged her to go to the presbytery without him. He had insisted, actually, even though she tried to explain how hard it would be for her to sit in front of a priest. "You *must*," he had said. "You're becoming paranoid, Lilly, you've got to get out."

She had been staying at home with Icilma while he went out, on her behalf, visiting with old people who knew or claimed to have visited Matilda, walking through Roseau and following leads from the casual conversations he was so good at making. He had come back both evenings looking tired, and Lillian understood that it was not really fatigue, it was discouragement, because although he only told her that people didn't remember very much, she knew otherwise from his whispered conversations with Icilma: Matilda had powers, everybody agreed, and she and Simon, the old people said, could heal people, yes, but they also used to work some bad, bad Obeah—for the right price, they would give you whatever terrible things you wanted of them.

Teddy's concern for her was deepening, she knew that, from his conversations with his psychiatrist friend every night. She could hear every

word, and she thought that Teddy was unable to judge the way sound
traveled near water. She did not know that his indistinct murmuring
was out of range of normal hearing. She, because people had never spoken freely in her presence when she was a child, had developed a keen
ability to separate out whispered words—like a deaf person's sense of
smell, a blind person's sense of touch.

L illian was not able to keep the surprise off her face when he entered
the bare appointment room of the presbytery. When she lived
in Dominica, priests were, by definition, bald, elderly white men with
strong European accents, and her assumption had held over the years.
She was not expecting a Black man in jeans and a "Choose Life"
T-shirt.

"Father Okeke," he said, shaking hands. "From Nigeria."

"Igbo?" she asked.

"Very good. You know Igbo names?"

"Small," she affirmed, delighting him with her use of West African
pidgin, his reddish-brown mahogany face opening up with his laughter.
"I work with a few Nigerian women in D.C. Mostly Igbos."

He seated her at a small table, and after she introduced herself they
sat smiling, the seconds going by. She had enough working knowledge
of African etiquette to know that he would never insult her so blatantly
by getting straight to the point.

"How are you liking Dominica?" Lillian asked, feeling much more at
ease with the Nigerian priest than she was with her own country people,
and now she found herself speaking again, even able to make small talk,
asking about little things, about the well-being of his family in Nigeria.

Then the priest left the room and came back with a glass of water
and a kola nut in his palm, and he broke it and said, "Take this, Lillian,

and eat. This is—" He stopped, reaching out to touch her arm at her reaction. "What is it?"

It took her some time to answer. Things like this were common now, moments when she confused what should have been memory with what was happening in her present. He had offered her the kola nut using the same words used when bread became body. *Take this, all of you, and eat. This is my body…*

And as easily as that, she was seven years old, back in a cathedral with the body of Christ on the floor, not once, but twice—where, for her, the torment had all started.

"I can't," she said, looking at the kola nut. "Consecration…" Father Okeke immediately understood. The ritual connection between the Igbo's ancient ceremony and that of his adopted faith was obvious; and this woman's story was a well-known one in the Dominican religious community; in fact he had been given the details within a day of his arrival on the island. He had also once held a conversation with a very old man called Pope in the lunatic asylum. He came from a culture where a different understanding of lunacy prevailed, where the ranting of a crazy man might be accorded more weight, given that it could well be a prophecy or some other message from beyond the reasoning of ordinary people. He knew that Pope's story was no delusion, it had been based on a real event.

He left the room again and came back this time with a glass of sugar water.

"My mother," Lillian finally said, after she drank the entire glass, "she said you were interested in the village where my grandmother lived."

"Noah. Yes." Father Okeke nodded several times. "Yes." Now, as if in the confessional; patient, not pushing, but still encouraging. "Strange name, Noah, so biblical. And so strange, what happened there."

"She said you were asking questions about how everybody just disappeared like that."

Without any indication that he might be curious about her interest, he nodded again. "It was the scars," he said. "On very old people, I was seeing these scars." The first time, he had almost missed it, the woman so old, the scars so faded, so faint, as if time had buffed and sanded down her skin. She was dying, and the neighbors had called him. He had been trying to give her the last sacrament, but she refused him. It had been disconcerting for him, her rejection. It had been a first—the first time anyone had refused the chance to ensure free and clear entrance into heaven, refused the best sacrament of all, the one that could arrive at the very last minute to forgive all sins regardless, and all one had to do was say sorry and mean it. But not this old woman, who turned her head away from him and died.

Scars from fighting the police, Lillian thought. From when the police went to arrest Matilda. Cutlass wounds. Bullet wounds. Stabs. Chops from hoes, scythes, other agricultural instruments, perhaps. And then she settled her mind on bullet wounds: the police would have used their guns. But wait, she thought, what about the fire the next day—burn scars. That was it.

The priest continued. "I wasn't really sure, though, if that's what they really were. I had just come here. I thought maybe I was homesick. But then I saw it again. Not often. But every now and then. Maybe less than ten in all."

"Aah. Scarification," Lillian said. "Tribal marks."

Father Okeke nodded. At first he had not thought much of it, assuming that it was yet another African tradition that had been handed down intact, something that was now, as in Africa, a dying-out custom, and therefore mostly seen on the old—there were the small indented ones that looked like fine engravings, those that had been treated with irritants—charcoal, gunpowder, ashes, even pebbles—to ensure that they would heal as raised keloids, some exquisitely rounded and worn like strings of beads along the upper torso.

He did not think it unusual, after all, West Africa was all around him in Dominica. The features of the faces, the food, the *bélé* dancing, the *peau cabrit* drums, the masquerades. The satire of the *chanté mas* songs. Storytelling. How people walked, how they balanced loads on their heads and walked up mountains with straight backs. How they opened their mouths wide to speak their Creole, how women sat in the market next to their produce, heaped into piles on bare ground. How they gesticulated when they argued, it was all straight from West and Central Africa, even from as far south as Angola. It made sense to him that the slaves, coming from all parts of Africa, would want to keep that connection to their lineage by marking their faces and their bodies with the identifying patterns. Their identity cards, so to speak.

Father Okeke would have continued to assume that this was a custom that had survived in the New World, he said, had he not come upon the old man walking naked into the river for his morning bath, his back beautiful with a linear pattern of raised dots. "It was how he reacted when I admired the pattern," he said. The man had abandoned his bath and got dressed immediately, refusing to speak. "It was the *not speaking* that struck me. The deliberate way he ignored me. So out of character with how Dominicans behave."

Father Okeke began to ask around, and found that either nobody knew very much about the people with the scars, or they did not want to talk about them. "They would say, 'So-and-so is not from this village. He came here long ago.' Well, of course I would ask where they came from. And they would just shrug." Over time, though, he had been able to determine that they had all shown up sometime in the mid- to late 1940s.

"So…" Lillian closed her eyes, acutely conscious of how hard it was for her to think through all the noise in her head. There was something here, something she should be understanding about these people with scars, but she was coming up against a wall.

Father Okeke came to her rescue. "They showed up after Matilda's village burned down," he said.

Lillian's voice caught. "You know this? You talked to them? You asked them about her?"

His smile was a sad one of regret that he could not help this woman, who was so obviously disturbed. "I tried," he said. "But when I mentioned their marks"—he shook his head—"when I asked them which village they were from or where their parents were born?" He showed her his empty palms. "Nothing. As if they had taken a vow of silence."

40

VOICES, MEMORY

On the day before they were due to leave Dominica to return to D.C., Teddy and Lillian climbed up Matilda's mountain.

"I want to go up to Noah," Lillian had said. "I've got to go Up There."

Mary-Alice tried to dissuade them. "You won't find anything," she had told them. "Ashes, that's all that was left. Ashes and the skeletons in the forest. Now the regrowth will make it impenetrable."

But as much as Teddy did not care for heights, it was something he knew had to be done, it could be good for Lillian.

New roads had given them an easy approach. Their rented vehicle, a four-wheel drive that Lillian threw carelessly into deep semifishtails around mountainsides, had taken them part of the way up the mountain, and when they reached the point where the road ended, they began their trek already several hundred feet above sea level.

Teddy expected that perhaps an old, overgrown footpath might let them up through dense vegetation of waist- or chest-high bush and grass. He'd worn a long-sleeved shirt of thick cotton and jeans against the anticipated bramble, and his darkest shades, imagining two or three hours in strong sun. But this was no jungle of secondary growth. He stopped to take it in: they were in the middle of a genuine virgin rain forest, with all the shadowy mystique that came with the dark and the damp, with leaves the size of a child's body, pointed tips dripping beads of water, with its wide-open understory allowing them to ascend the mountain freely, unencumbered: the little sunlight that managed to penetrate the dense growth allowing only ferns, palms, and thin-trunked trees that did not branch until they reached up to the canopy. Beneath them, the grassless forest floor was padded, soft, and springy with a deep layer of rotting vegetation. And then, looking up, a hundred feet up, seeing for the first time in his life the sign of a true rain forest—the latticework of green forest roof, unbroken, through which here and there bits of bright light penetrated in flashes of silver, but not the smallest blue of a sky anywhere to be seen.

They climbed for over an hour, Lillian in the lead, and approached a point so steep there were steps cut into the mountainside. They stopped to examine them, digging their fingers down into the four-inch-thick layer of vegetation carpeting the stairway of solid rock going up farther than they could see, cut by hand probably more than a hundred years before.

"Let's take a minute," Teddy said. "Catch our breath. From here on it'll be tough going." But Lillian did not rest, she stood with her back against the mountain wall, unbuckled his belt, and left more bite marks on his shoulders, more deep scratches on his back.

"Well, yes, maybe, that could be part of the trauma syndrome," Wallace had agreed, "but it's hard to say . . . could be something from her childhood, too." But it was all fitting together now for Teddy. What had so surprised him then, shocked him even now, made sense, that she'd be that way with sex. It was a feature of her illness, he believed. The only outlet she had. Here in Dominica, in the six days since their arrival, she had at first seemed to be doing well, but then she steadily began to deteriorate. Trying to reach out to the market woman Myrtle seemed to have thrown her into a tailspin (although it seemed obvious to him that the woman wouldn't have wanted to see Lillian). He could see her struggling to stay connected—she had, except for her visit to the African priest, practically stopped speaking, letting him do most of the talking; and as her disconnect intensified, so had her appetite for hard-core sex.

They were climbing again, but it was now much more strenuous, and the forest was gradually changing, the canopy beginning to open up, trees getting shorter, the moisture beginning to take the form of occasional mist. It was wetter now, dripping moisture, and chilly. Teddy put back on the shirt he had taken off earlier in the steamy heat.

At first the steps were shallow enough to manage, but within twenty or thirty feet it was no longer possible to simply raise a leg and step, they had to pull themselves up by their arms, bracing, then a short jump to swing one knee up to the next step. Although it was not possible to see the apex, Teddy was sure they were close—the rain forest was morphing into cloud forest, and it was unlikely that a village would have been established beyond that altitude.

And then he remembered something he'd read about the island. Dominica's mountainous terrain was so extreme that villages were established wherever flat land could be found, and until quite recently, twenty or thirty years, many villages were almost completely isolated, because the mountains were impassable.

Still, Teddy thought, this was a hell of a way to go for some flat land. He stopped for a moment to clear his ears, glancing down at the same time. What he saw made him forget how easily Lillian startled, and he shouted out her name because he saw, too late, that this was the kind of climb that should have been undertaken with harnesses, ropes, and anchors, at the very least. He had been too busy hauling himself up to notice that the slope was now only a degree or two away from vertical; one slip and the fall would be to death.

"Lilly." Now he controlled his voice, made it soft. "Wait for me."

"Almost there," she said, and he now had even more reason to fear for their lives, because it was just occurring to him that he didn't know what she would do when she confronted what was her grandmother's legacy. Twenty-five hundred feet above sea level on the bare face of a steep mountain was not a good place for an emotionally disturbed woman to be.

I t was sudden, the opening up, the way there was light, the way the last step had twisted, and from one hoist to the next they could now see the flats, the place where people once had lived and then had ceased to exist, a place where something terrible had happened, although now there was nothing to see but overgrown bramble.

They had come to a ridge, a flat sliver of land that was perhaps three feet wide, maybe a hundred yards long. They would have to walk across it to access the final hundred yards or so up to the plateau. At some point in the past, it seemed, the natural bridge had been reinforced, made into a narrow pathway with cobblestones and some kind of cement. But now it was crumbling and loose, heavily eroded. In several spots, only a few feet beneath the surface of the ridge, wind and rain had eaten all the way through to the other side of the mountain. It was no longer passable; it was beginning to cave in on itself. It would not support the weight of an adult.

Lillian stood up. She took a small step, then another. She stretched

out her arms for balance. Teddy weighed his odds and determined that
she was more likely to fall trying to walk across the ridge than from a
struggle with him. He was calculating the angle at which he would need
to pull her, figuring out whether a tackle to her waist would bring her
down cleanly or if he had a better chance if he first immobilized her
arms and then pulled her backward still standing. The latter, he decided.
Behind him, the mountain continued to rise, and if he braced well, he
could keep his balance by falling back against it.

But Lillian did not move after her first two steps. What she felt
when she stood at the start of the bridge was a thickening of the
air around her, and the noise in her head was nothing compared with
the sounds that were in that air. At first she thought she recognized the
tonal sound of talking drums, but soon she realized that she was hearing voices, so many of them, all speaking together, in a language she did
not understand, although the urgency and insistence of their calling
was clear. She thought, *Oh, so I am finally going crazy,* but she somehow
did not feel as if she were losing her mind; on the contrary, her mind was
becoming clear and quiet, and she was in full control of her thoughts.

And the thickened air was not still, there was much strong movement, as of wings beating around her, and she felt about to be lifted up.
She raised her arms and held them out at the level of her shoulders. But
even as she turned her arms into sails so that the air might catch them
and pick her up and transport her across the bridge, in the quietness of
her mind she was thinking of Teddy, remembering that he was standing
right behind her. As she turned around to go back to him, she looked
directly into his face.

When she saw the love and the anguish, she thought of her mother,
Iris, and of her mother Icilma, and could see both of them together, in

her mind, at the same time, and she thought that those two things, love and anguish, inevitably seemed to end up together.

Teddy reached out and grabbed her savagely, pinned her arms with one of his and circled her waist with the other and dragged her away from the bridge. And the voices in the air stopped calling to her, and the noise in her head began again, but not before Lillian found a memory, one she didn't even realize she had been looking for.

41

STONING COWS

"Out! Out! Out! Out!"

A five-year-old Lillian opened her eyes. Even though she was not fully awake, she began timing the pauses in between each identical word she could hear her stepmother shouting out in the yard, and every pause corresponded to exactly the amount of time it would take Icilma to bend down, pick up a stone, and throw it after the animals. Lillian jumped down from her bed and pelted outside, not stopping even to wash her face. From the amount of energy Icilma was putting into the shouting, the volume of Icilma's grunts as she threw the stones, and the kind of anger in her voice, this would be a big herd of cattle, most likely, trampling through Icilma's beds of exotic flowers or ground provisions.

Chasing stray animals out of the yard was one of Lillian's favorite things to do. Cows were less common, and so much more thrilling than the goats, because there was always the chance that a cow could turn around and chase you back. She ran to Icilma, a stone ready in her hand, and hiding behind her mother's skirt in case it was really a herd of cattle, she pitched her stone, without looking, in the direction Icilma was facing.

When she peered out from the back of her mother's thigh to see whether she had come near her mark, the animals all seemed to have disappeared, and she stepped out in front of Icilma for a better look at where they might have gone. It was then she saw that Icilma had not been stoning a herd of cattle or goats or donkeys, she saw that this was just a single woman, a beautiful red-skinned woman, who seemed to be shining in the morning sunlight, and without knowing why, Lillian ran to her.

The woman picked Lillian up, scooped her up as if she were expecting her to do exactly that; and she turned and ran with her, and the woman's smell was a very familiar one—several different notes, combined to make a single identifying scent that reminded Lillian, oddly, of milk.

There was the moist sweet-and-sour smell of the woman's breath as she panted from the exertion of talking at the same time that she was running with a child in her arms, a smell Lillian knew was connected to a flat glass bottle in a brown paper bag from which the woman regularly drank.

There was that same smell exuding from the woman's damp skin, along with other smells; musky, earthy ones that came from the leaves and bits of bark in which the woman bathed. Lillian, not knowing she was drawing on the memories of the first two and a half years of her life, could picture the woman naked in an outdoor concrete bath, her lower body submerged in the water on which the leaves floated. She remembered the baths, taken several times each day, taken each time one of the men departed, after the men had clambered on top of the woman and had lain the length of the sweet-and-sour-smelling, glowing skin, after there had been the tumbling and the men's shouts of pain, because the woman would hit the men, and bite them, and claw them; this she knew because she had often seen it with her two-year-old eyes, when, tired of sitting outside in the rain or the sun, she would climb up the few stone steps at the front of the one-room house, quietly sitting in the doorway waiting for the infliction of pain to be over, watching, and learning.

Lillian closed her eyes and tried to put her cheek against the woman's, but they were bouncing around too much for their faces to remain touching. She wrapped her legs tighter around the woman's waist and her arms around her neck to stop from sliding down, and she tried to listen to what the woman was saying, but she could not catch the words at all because they were coming out jagged, and also there was too much shouting to hear properly. Lillian opened her eyes to see who was making such noise, and she was looking straight at Icilma, behind them, her face so distorted that Lillian did not immediately recognize her.

She felt Icilma's hands grabbing her arms and then circling her waist and pulling her away. Even though Lillian did not really know who this familiar stranger woman was, she did not want to leave her, not, at least, until she could hear what she was so urgently saying, what she was trying to say, but Icilma was not allowing it, she was dragging her away. The woman was trying to hold on to her, and all the while she was still talking to her, but there were other people who were coming now, swarming; women straight from their beds, still in their nightgowns, with their loosened breasts dark under the thin nylon and their hair sticking up in the air and their breath rancid from the night; and they were all helping Icilma. A strong, tall man plucked her easily out of Iris's arms and swung her in a semicircle high over the heads of the people in the crowd into the arms of another woman, a neighbor, who carried her away, to her house, so that she would not see any more of the commotion on the street, so that she would not see when the police came and took her mother away.

42

BLACK MAGIC

They went on the balcony to talk in the late afternoon. It was nowhere near sunset, but beneath Morne Diablotin already it felt like evening, the green gone darker, the river water browner, the boulders turned an opaque slate without the silver sheen from the sun that had fallen behind the mountain. Around their cottage, dusk came early.

Lillian took her usual position, placing all her weight on the balcony railing, her back angled past the point that Teddy would have considered safe from the perspective of balance, her right thigh resting on the railing, her right leg dangling high, with only one foot securing her to the floorboards. He was jittery; deeply shaken by what had happened only a few hours earlier on the edge of Matilda's mountain; afterward, he had barely been able to summon the confidence to make it back down the face.

Lillian had started off by saying that she wanted to stay another week in Dominica, and he had not answered. He was drinking, to steady himself; a full juice glass of rum, without chaser or ice, and she was leaning back in that casual way that said she had been raised to be unafraid of heights. Sitting on a deck chair, watching her unfold her arms to gesticulate, he had to deliberately fight the feeling that she was constantly on the verge of tumbling backward. She was exuberant. She kept jumping on and off the railing, sometimes pacing in tight circles in front of Teddy.

"Icilma thought that Iris came to take me back," she was saying. "But that wasn't it. Iris knew she was dying—she died that night. She came back to tell me about Matilda."

Emotionally exhausted and physically drained, Teddy was losing the ability to stay focused. He wanted to tell her that they should go to bed, that she should let him make love to her—and she should let him do it his way, something quieter, something tender, something that would tell her that he'd take care of her, he would help her to get well. He wanted to tell her they should leave the next day as planned. She was deteriorating in Dominica. "Lilly," he said, "you just told me you couldn't understand what she was saying."

She stopped pacing and stooped down in front of his open legs, getting to his eye level, one elbow on each of his thighs. "You're not listening to me, Teddy. I told you, I caught some of the words. She said 'Matilda' many times. She kept saying a word that sounded like 'magic.' I remember that word, a five-year-old would remember that word. She said it in Creole, *magie*."

He nodded, and Lillian could see the indulgence in the way he smiled at her, and she could guess his thoughts—he would be thinking: You remember a few nonsense words your crazy mother supposedly whispered to you; and you happen to remember them right after you hear voices calling you; you also happen to remember this right after you try to fly across a precipice.

"Iris told you 'Matilda' and 'magic,'" he said with kindness. "And this proves to you that Matilda was innocent?"

"You're speaking to me like you'd speak to an idiot. Or a lunatic."

Teddy toughened his voice into normalcy. "Okay, Lillian, listen to me. Right now we don't have any indication that Matilda didn't kill those people. Sweetheart, I'm not saying she killed them, there's no proof of that—except that she confessed—but honestly, I don't see how—"

"*I* have proof," Lillian said. She got up from between his legs and went back to the balcony rail. Her arms were tightly folded. "I have the expression on my mother's face when she was running with me. She was trying to tell me something about Matilda, I know that, she kept saying her name. And it was something *good*."

He said, "But she was an alcoholic. You yourself said she was drunk that day. And Iris wasn't well, Lillian. She was mentally ill. She could have said anything, she—"

"My mother wasn't crazy. She was destroyed."

"Lillian. Matilda confessed," he pushed, his judgment impaired by the alcohol.

Her body reacted as if he had hit her with a physical blow. "You of all people," she said, looking straight at him, "you should know that means nothing." She closed her eyes. "I know it, Teddy, you have to believe this, I *know* Matilda didn't do it."

He would think back on how he spoke with such expansiveness, so lightly: "Well then, if this is your proof—there we have it. Mission accomplished. We did what you came here for, you know she didn't do it, so no need to stay another week."

Lillian could tell Teddy was drunk, his voice was slurred, his speech sloppy and careless. She knew she should just send him inside, let him go to sleep, but he was all she had: Icilma and Mary-Alice would be even more convinced that she, like her mother, was once again losing her mind—because, they believed, it was inherited madness that had sent her to dig up Iris's grave that night, and madness that made her cut her wrist open. Madness, and Matilda's hand from hell, intervening in her conception; and do not forget the mark God put on her soul, her magnified original sin— What a combination, Lillian thought suddenly, *what a hand I was dealt.*

She moved away from the edge of the balcony, she saw how nervous that made him, and she sat next to him, at his side on the long seat of the chair. She thought of telling him that she had heard all his conversations, with Icilma, with the psychiatrist; that she knew he was planning to ease her into some kind of program when they got back to D.C., some kind of therapy. She knew he was doing it for love, but she also knew that she would not leave Dominica without all the answers.

"But the dead people," she said to him, pressing her forehead into his arm. Days before, Teddy had spoken to the son of the coroner who had performed the analysis on the skeletons. The stories of the dead in the forest could not have been a simple lie, nor could they have been dug up from graves and planted there to frame Matilda: the skeletons showed traces of the same poison, they had all been killed by poisoning. "I need to know why they were there. Who poisoned them. Why they were poisoned."

Teddy did not answer. Instead, he got up and began to walk away from her. She tried, then, to hold on to him, she reached out and took his arm, but she felt him deliberately pull away. He stood with his back to her, facing the river.

"You think she did it." It wasn't a question and he did not deny it, he said nothing. Lillian raised her voice. "So you think she just had a taste for it?" She didn't want to speak to him that way, she didn't know why she was using that accusing tone, as if he were the one responsible. "You think she just brewed up a poison and fed it to somebody every time she felt like it, or what? Or she was crazy—you think she did it because she was a madwoman?"

And Teddy, loose-tongued and longing for it to be all over, did not turn around when he said, "No, I don't think that's what happened at all. It wasn't senseless killing. I think she killed them as part of the Obeah." He had been hearing the same thing over and over for a week now, that Matilda and Simon had worked the kind of Obeah that was more in the realm of heavy devil business: "Black magic," people said—and Iris in her craziness was probably trying to say exactly those words to Lillian. Matilda killed for profit, Teddy told Lillian, using the worst kind of Obeah. They killed in order to increase the power and wealth of those willing to pay her for the most powerful medicine of all.

His back was still to her, he was looking at the stones in the river. It was now beginning to get dark, the sun had not just fallen behind Morne Diablotin, but was by now slipping into the sea. Then he turned around, and he immediately knew he should never have said that. In his drunken state he had forgotten about the campaign Lillian had worked on with a British group, when the body of the African girl was found in London's Thames, when an autopsy by experts flown in from Africa confirmed that she had been murdered in a way that was consistent with what in the twenty-first century was now called ritual homicide. Lillian knew more about it than most, she had researched it in all its horrifying detail: she knew that vital organs were cut out when victims were still alive to increase the potency of the medicine that would be made from them; she knew that the screaming was supposed to increase the energy that would be transferred from the victim's body to the person who would pay for the power, the protection, the success in business or in politics.

Lillian walked up to Teddy and he thought she might hit him, but instead she went past him. She sat on the railing and took off her shirt, and in the same place where they had made love the first night, Teddy let Lillian punish him.

In the morning, when they woke up, she would not speak to him, but the bright light allowed Teddy to revise his memory of what had happened. In the intense sunlight, with the river making friendly sounds, looking inviting outside their window, in his recollection of the kind of love they had made the previous night—love that held desperation; love that spoke of destruction—her spine had not bent backward over the railing and down, her head had not hung suspended above the river's boulders, and her legs had not gone rigid, had not lost their grip around his waist.

The memory of the panic, the terror he had felt, the sense that he was out of control, pushing her farther and farther over the rail, that was all blotted out in the light of morning, and Teddy had no memory at all of when he fought hard to lock his knees, to hold on to her legs, and just a vague impression that he had called upon an unknown reserve of strength to reach down, grab her arms, and pull her up.

When the sun woke them up the next morning, Teddy just remembered it as the fuck of his life.

43

REVELATIONS

Teddy sat by himself at a window table drinking the juice of a fruit he had never heard of. "Sapodilla," the waitress had said, and the sound of the name had made him choose it over the long list of juices that were prepared from fresh fruit only when the order was placed.

His back was to the sea. He was trying not to think of Lillian hearing voices on the cliff of the mountain, Lillian with her arms spread like wings, ready to fly. He was trying to plan his next move, wondering how much longer he could stay in Dominica, how long it would take to win back her confidence after the previous night's fiasco. He was sitting in the window of the oceanproof three-hundred-year-old building, the deep sill of which had been cushioned and turned into a seat. Surrounding him, the walls of the waterfront café were solid stone, three feet thick, built to withstand hurricane-generated waves and seas that might, at any point between August and November, cross the road and cover the roof for days on end, when the swollen wood of the doors and shutters would seal the building tight.

Leaning sideways to feel the warmth of the stone, Teddy was about to send back his drink. The flavor was rich and deep, but it was pungently sweet, too thick, too granular, too brown. He liked his drinks thin, he liked them to go down smoothly, and he liked them in bright colors. The yellow-orange passion fruit juice the people at the next table were drinking looked more like it. He was looking around to find the waitress, and when he turned his head back to the table, he was not exactly surprised to see that the typist from the archives was pulling up a chair to his table, her ultrawhite teeth shining against her dark skin. It was with the clarity of hindsight that he checked his excitement and stood to offer her his hand and say his name.

"Sylvie," she answered, sitting down.

Had he been anywhere in the world except this olden-days throwback island, this place where his sense of who he was, his place in the world, was gone, he would have noticed that her apparent disinterest, the studied concentration of her rote typing, had been overplayed, and that there was an alertness, a slight turning of her head that angled her ear to best pick up their conversation above the sound of the keys hitting the carriage.

"I remember you," he said.

"I've been looking for you for two days now."

"Lillian's with her mother. Stepmother. We can take a taxi."

The young woman shook her head. "Not necessary." She thought about what she would say next. "She looks like she's not . . ." and then changed her mind. "Like you in charge anyway."

Teddy hesitated, wondering if her last observation hid a feminist reproach, then decided that this Sylvie was to be taken at face value. He made a guess at the news she had for them. "Tell me the hurricane didn't destroy the documents after all."

She shook her head. "Sorry. David took them all right." Her drink came. "But never mind. You wouldn't have found out anything from those notes, anyway. Nothing in the police reports, either. They covered everything up."

There could only be so many options. He guessed again. "Someone from the trial is still alive. Or a police officer. Someone who was there."

"We have the highest ratio of centenarians in the world—yes, that's a fact. But a small country like this, all these hundred-year-old people about the place, and not one was at the trial." She smiled at him for a moment, and then she was truly serious. "Look. I don't have any great revelations for you. Just a few things my grandfather overheard. It mightn't be helpful at all." She stopped to drink her nectar, thinking about how she would express her sentiments. "I've always heard your girlfriend's story, from the time I was a little child—Matilda, Iris, then they say she went crazy when she found out—digging up the grave ..." She raised her shoulders, turned up her palms. "I don't know. Anything that might help her to get a better picture ... might be worth a listen." She hesitated. "Or you might think she doesn't need to know. Up to you."

Her grandfather, she said, was a manservant to the governor. A lowly servant, but one who walked freely through Government House, one who served drinks and meals to people so high above him that they didn't really imagine he had the capacity to understand what he heard. He was known and liked for his deference, his respect for his master, though, like all people born to servitude, he kept his head bowed to make sure no one saw his eyes, which would have given him dead away.

He had kept quiet about what he heard that night in Government House: the police inspector, who had left his men in Colihaut, sneaking into Roseau without the knowledge of even his wife, he and a priest coming well past midnight through the servant entrance in the back. He had served them brandy and then fed them, and when the inspector could finally speak, he told Sir Lawson and the priest about the village.

"It's not like they were just another remote village," Sylvie said. "They had set it up so they were deliberately hidden."

Teddy waited for more. This much by now was obvious.

"They had people at the foot of the mountain, lookouts. Some ran up to warn the others. The rest attacked the police with hoes, killed three. The police shot them all dead."

"How many is 'all'?"

She didn't know exactly how many people had been at the base of the mountain. "But when they reached up to the top, my grandfather said, they found more people, a whole village. Hundreds and hundreds, maybe even a thousand."

From behind the kitchen door the servant had listened to the police inspector describe the scene. Even though it was the second day of Lent, when Masquerade should have been long over, the people they found in Matilda's village, the inspector said, had extended their Carnival spree and were still carrying on like it was Mardi Gras. There was heavy drumming, *bande mauvais* masquerades stomping the bare earth, and costumed people dancing. "The inspector kept saying how wild they were jumping up, but still everybody was doing the same kind of movements. And he said how black everybody was." She stopped to clarify. "Not African-American kind of Black, you know. He meant dark-skinned, black like me." She quoted her grandfather's exact words. *"Tout moun ka noir-noir-noir."*

"Noir." Teddy repeated the word slowly.

"Black," she said, drawing the word out.

"I know." He could see her suppressed smile, and he knew why. "Noah. Noir."

They sat in a few moments of silence, Teddy absorbing the fact that when Matilda told the court the name of her village, it had been recorded as its nearest anglophone sound, but in fact she had lived in a place named after the color of its people. He thought of what Lillian had told him, the African priest's story of the people with the scars, and something in the back of his head began to take form. He did not try to work it out then, he left it alone to concentrate on whatever else she had to tell him. "Okay. So the people up in Noir were dancing in costume. Maybe they were celebrating because Matilda had killed John Baptiste. Like a town-country blood feud."

"Maybe. That's what the inspector thought." She had a way of keeping her smile from breaking through, of pulling in the edges of her mouth, and now Teddy could see that she had understated her case, that she was not relaying a few overheard pieces of information. She had a theory, and she did not buy the inspector's interpretation of what he had seen. She did not think that the people were extending their pre-Lenten Carnival revelry to celebrate a victory over the bourgeoisie. He waited for her to continue.

"He spent a lot of time talking about their costumes. Only the *bande mauvais* masquerades were masked." Her pause told Teddy that something important was about to be revealed. "Everybody else, bare-face, and running *mas* half naked." The moment of silence again, and Teddy waited. "Women, too. Women were topless."

"It was Masquerade, right—what we call Carnival today? I've been to Rio. Couple feathers here and there, but pretty much naked, no?" He was speaking facetiously, understanding what it would have been like for the police to come upon a sea of jumping breasts, but she mistook it for a question.

"No. Nineteen-forties Masquerade in Dominica would have meant every inch of skin covered. Gloves for the hands, masks for the faces."

"All right, Sylvie." Teddy was playing a game with her, they were both enjoying what they were doing. "So it wasn't exactly Carnival, was it?"

"Not Carnival at all."

"So what were they dressed up as anyway?" Teddy asked, and then, quickly, to show her that he was with her, ahead of her, he answered it himself. "African warriors preparing for war."

He watched her put her drink down carefully. "So you knew," she said.

"No. It's just now coming to me, as you're talking."

"Impress me," she said. "What happens next?"

"There was a massacre," Teddy said. "The police massacred the villagers."

"Right. A whole lot of people died Up There. At least fifty, sixty. But nobody ever knew that—rumors, yes, but you'll never find that in any report."

"Okay. So what next?"

"The police kept shooting until Matilda took off her mask and gave some kind of order, and then people started running away."

"So that was the reason for the cover-up?" But Teddy only asked the question as a conversation tool. He knew there would be more. There had only been maybe a dozen police; three had already been killed at the foot of the mountain. There were at least several hundred villagers, armed with spears or knives, apparently, and more than able to overpower the few police. There would be no doubting that the police acted in self-defense.

She raised her hand, shook her head. "I don't know," she said, "I'm just recounting an overheard conversation." Then she gave herself away with her laugh, and she told him the rest of her grandfather's story, exactly the way he had heard it from behind the pantry door.

The inspector admitted his error in climbing the mountain, confessed his culpability for the additional deaths suffered on the plateau. There were five dead in all, more wounded. He tried to retreat. They had Matilda in handcuffs, they would return later for the rest. He gave the order, but his remaining men had grown bold when the people all ran, realizing that the villagers had no firepower. They defied him and ran toward the tight clusterings of abandoned *gaultay* houses, rampaging as they went, easily breaking down the walls, sending dried mud flying as they kicked through the latticework of twigs and saplings with their heavy boots and tore off the straw roofs. In the wake of their destruction, they uncovered the fact that this was no ordinary remote village, that this was a place where people kept themselves deliberately hidden from the rest of the island so that they could, each and every one of them, openly engage in their devil worship and aberrant sexual practices.

The Catholic police were well accustomed to altars in homes, shrines adorned with statues and rosaries and crucifixes. They were used to candles burning to saints in perpetual supplication for one favor or another—they expected these things—and they certainly accepted the need to mix in a little Obeah on the side to cover all the bases. At some point in their lives, they had each gone to an Obeahwoman, or had a mother or a lover go on their behalf, and they had taken their prescribed bush baths for the expulsion of the evil that had been plaguing them. They at some point had worn their amulet for protection or hung something outside their home to foil an ill-wisher. That was just a little backup, a little side bet put down on the likely loser, and it did not interfere with the worship of their one true God, in his only possible manifestation as Father, Son, and Holy Ghost.

But these villagers did not worship God, said the inspector. Inside every house, the big holes in the wattle-and-daub walls revealed that the people worshiped squat devilish idols carved out of wood, devils sitting on altars with protruding eyes and protruding lips. He-devils with obscenely sized genitals and she-devils with long, hanging breasts. Fed with plates of food and bowls of blood, some fresh and red, some thick, congealed, darkened.

And the signs that one man lived openly with three, four, five women at the same time were spread there for them to see when they broke through walls and looked at the clothing and personal effects in each room. They saw that in each household there was a central man's bedroom-hut, surrounded by the rooms of his women and their children, and they were sickened at the same time that they were envious of what they imagined would take place here as a commonplace part of the devilry, given the public nakedness and debauchery they had seen with their own eyes before the people ran away.

With the realization of where they were and what they were facing, most of the men hoisted their two new dead and began running back across the narrow ridge, back down the steps of the mountain. But some of the policemen, the ones who had not just wanted to feed their rage by breaking down mud huts, but who truly had the taste for their work, who wanted to feel the yield of flesh to boot, who enjoyed the buck of the barrel as the bullet left, had gone valiantly looking for the vanished people and had rushed into the dense thicket of forest that surrounded the cleared circle in which the *gaultay* homes had been constructed. These, too, came running back, running out faster than the others, not stopping to assist in hauling down their dead, and it was only when they were all once more at the foot of the mountain that the men who came out of the forest were able to speak, to explain that, in there, with fog shrouding and clouds descending, they had seen them. Through the hanging vines and ferns and orchids, the police had seen them all, so many of them, some sitting with their backs supported against the deep green of the moss-covered tree trunks, some lazily lounging on the forest bed, some reclined on their sides, others spread-eagle on their backs, gazing up at the canopy.

The police had seen that the forest was heavily inhabited by skeletons—many, many more than the number that was eventually made public: eleven skeletons, the authorities decided in the end, was enough for Dominicans to handle, would give a sense of a serial killer but would hide the true nature of the killings. And in the same way they reduced the number of skeletons to manageable proportions, so also did they tell the rest of Dominica that Matilda only lived with a few derelict outcasts, a few drunkards and layabout types, in a place she called Noah that was not really a village at all.

S he was looking at him, and he did not realize at first that she had finished giving the inspector's story, that she had stopped speaking and was waiting for him.

"Maroons," he said at last. "A Maroon community, undiscovered for two hundred years."

"Of course." Her laughter was the same stifled breaths she had made sitting behind a typewriter reacting to his ignorance of the fact that Caribbean people and their hurricanes were on personal terms. "That's self-evident." Impatience clipped her voice. "But the skeletons. Tell me about the skeletons. Let's see if you're as smart as they say you are." She smiled when his eyebrows went up. "I watch CNN, you know. You looked familiar but I couldn't place you until you said your name."

Teddy took a breath and clasped his hands on the table. "In the practice of some African religions," he said formally, as if it were the opening sentence of one of his lectures, "human sacrifice often constitutes an important element."

"Yes indeed" was all Sylvie said before falling silent, satisfaction setting her face into a half smile and causing her eyes to glaze slightly as she stared out over Teddy's shoulder at the tourists walking along the Roseau seawall.

Teddy stood abruptly. "I have to go," he said, startling Sylvie.

"One other thing he told me," she said, forcing him to sit again. "Lillian's grandfather on her mother's side was Carib."

"Right. Simon. Matilda killed him."

"No she didn't. People said so, but he came back for the trial. I'm pretty sure he was in South America all along." In 1997, she said, a group of Dominican Caribs had made a trip by dugout canoe in search of their ancestral home. They came back with many stories, one of which included the tale of a Carib from "a small island." He had undertaken that same journey, by himself, in the early 1940s, and had lived among the South American Caribs until he died some ten years earlier. Sylvie was sure it was Simon—the man called himself Diablotin. "You understand the name?" she asked Teddy. "A bird that's supposed to be extinct, but isn't. The Caribs, the Maroons—"

Teddy relaxed his jaw, knowing his tendency to clench it when he was out of patience. "So Simon came back."

"My grandfather told me he was there all right, the first day. He came in a canoe by himself."

"Did he testify?"

She *chupsed*. "A half-naked Carib, stinking, sweating, sunburned, hair all tangled up, shouting like a crazy man outside the courthouse? Remember it was a closed trial. He couldn't even get in. In any case people didn't know it was him, because they had been saying for years that Matilda had killed him."

Until he was arrested for disturbing the peace after a few hours, Simon had stood near the door of the courthouse, even after the police had cleared away most of the crowd, calling out to the judge inside, proclaiming Matilda's innocence. "My grandfather said he just kept shouting the same thing." She raised her voice to imitate him, quoting in Creole: "*'Magistrat! Magistrat! Magistrat! E pa ka tué. E pa won mordarar!'*"

"Translation?" Teddy asked.

"'Judge, Judge, she didn't kill—she is not a murderer.' After hours of that, the judge got tired of hearing Simon shouting to him, *'Magistrat! Magistrat!'* He locked Simon up until it was over."

It looked like Sylvie wanted to keep talking, now that she had tapped into her old memories of her grandfather's stories, but his need to get to Lillian was now uncontainable. Yet she was not finished. "Careful what you say to Lillian. She seems ... emotionally fragile."

Teddy understood what she was saying. That day at the archives, Lillian had been fresh from the market where Myrtle had made the sign of the cross at her. And after his own experience with her the previous night, he fully understood the extent of the fragility Sylvie had seen. But this was good news, this was about genuine African religious practice. "It'll be okay now," he said, suddenly knowing he would never see Sylvie again and feeling that he owed her as much of his time as she wanted. "Lillian's whole"—he chose his words carefully—"her psychological issues. They all turned around Matilda—how she was evil, how she killed senselessly. Basically, Lillian didn't want to believe it. When we got here—up till this conversation, actually—there wasn't any reason to think the story would be any different from what it's been for the last fifty years. But now, now, it's a *not guilty,* after all."

They were walking out into the sun, Sylvie waving at a taxi driver she knew. "Okay. But make sure you tell her that Simon came for the trial.

It's just a little detail, but it might help to humanize Matilda, that the man she loved tried to save her ..."

They hugged finally, Teddy saying goodbye to the woman he had dismissed, not even noticed, when he saw her, plump and plain, hunched in a corner typing.

44

MATILDA SWINGING

From the moment her daughter left Noir for good, Matilda could think of little else, because what happened to Iris was her fault. For almost a year she had planned her legitimate vengeance, with the blessing of the forest spirit she represented and the full support of each citizen of Noir—they had killed John Baptiste. They had done it with full understanding of what could have happened next, but justice had to be served.

They knew that once they showed themselves, the modern-day slave masters could well come after them—as they had. And so Up There, they had followed the law laid down by the founders of Noir: when they come (the founders had not said *if*, they had said *when*), fight your best fight, but do not let them take you.

The police had wanted her alive, though; they had taken her alive so they could kill her themselves.

Now, just minutes away from her death, her daughter's father was on her mind. She had not killed Simon; she had been very careful with the proportion of the medicine she had given him fifteen years earlier. She had put him at the very edge of life, where he stayed for five long days. During all that time he only appeared to be unconscious but was fully able to see down into the abyss that was death, before she pulled him back and offered him a second chance, one that he had not squandered. He gave himself a new identity, naming himself after a bird on the brink of extinction, and he had gone to South America, proselytizing to the mainland Caribs he found there about the few Island Caribs who still remained. He had, without knowing it, planted the seeds of a Pan-Carib movement.

From a month-old newspaper from Trinidad, found in a trash can in Guyana, Simon had read of her trial. He got into his canoe, with only a five-gallon jerrican of water and a crude sail, and used the wind to help him paddle up the Caribbean Sea without stopping, eating whatever raw sea creature he could quickly spear.

The day he left Dominica, Matilda had warned him that she *would* kill him if he ever returned, but he had come back anyway. It was in the name of love, a futile attempt to save her life.

His effort had, of course, been in vain, but it had done so much for her. She had seen him two years before, the day her trial began, a glimpse of him, the one man she had ever loved, looking like a lunatic, unbathed and almost unclothed. He had been an overambitious fool to have become involved with such wicked quackery, claiming to be able to kill without touching, claiming that he could make his clients prosper without them having to lift a finger for the wealth he could bestow. He claimed powers he never had; and she had been right to banish him.

When she saw him, the prison guards had been walking her from her cell to the place where they dispensed their justice. Just that flash of his face, so anguished, as she climbed the steps of the courthouse, was enough for her to remember that there had been love, and it had made a difference to her, that there was, in a sea of people shouting for her neck, there was one single man who had traveled half the length of an entire sea to proclaim his love, to proclaim her innocence.

And she forgave him for his ambition, even though it was his ambition that helped Dominicans to turn on her. He had used her name when he made his awful promises, when he took all their money and gave them his lies.

S he was ready for it to be over. They had lived good lives, the people of Noir, and they had survived far longer than their founders would have ever imagined. They had lived by the laws those original women had laid down, those Maroon women snatched from Africa who had fled from their so-called owners, only to be left behind by the men at Jacko's Flats when the British raided—the few who had escaped, while the others were dragged to the very same courthouse where Matilda had been put on trial.

Matilda had said nothing about Noir, not a word of explanation; she only said that she was responsible for the dead in the forest. She had not clarified what she meant by "responsible," and they called her a murderer.

So be it, she had no fear of death. If anything, she and all her people in Noir lived in anticipation of it—the beginning of their everlasting lives as ancestors.

B ut her child. Matilda had been groomed for other things, she had not been prepared for motherhood. Her judgment, so keen, so precise, when it came to other matters, had failed her daughter. She should have overruled the Council and prevented them from sending Iris away. She should have listened to the nun, who was, after all, only trying to save her daughter.

And justice had been served, the life of John Baptiste had been exchanged for the destroyed spirit of her child, but what did that matter? It offered nothing, nothing to Matilda, and it offered less than nothing to Iris.

Matilda, just a few breaths away from her last one, suddenly wanted to break free of the iron shackles around her ankles, of the rope holding her hands behind her back, to jump down from the wooden scaffold. She wanted to run past the somber officials lining the courtyard, run away to find her daughter.

Then she heard footsteps. A man holding a black hood was approaching, and a calming thought came to her, the same thought that had sustained her since the day of her arrest: she reminded herself that on this earth she was only a woman with healing hands, able to do nothing more for her daughter; but as an ancestor, she would finally have the kind of power they'd always believed she owned.

She offered the man her neck.

45

SACRIFICE

Teddy waited until they were in bed that night to offer his apology, and to give her Sylvie's good news, but her reaction was the opposite of what he expected.

"A government and church conspiracy? A cover-up because they found evidence of *human sacrifice?*" she kept saying, her hand held out to him, beseeching. "Don't give me that. *Human sacrifice?*" She was spitting the words.

But Teddy was very sure. Neither the British colonial administrators nor the Catholic Church would have wanted the story of a devil-worshiping community to get out. What they saw—how they interpreted what they saw—went far beyond mere Obeah: men and women dancing together naked, fornicating in openly orgiastic wildness, and the evidence of human sacrifice.

If Matilda and a family or two had been found Up There, it would have been different. But there were hundreds of them. And the Church had even more incentive to keep things quiet, there in one of the Caribbean's most devoutly Catholic countries, a country that, despite the presence of British administrative rule since 1770, had held tight to its

French foundations and was one of the shining examples of the success of the Church in the region.

The authorities, Teddy told Lillian, had fed Dominicans what they wanted to hear. A mass murderer was so much more modern and thus acceptable than a woman sacrificing human beings to African deities, to the devil—there was no difference to the Dominican mind, it would all be the same slavery-based backwardness they were on the verge of escaping. But that kind of a killer!—England had them, America had them, it didn't sound too bad to a people who could see self-government on the horizon. There was some status to be gotten out of it, a sense of advancement. People were happy to accept Matilda's confession; to re-create a woman primarily known as a first-class bush doctor.

Lillian shook her head. "I've heard you talk a lot of nonsense, Teddy, but this beats all."

He backtracked, started again. "Mary-Alice got it all wrong," he said. "Matilda came from a polygamous society. A place that was still operating like an eighteenth-century African community. Women married early. Second wives were usually very young. Remember what she told Nen Allie, that Iris was better suited to 'that arrangement'?"

Lillian had turned her head away from him, and the set of her jaw in profile showed that she was not going to answer.

Once Lillian understood that Noah was Noir, was a Maroon settlement, it should have been clear that Matilda believed her daughter would have been the equivalent of a well-taken-care-of second wife of a powerful man, nurtured under the tutelage of a senior cowife who would have assumed authority over her, treating her like a younger sister, training her well, teaching her. Matilda's interest in the man's wealth, and whether he was providing her daughter with her own home, were meant to determine what measure of financial independence he was willing to offer Iris. Lillian *knew* this.

And the question that had cemented Matilda's corruption in Mary-Alice's mind, the question about what had John Baptiste sent for Iris's family in exchange for their daughter, that should have been the most obvious of all, that question was about the all-important bride-price. If *lobolo* had resisted all efforts of progressive modern-day African governments to stamp it out, if it was still actively practiced almost all over the world, how could Lillian not see that Matilda was only asking the one question that any good mother would have asked?

His words went unacknowledged. Still he tried, getting off the bed to walk around to her side, to bend down and speak close into her face, taking each piece of the story and holding it up to her for her examination, turning it around for her with his explanations, his elaborations of things she already knew.

"You remember, you don't remember," Teddy said, "how Mary-Alice talked about when Matilda dropped her dress? When she hit her in the face?" Even though Mary-Alice had tried to speak impartially, to describe only what she considered to be fact, her interpretation of the incident as something disgustingly immodest and sexual had come through. But there had been nothing sexual about it at all—it had been about everything else.

Mary-Alice had never before experienced the attitude of a Black person who came from ancestry that had succeeded in an early escape from slavery, a Black person who had never lived in that subjugated place under the double authority of the colonizer and the colonizer's religion; a Black person who knew herself to be superior to a white one. Mary-Alice had never experienced a woman from a culture where fertility and sexuality were intertwined and celebrated, one where the greatest significance of a woman's breast was its use for the nourishment of children, a culture where breasts were covered only for practical purposes, to keep them out of the way when at work. And so when Matilda had seen the nun's shock, seen her turn flustered and unsure of herself, seen her fear in the face of blackness that had not yet had the beauty trampled out of it, she had simply consolidated her position of power over her, she had gone up to her to strike her down. It was the slave whipping the slave master, Teddy argued to an unhearing Lillian, and indeed, hadn't it brought Mary-Alice to her knees?

Teddy moved around the bed in a constant semicircle, speaking into one ear, then the other. But he still wasn't getting through, he could tangibly feel his words bouncing back at him.

"They were very religious," he said to her. "They were devout. There were shrines in every single home." He thought of Sylvie, intuitive enough to tell that Lillian would not want to hear that Matilda, in her role as whatever she was—healer, overall ruler, supreme spiritual guide of her village—was responsible for the placation of their gods through the sacrifice of human beings.

She kept ignoring him, and he kept up his bombardment of explanation. He reminded her of Dahomey, of the thing that had fascinated the Europeans as they set out to subdue West Africa's most powerful kingdom: the infamous Annual Customs, the sacrificial killing of nearly a hundred people each year. Their Grand Custom, at the death of their king, of sending five hundred souls with him into the next world. "Even today, you know it's still done. Illegally. All over Africa. In India. All over the world."

When she finally spoke, she said, "So you bring this to me as my happy ending?" He had used that phrase, *happy ending*. He had truly thought that the information would have freed her, the knowledge that the skeletons in the forest of Noir were put there because Matilda and her people had remained two hundred years back in time, two hundred years back on another continent, where the sacrifice of a human being to placate an irate god was simply the correct thing to do.

And Lillian should have been happy to get this news, that it was religion and not psychosis and not Obeah or black magic, because sacrifice was the only thing that made sense when it came to God, anybody's god. Wasn't the concept of capricious and careless, vicious and vengeful gods more accurate than that of a single one with his eye on the sparrow? And hadn't even that so-called caring one given up vengeance only in exchange for the human sacrifice of his own son?

She spoke again. "You think it's a good thing, to stand there and smile at me, and tell me that kind of a thing?"

"It was their religion." He felt powerless. "They were hiding out for two centuries. They would have offered sacrifices for their freedom. For—"

"Shut up," she said quietly. "I beg you. Just don't say anything else." She turned over and closed her eyes, and within a minute she was asleep.

46

TOO MUCH BRAIN

When it hit him, Teddy was unable to figure out how he could have missed the obvious. From a deep, dreamless sleep, he found himself suddenly alert, staring at the ceiling. He left Lillian asleep on her belly, most of her back covered by her hair, her inheritance from her mother.

When Teddy entered the house in the semidark of 5:45 A.M., Mary-Alice had already left for her fields. He made a simple statement. "They were Maroons," he said to the wide-awake old man, whose face had caved in on itself, flattening the features and blending them into something representational, so that Teddy had the impression he was looking at an abstract painting of a human face, matted by the stark contrast of white pillowcase. "They practiced West African religions. The bodies in the forest were not murder victims. I know that. You were part of them. I know that."

Bird had not aged well, and could only leave his bed with assistance, but under Mary-Alice's supervision, children and grandchildren came in and out all day to keep him comfortable, to change him, clean him, feed him, take him outside to sit under a tree in the breeze, but it was still early and no one had come yet. The smell of an old person's diaper was high. Teddy opened up the shutters, held back the front door with a stool, letting in air. He put extra pillows behind Bird's back, and went to the gas stove to strike a match and boil water, adding the bundle of leaves that Bird indicated.

Bird had not yet spoken. Teddy was moving around the room, following the instructions Bird was giving him—showing him what to do by pointing a finger that shook in slow left-to-right movements, inclining his shrunken head, blinking oozing eyes with browned whites that had merged with the brown of his irises, from which his black pupils shone. When the tea was drawn, Teddy poured two large cups and put one on the nightstand next to Bird. The smell of urine in an otherwise clean space was manageable after the first sting. He pulled a chair close to the bed. "Why didn't you tell Mary-Alice?"

Bird's voice had a strained, hoarse quality, combined with a thick Dominican accent. His English words were pronounced as if they were French, making it difficult for Teddy to understand. "She is a white woman."

"She was your wife. She is your wife."

"An oath I take, *oui,*" said Bird. "How for you to understand that kind of thing."

"I understand. I understand."

"You understanding what?"

"Everything."

Still Bird wore no expression, and Teddy said, "You are sworn to secrecy. You drank a damnation oath, unbreakable." He knew about West African oath-taking ceremonies, how the word *oath* could not even begin to convey the full significance of the religious pact. "You cemented it with a drink of alcohol mixed with dirt from an ancestor's grave. And blood from a sacrificial animal."

Bird began to bring his cup to his lips. The pale green liquid sloshed gently inside the teacup as the hand went back and forth with a tremor that took its time. No rush, no suddenness, just back and forth, like the even movement of a lie detector's needle when truth is being told. It suddenly became very obvious to Teddy. By not responding, the old man was confirming the story. If he had been talking nonsense, Bird would have been able to say it wasn't true. But to confirm the truth would break his oath.

"Noir was founded by the women who escaped from another Maroon camp—a place called Jacko's Flats," Teddy said. He waited for a response. There was none. "I know this because Noir was a place where all the rules of an African village were in place—except when it came to women and power." This time, definitely, Teddy saw a relaxing around Bird's eyes, a softening of the mouth area. He was sure it was a smile. "Women can have power behind the scenes, but with one or two exceptions, women can't represent a spirit—they can't dance the masks. But Matilda did. Matilda was out-and-out Boss Man, openly so. When the police raided, she was the one who ordered the retreat."

The sound of Bird's voice made him drop his own cup, enamel clattering and rolling around on the wood floor, one leg of his jeans soaked. "If you so know, then what you doing here? You just like to smell the morning stink of an old man?"

It was impossible to read Bird and his impassive face, a raised eyebrow, a quiver of mouth impossible for him, but Teddy thought there might have been an opening, in spite of the words. He tried. "Lillian. Matilda's granddaughter—"

Bird interrupted Teddy. "I know Lillian long before you."

"Then you should want her to know. Matilda's own granddaughter should know what you know."

"Is her man you be?"

"Yes."

"And you don't tell she all these things you say you know?"

"It's hard for her. The idea of human sacrifice, it's not going down so well."

There was a jumping inside Bird's eyes, and then he turned away from Teddy.

"She can't see it in religious terms," Teddy said. "She's seeing it as worse than murder."

There was silence in the room that stretched long enough for Teddy to think that Bird had chosen not to speak to him, and then Bird suffered a violent coughing spasm before he finally spoke, in between the heavings of his body. "Human sacrifice, eh? Tell me how you came up with this human sacrifice story."

"The process of elimination. It was the only thing that made sense, once I knew more about Matilda and the village."

"Tell me about this process of yours. Tell me what made sense to you."

Teddy had not been in Bird's presence long enough to interpret the distorted tone of the old man's voice, he had no way to read the sarcasm and the irony buried in his questions. Earnestly, he laid out the process by which he had come to know that human sacrifice was practiced in Noir. He kept track of his checklist for the attentive Bird: that they were Maroons was obvious from how they kept themselves hidden, and the unchanged African culture they maintained.

He adjusted his position, thighs stretched too tight for too long between hip socket and knee, the burning sensation so intense it seemed that the muscles would snap, but he knew he could not stand, unwilling to risk losing Bird's attention. He raised a new finger. It was clear, from the way the skeletons were found, not far from where the villagers lived, that the entire community was aware of them. In addition, there was the reaction of the villagers to Matilda's arrest. Their disappearance went against the norms of social psychology. If Matilda were a killer unknown to them, the trauma would have led them to move en masse, sticking together. But they were culpable, too, they were part of it, and to protect themselves from further scrutiny, they had to disappear. "They probably scattered after they burned down Noir," Teddy said, "slipped into villages one or two families at a time." He paused. "So now we end up with two possibilities." Teddy lowered his hands, tucked his fingers back into their fists, and stood, massaging his thighs. He walked back around to his chair on the other side of the bed. "Either an entire village of senseless killers—and from a sociological perspective, there could be no such thing—"

Bird took it away from Teddy. "Or a whole village sacrificing people to gods."

Now it was coming through, the mockery in the voice; Teddy could even begin to see it in the curl of lip against gum. This time, when the hacking cough started up again, Teddy could see that the man was laughing at him. He stood to walk out, but Bird had anticipated that and his hand, the lie detector needle when the lie had been detected, spastic and jerking fast, reached out to catch him at the waist of his jeans, pulling him back down hard onto the seat of the chair. "Is only people with too much brain could come up with a story like that," Bird said, and Teddy accepted the task of humility, put down his head, and shut his mouth.

47

THE STORY TOLD

"I am going to tell you a true story," Bird said to Teddy, knowing that the oath he had kept for eight decades was about to be broken.

And Bird told the story that had been famous among the people of Matilda's village. It was famous, too, among the few families in Colihaut, those who had been the liaisons between the Maroons of Noir and the rest of the island, who had helped to keep them hidden. Bird had been the last of them.

"She was a very young woman when this happened," he said, "a girl. Still in training, still learning from her mother. She had not yet met Simon."

At that early point in her career, Matilda had little experience with the dosing of aphrodisiacs, and even less of an understanding of the sexual protocols that should have governed her decision as to whether to give a certain client the treatment he requested. The man was old—he was *aged,* but his third wife, for whom he had paid a magnificent bride price, had left him, scandalously, for a young man; and his second wife had passed away. That left him only his senior wife with whom to salvage his pride—he did not want people to know that his young wife left him because he could not perform.

But his first wife was a woman as old as he, who had long retired from regular sexual activity, as was her right, and she guarded it carefully, even approving of the exorbitant price requested by the family of her young cowife.

Eventually, following weeks of unwanted sexual intercourse—something she later described as torture—the old woman killed her overprescribed husband with long strokes of a razorlike cutlass. When the old woman realized what she had done, she had announced that her husband had disappeared, and enlisted her children's help in surreptitiously burying the body. A few days later, it was dug up by dogs.

In those days, Matilda's mother headed the Council. Matilda was present at the trial when the old woman explained that she had enjoyed the companionship and occasional lovemaking of her husband, but that he had suddenly turned into a monster with a baton with which he relentlessly attacked her, daily and nightly. The old woman testified to the Council that she tried her best to direct him to other women who might have been interested, including an old widow who had just ended her celibate mourning period and would certainly have been in heat. But even the starving widow rejected him, unable to disassociate the decrepit face and body, exuding the aura of those close to the grave, from the lusty promise in his pants. She was an elder, she argued, she had lived long enough to command the respect of her neighbors, of the entire village, but he was shaming her every night with his overdone loudness, abusing her old body for the sake of his pride. On the sixteenth straight day, she testified, she simply could no longer stand it and went for the cutlass.

Matilda also gave testimony at the hearings, admitting that she had indeed given the man a strong aphrodisiac at his request. Her mother and the other women of the Council inquisitioned her brutally, accusingly:

"Did you imagine that he wanted the treatment for the benefit of another woman besides his wife?" they asked, and the young Matilda had to admit she knew that, based on his age and the condition of his body, he could not attract someone new.

"So then did you make any inquiries of his wife to discover whether she would welcome the effects of the medicine at her age?" they asked. She had not.

The Council, which by the founding laws of Noir deviated sharply from African tradition and was made up exclusively of women, spent several days behind their masks in close consultation with the elders, debating the finer points of their legal system and the nuances of culpability. In the end, they agreed that the old woman should die—but not for killing the man. That was self-defense and was fully justifiable under the circumstances. And not for trying to hide his death, as the law allowed for the panic of one who had never killed before. She was sentenced to death for the abomination of involving her children in the cover-up of their father's murder, her body to be thrown, unburied, into the part of the forest reserved for those whose lives had ended in the disgrace of the death penalty.

Her children, on the other hand, went unpunished, as it was obvious to the Council, to the other legal experts, and to the people at large that it would have been their duty to comply with such a desperate request from the woman who had given them life.

And Matilda was punished, too, with a year of hard labor in service to the village elders, for being too conceited, too sure of her capabilities, to recognize the complexity of the case. She should have refused the man, or referred him to a more experienced healer.

All this had happened quite some time before Matilda took over from her mother as the chief justice, as head of the Council of Noir.

A nd as Bird drew to the end of the story, Teddy sat still, breathing such shallow breaths that his head became light. He was hearing Sylvie's voice, seeing an image of her sipping her sapodilla nectar and telling her grandfather's story. It was the last part of her story, the part about Simon, how the Carib man had shouted outside the courthouse. Teddy had become too impatient by then to listen to her carefully.

"Magistrat! Magistrat!" Simon had said. He had not been calling out to the judge inside, after all. He had been shouting to the people outside. "She is not a murderer," he had been trying to tell them, she was a *magistrat.* She was a judge.

And Teddy was remembering how Lillian stood on the balcony over the river, so happy after she had heard the voices on the edge of the mountain, after she had found the memory of her mother. "A word that sounded like 'magic,'" Lillian had said, and he had been so sure that she was losing her mind, he never considered that he could be dead wrong; that Iris had not come to tell her child that Matilda was involved in black magic, in human sacrifice.

Lillian was right, but her child's understanding had only allowed her to register the part of the word she recognized. The word Iris was saying was not *magie,* it was *magistrat.*

T hrough his window, Bird watched Teddy go. He lay back against his pillow, waiting for Mary-Alice to come back home for their morning tea so he could finally tell her the truth about Matilda.

The professor had done well; he had got it mostly right. He understood everything, except, of course, the foolish human sacrifice part,
and the part about what had happened to the rest of the people of Noir.
Had he not fled so quickly, he would have told him what really became
of them. He was a smart *garçon*, but he dropped points for that—a handful of people in a small island might be able to appear at the same time,
full grown, with no explanation, but not a thousand of them.

He would tell Mary-Alice, and she would let Matilda's granddaughter know what really happened to the villagers after they burned down
Noir. He would tell his wife how they had all jumped, all except the few
who remained behind to prevent an abomination, because, according to
their customs, an unburied body was the punishment for a shameful
death.

A few of the people of Noir had voluntarily postponed their home-
going to give the thousand bodies down in the still-uncharted forest a
proper interment befitting their noble lives and glorious deaths, and
then they had quietly waited out their time, undetected except by Father
Okeke's African eyes, with only their beautiful scars to mark them as
holy.

I n the distance, Teddy was growing smaller and smaller. It was an
odd sight. Past a certain point in life, people might jog along, lope
toward a car that had stopped to give them a ride, clip at a faster pace to
catch up with a waiting friend. But adults only ran like Teddy if life was
threatened, or if they were bringing certain kinds of spectacular good
news. That was how Teddy was running, flat out, like a child.

48

CHANTÉ MAS

Teddy had left the room without making a sound, but the absence of his warmth woke Lillian up even before he closed the door. She listened for the engine of the Jeep, but he did not take it; he was afraid of Dominica's mountain roads. He would be standing at the roadside—rides were easy to get, especially if one was willing to sit at the back of a truck with some bananas. He would be going to town, most likely, to continue collecting his evidence against Matilda. She could not blame him. She had asked him for his help.

She knew when she had begun to lose him: it was when she ran from the market, from Myrtle making the sign of the cross. That was when he had begun to treat her differently, to speak with his friend on the phone about "treatment." And then, after there had been the voices at the precipice, it was over. When they came down from the mountain, he walked away from her, he stopped believing in her sanity.

Lillian agreed with him, with what he never directly said to her but had said repeatedly to the psychiatrist, that her mind was somehow disabled, but it was not because of any mental illness. She was not crazy, of that she was sure. She herself had done it, had built so many blockades that there was little space left for thinking. The sounds in her head were there because she put them there and had unwittingly locked herself out.

Once, only once, just the day before on the mountain, she had thought for a moment that she was losing her mind, but almost immediately it became clear that they were real voices, and Lillian now knew who they were and why they were calling her.

She dressed quickly, made up the bed carefully, and then hunted in her suitcase for a small silk pouch, which held the contents of her jewelry box. The long chain with the heavy cross went around her neck; the Adinkra cuff links she placed on the bed. Their weight made an indentation in the taut stretch of sheet.

She left the cottage without closing the door, got into the Jeep, and started the engine.

S uicide was not something Lillian had ever spent time consciously considering. Even when she had tried in vain to open up the artery in her left wrist, there had been no premeditation, only a sudden urge to get answers to her life from two dead women. It was not unusual or superstitious for her to believe that in death she would be able to speak with her mother and her grandmother: it was more than a fundamental tenet of her faith, it was logical.

And now, as she drove almost by instinct, her intent was the same. She would go to get her answer, because Teddy was wrong. When Iris had come for her at Icilma's house, the expression on her mother's face was not the look of a madwoman, it was just a look of love. Lillian knew that her mother was not using her last few breaths to tell her child anything about human sacrifice.

For the details, though, she would go back to the voices that had called her, to the place in the mountains where she discovered that most of the people of Noir, the Maroons, had jumped to their heaven, as people were wont to do when enslavement was not an option. She had not only heard their voices calling to her, she had *felt* it, the sensation of a thousand pairs of wings, beating like butterflies all around her.

⊗⊗

She could have ended her life anywhere, anyhow, she knew. It had been so tempting, the last time she had made love to Teddy, the night she lost him—she had almost let go and fallen over onto the rocks. But she had not let the weight of her body tumble her over the railing that night, just as now she kept the wheels of the Jeep on the road, though it would be so easy to go over the side of any one of the ravines along which she was driving.

She had spent her life in atonement, practicing self-sacrifice and self-denial, in the hope that she would one day pay for her inherited sins. But now she was going to allow herself an indulgence: she would do this for herself. In the public aftermath of her death, she would not disappoint the people of Dominica. Let them sing another song about another woman whose life had not fulfilled its promise. Let them sing on her— she wanted her own song, it was her birthright. A *chanté mas* to guarantee her place in history, alongside her grandmother and her mother.

She had put time and thought into it, over the last day, to help them with her song. Should they find her floating faceup in a river, so that they could agree finally that she, like her mother, had been a *Mama Glo*, the West African *Mami Wata*, the seductive, long-haired water deity, because one of the songs said that Iris had been seen regularly, by sane and credible churchgoers, standing on top of the deep and rushing water, walking in a circle around a river pool as if it were a road.

Or should she just lie down across a mountain path dressed in Creole finery to rot, her wide-brimmed hat hiding her devil-eyes, so they could say, "Yes, look: a *La Diablesse,* we always knew, like Matilda," who some songs said had lived, cloven hoof and all, with her fellow devils in a forest of clouds at the end of a magic road in the sky.

But Lillian had decided that it would be best to be the worst of the lot, a *soucouyant:* a woman who takes off her skin at night and flies around in search of victims whose blood she sucks. Yes, she would give them that pleasure, and it made sense for her to go back to where the Maroons had jumped; she would fly through the air for her country people—and at the bottom there were enough trees and branches to tear off her skin, so that when they found her she would be exactly what they wanted her to be: their nightmare come true, a *soucouyant.*

It would be perfect for her song.

Acknowledgments

In the process of writing and researching this book, so many people were involved in so many different ways that it's impossible to call each by name. I offer my heartfelt thanks and gratitude to all, including:

Eric Simonoff, my agent, for picking a rougher-than-most manuscript out of his slush pile and for his confidence in my ability to make it as good as all that, for patience and especially kindness and for having my back; Dawn Davis, my editor—taking on *Unburnable* was an act of courage; transforming it into this fine work is pure talent.

Early and late readers and flag-waving friends without whom I might not have kept going: Eileen Pastora (first written critique), Abby Richardson, Alison Stewart (eleven single-spaced pages of feedback at one go, and three years of hilarious e-mails), Natasha Gonsalves, Yvonne Armour Shillingford, Marita Laurent, Mae Hwa Huang Brooke (and we've never even met!), Jackie Bryant, Kim Nickens Randle, Kristin Wells, Joan Fonseca, and Charmaine Werth.

Huguette Njemanze Fafunwa who read every version and made long, middle-of-the-night, analytical calls from the Philippines full of unbridled enthusiasm and dead-on critique; who for the sake of this book finally came (five-strong!) all the way to Antigua after twenty-three years which all began on a University of Nigeria campus. Yvette

Noel Schure, best friend, for always finding time for me, even in the face of the world's biggest superstars, and for helping me figure out how to fix the ending. Margaret Morton and Sabiyha Prince for "getting it" early on and for selflessly sharing all their incredible contacts and well-connected friends. Kaye McDonald for good vibes and for stopping by to encourage over those coffee sessions.

Diana Loxley for the professional analysis that helped put me on the right track, and for continued interest, and Gwendolyn Mikell for research direction. Dominican historian Lennox Honychurch, whose book, *The Dominica Story,* I drew on heavily, for preserving the cultural legacy of my great-aunt, Mabel Cissie Cauderon. Thank you to Jennifer Hector for arranging the interview with her husband, historian Leonard "Tim" Hector, who passed away just weeks later.

In Dominica, Athene Shillingford and Myrle Shillingford Swift helped in many ways with the research, as did others who answered my questions about Masquerade, including Aileen Burton and Pearle Christian of the Dominica Division of Culture. Special thanks to Sylvi-anne Nicholas of Goodwill for recounting her own *bande mauvais* experiences. Special thanks to Patricia Linton for such energy and spirit and for our climb to Jacko's Flats.

I'm grateful to the kind *chef de village* at Club Med Caravelle in Guadeloupe, Gilbert Burgio, for the room upgrade that allowed me to keep writing while the children had their best vacation ever thanks to the Kids Club.

My family, especially my mother, the indomitable Marcella John, for faith (this book took faith and is about faith), and giving me such a clear picture of Dominica in the 1940s, and her sisters Irma Byron and Judith Blake for their Auntie Cissie conversations, Masquerade, and wedding-watching reminiscences and *chanté mas* songs. Donald Boyd and Alex

Lugay for a place to stay in Dominica, transportation, and good books. My father Victor John gave important encouragement in the form of things like kibbeh and the best mangoes. Sonya John for being a one-woman book club and critiquing all drafts through pickney and pregnancy; Laurie John for moral support and the open-door warmth of her home. My sister Mary John and my brothers: Joey John for telling everybody it's a masterpiece with the kind of exuberance only Joey John is capable of, and Michael John, who somehow without reading a word was able to give great plot suggestions. Justine Byron also never read a word but supported in technical and many other ways. Doreen Boyd for reading, for Helpful Friends, for general inspiration and spiritual encouragement. Suzanne Boyd, what fortune for a writer to have a cousin who is also an editor extraordinaire, thanks especially for The Missing Chapters. Carina and Victor John for believing in Auntie Mar and for your college connections.

Thanks to all the in-laws who never failed to ask about The Book and to wish me well—the Woodard and Smith clans of Wilson, North Carolina, now spread into the D.C. environs, and beyond; and to the Delany family of Mt. Vernon, New York, via Harlem, who were always so good to me and who began encouraging me to write more than twenty years ago.

I acknowledge the influence and perspective and love of two departed and very different women on my life, and also on this book: Martha Henrietta Lee, my nanny, and Nellie Jean Sindab, Ph.D., my mentor.

I saved the best for last. My deepest thanks and love to my husband William Smith, for immediately saying, "I think you should" without so much as blinking when I suggested I would stop working for a year to write a book, for still believing when one year turned into four, and for never doubting it would happen with no evidence that it could.

And thank you to my heartstrings Trey and Elyse Smith for trying to keep quiet all those afternoons, for patience. The biggest thrill in the early writing days came from your social studies exercise books—the stick-figure woman with crazy hair and a laptop, under which you wrote, "My Mommy is a writer."

HALIW   JOHN

JOHN, MARIE-ELENA
UNBURNABLE

ALIEF
07/06